# SINGLE GIRL IN A

# 40 SOMETHING WORLD

## BY LUNA PEARL

Cover design by Ben Hunter

First Published 5th April 2020

This book is dedicated to my special friends Yoko, Louisa, Claire, Shelley, Helen, Maria, Lisa and of course my mum. Thank you for being there.

# CHAPTER ONE

Teenage single life had been very very different. There were single men at college, in bars, at Saturday jobs. In your 40s, the pool of available men seemed very much restricted, and much shallower. So how to find the available men? People often suggest that you would find love in "every day life" and that "Love doesn't come when you are looking for it". Of course all this advice is fantastic coming from people who had been settled down for years, and no longer had any idea of how the whole dating thing worked any more. It used to be that guys would ask for your number, they called, you went out and had a fun time and if you liked each other, you'd see each other again. Nowadays you had no idea if a guy was available, if he was indeed interested, if he was a cheater/married, the list of pitfalls was never ending.

Josie worked as PA in an office in a modern business park set in rolling green fields, close to a small airport. She was studying to try and get a degree and hopefully a career change, but the office job was what was paying the bills for now. All the buildings on the business park were two-storey and surrounded a circular red brick walled fountain which was rarely turned on. The buildings on the business park all looked the same, with rows of endless windows and parking bays lined up outside. The reception area in Josie's offices had a high ceiling with shiny marble tiles on the floor. At the back of the reception area was a grey carpeted mirrored lift to the second floor which only the Chief Executive and her assistant seemed to use. In the office space upstairs, each department's area was open plan and the desks were pooled together in groups of at least 4. Privacy whilst working was a rare thing.

Josie walked through the reception door and Bridie the receptionist greeted her with a huge smile. She was in her early 60s, and had black dyed hair which was 'set' with curlers each day and she wore thick black round glasses. Bridie had wide blue eyes that took in everything around her. She spoke with a deep Irish accent and always seemed happy. In the morning she called Josie 'Josie' but in the afternoon always called her 'Jenny' - someone suggested maybe Bridie thought Josie was a job share. Either that or a little bit mad. Josie favoured the second option.

Josie smiled back at Bridie and made her way up to the second floor, then sat next to her desk ready for another day of administration work. Nic, one of the admin assistants, was already there.

"Hi Josie! Good weekend?" Nic grinned whilst Josie shrugged

"It was ok" replied Josie "Although the divorce stuff came through. Pretty quiet really".

Nic was always quick to give advice. It might not always be the best advice, but she was always keen to give it. She'd been married to the same man for over 30 years, and whilst it wasn't the stuff of romance and dreams, she'd always said "I know it's better than the other stuff out there".

"You need a man!" exclaimed Nic as she tidied her filing pile which she took in and out of the same drawer every day. Nobody knew if Nic actually filed anything anyway as the pile always seemed to stay the same height. Josie wasn't sure whether 'needing a man' was such a good idea. She hadn't been on a date in a long time and the thought of showing her naked, child bearing body to someone new didn't bear thinking about.

"A friend of mine was divorced once" said Nic "She worried like you did. She had loads of stretch marks but she found a boyfriend and got naked with him. And do you know what he said about her stomach??"

Josie looked up from turning on her computer and looked over at Nic, hoping that his response had been good.

"He said it looked like her stomach had been run over by a tractor!" laughed Nic.

Josie didn't know whether to laugh or cry, so gave a meek smile and carried on logging to her computer.

"Morning babes!" came a loud but smoothly sexy voice. It was Helen, the other admin lady who sat on Josie's desk group. Helen was well versed in the whole marriage, divorce and dating game. She'd been married twice, divorced twice but was now playing the dating game hard. Her first husband was a complete washout but she still had the odd liaison with husband number two, despite the fact that he was now engaged to someone else.

Helen was doing the online dating thing and was constantly going on dates, or so it seemed. Helen didn't seem to worry about any tractor tyre scenario.

She was always telling stories of her sexual adventures, some words from which Josie had to look up on the internet to find out what they meant. Helen was not your usual sex goddess. She was reasonably short at 5'1, a rounded size 16 and favoured fake eye lashes and dark, but very fake, tans. Helen had beautiful long, curly dark hair which was her best feature, with a round face and small brown eyes which were usually decorated with a shade of bright blue eyeshadow.

"Guess what happened to me last night..?" said Helen raising her well manicured eyebrows. Helen was often seeing 3 guys at a time, so what she actually did would of taken some guessing. Nic pulled a face. She wasn't a fan of Helen's bedroom activities although she was intrigued even if she didn't like to admit it. No one responded but Helen continued with her story anyway.

"I went to see that Robert and met him at that pub by the river near the bridge, it was really nice. But then he said did I want to go to a lay-by and have sex in the car!"

Josie looked briefly away from her emails and caught Helen's eye "And what did you say to that Helen?" asked Josie. Helen laughed her raucous laugh and flicked back a thick strand of her curly hair "I said to him I wasn't that kind of girl! So I gave him a blow job in the car park, but the trouble was that every time a car came over the bridge, the headlights lit up his face haha! Anyway, does anyone want a cuppa?"  Nic went quite pale and looked like she might be sick and Josie shook her head. Taking a mug of tea from Helen's hands at this point didn't seem like a good plan. The day passed like any other, lots of meetings, typing, phone calls etc and as Josie drove home she thought that maybe she should try and make some changes with regard to her non-existent love life. Maybe not as wild as Helen's but perhaps not as staid as Nic's either . Josie's close friends outside of her work were very different to her work colleagues. Josie had a close group of 4 friends who lived in the same block of flats which is how they'd become good friends.

Their children had attended the same schools and they shared the highs and lows of their lives together. They were all single too so Josie thought maybe they could impart some experiences and perhaps some advice that might work. They met up at least once a month for a coffee or a proper drink, so it seemed like a good plan to share experiences and ideas of how to best to improve their dating lives.

Josie opened her front door and took off her shoes, kicking them to the side of the shoe rack which she had put together herself but was now leaning rather obviously to the left where Josie hadn't tightened the screws enough. She put her handbag on the floor and reached in her handbag for her phone to message her friend Aimii.

Aimii was a beautiful girl with exotic Japanese looks, and who had moved to England about 15 years previously. She still had a very strong accent mixed with a localised accent and often got her words mixed up.

*"Are you in babe?"* typed Josie, then waited for the message to go to 2 ticks .

Aimii responded quite quickly *"yeah, you ok?"*

Aimii was sat in her flat watching a film on Netflix. She hadn't actually paid for it, but was using her ex boyfriend's account as he hadn't changed the password since they'd split up. It was useful but a bit annoying if he hadn't watched anything that she wanted to watch - she realised that he must know that she still logged on to his account, but she didn't want to make it too obvious by watching more episodes than him of the latest box set.

*"Yeah, just thinking about doing the online dating thing, what do you think?"* messaged Josie. Aimii looked at the message and smiled then took a long puff of her strawberry flavoured vape. *"Come round"* she typed. Josie quickly changed into a jumper and leggings. She grabbed a bottle of wine, grabbed a key and put on on her slipper boots before making the few steps to Aimii's flat. Aimii opened the door and noted the wine in

Josie's hand with a smile. The two women sunk into the old leather sofa and Josie gave a sigh.

"Am fed up of being on my own so thought I might do some online dating, what do you think?" asked Josie.

Aimii took a long puff of her vape "Oh my god babe, just do it! I have done it before but oh my god, my first date was a disaster"

Josie took a big sip of wine, and placed it on the oak coffee table "And?"

"So" said Aimii, who began flattening down her already perfectly straight fringe with her fingers, "He was a fireman, I thought he'd be well nice. Took me for a meal then we went bowling".

"That sounds lovely" said Josie.

Aimii scowled and shook her head, displacing her straight fringe.

"Oh my god, it was awful, and he had no teeth, or I couldn't see them! And he was going bald, you know me, I don't like bald heads.  His voice was really high and squeaky, it was really weird.  He kept leering at me and I had to stay until we finished the bowling, and it was 10 games that we'd paid for".

Josie raised her eyebrows "Did he not look like his picture then?"

Aimii nearly choked on her vape "Noooooo! Picture was about 10 years old. He had no muscles and no fucking teeth babe"

Aimii grabbed her phone and showed Josie one of the apps that she'd been using.  As Aimii clicked on the app, Josie noticed that Aimii had alot of unread messages in her inbox.

"Aren't any of those men any good...?" asked Josie.  Aimii shrugged.

She was a beautiful girl with looks that defied her 39 years, and whilst at points she seemed to have quite high standards, she did seem to have dates with quite a few losers.  Or maybe that was a common theme with online dating, Josie wasn't quite sure.

Aimii looked at her inbox to see if there was anything interesting on there. Josie had a glance and it appeared that there were quite a few profile pictures with men stroking tigers, holding fish or in group photos with mates which made it very difficult to tell whose profile it actually was. How was any of it to make sense?

Aimii saw one message that she'd already clicked on and replied to.

"I've been messaging him, he asked me out. I think I'll go but I'm not sure if I like his eyebrows...."

This was Aimii all over. Didn't matter so much if the guy lived nearby, or was in the same age group or a decent job - did he have good hair and was he not too tall.

Aimii was tiny 4ft 11 and didn't want anyone too tall as she said it "Would look too silly". This guy in question was called John and he looked Greek or Italian. 5ft 8 was ok. But he did indeed have thick eyebrows that seemed to have no gap in the middle. Also known as a monobrow.

Josie then had a look at Aimii's dating profile which was quite sparse with words but had some lovely pouty pictures with a soft filter (not that she needed it) which seemed to appeal, judging by Aimii's plentiful inbox. Aimii made a few quick "like" clicks then went back to her profile. Her hobbies section was empty.

"I don't have hobbies!" said Aimii, finishing her glass of wine "Everyone else, they are skydiving and travelling and scuba diving...."

"And yet they have hours to spend on dating apps" laughed Josie "They probably do those things once a year when they go to Ibiza, these aren't things you do every week!"

Aimii took another puff on her vape and smiled "You are right! You join it and see how you go".

"But which app shall I go on, I just don't have a clue" said Josie, searching on her phone.

Aimii laughed "they are the same people on a lot of them so take your choice! Come back over tomorrow, I will ask the other girls over and we put our heads together!"

Josie smiled and gave Aimii a quick hug before leaving her flat

"I will definitely be back tomorrow, make sure the others come as I need help with all this".

Josie didn't sleep that well. Having made the decision to start dating again, it felt a bit overwhelming. Maybe she had been listening to Helen's stories at work too much, maybe tomorrow she would feel better.

The following evening, Josie made her way round to Aimii's flat. Katie and Mel were already there. This time it was coffee and tea rather than alcohol as they all had an early start the next day, or that was the plan.

Katie was the youngest of the friends, she was very well groomed and well spoken. She had beautiful long auburn hair and had a few freckles on her fair skinned nose and cheeks. Men were generally drawn to her whenever they all went out. Katie didn't look like she needed help but she'd had a her own bad luck when it came to dating.

"My ex cheated on me with a girl he was friends with and said was a lesbian" Katie took a bite of her biscuit "Total loser and what a twat".

The others agreed wholeheartedly.

"Question" said Katie "Do you think it's better to sleep with a guy early on and find out what he's like or leave it and risk it?"

Mel looked at Kate with a quizzical look "Risk it? Risk what?"

Mel was in her forties, blonde hair and very photogenic. She was quite large chested and always seem to attract the younger men, having been married to an older one previously.

"Well..." said Katie "if you didn't sleep with them for ages, you might end up really liking them but they might be useless in bed , or have a really small willy".

"Different positions help" offered Aimii, sneaking a gin into a glass.

"But what if it's a skinny one?" suggested Katie.

"Then that's no good" giggled Aimii "There's nothing you can do about a skinny one.  Anyway big dicks are always welcomed!"

All the girls laughed.

There was a knock at the flat door and Jo came in to join the girls night  in.  Jo was a loud girl with shoulder length brown hair and tattooed arms.

She was very much to the point and seemed quite brash but the others knew she was a softie at heart.  In amongst the loudness and humour, was also someone who was quite spiritual.

"Hello ladies, I've got myself some gin and my tarot cards!"

Aimii fetched Jo a glass.

"We were just saying, is it best to wait to sleep with a guy until you really know him and risk finding out he's rubbish in bed, or do you sleep with him sooner to find out if, umm, he's got skills?" asked Josie.

Jo took a large sip of gin and tonic and starting laughing "Buy a strap on, solves all problems, I'll give you all a go!"

The others burst out laughing as Jo started shuffling her tarot cards

"Right, who's first?" asked Jo looking around at the friends.

There was a pause whilst they tried to work out if she was referring to a strap on or a tarot reading.

Josie broke the silence "I'll have my tarot cards read". Josie took some cards and Jo laid them out in a sequence. After looking at the cards for a while, Jo started her reading.

"Ooooh you've been hurt before, looks like you'll have to put your armour on and move on from all the hurt".

Josie politely nodded and finished drinking her tea, not really being in the mood for having her fortune read.

"Right ladies am off home to do my wonderful and amazing dating profile" declared Josie standing up "I'll let you know how it all goes".

Josie refused their offers of doing it for her and went back to her flat to start the online dating process. One of Josie's friends, Jane, was already doing the online thing but was paying for the whole process. She'd said it was her aim to log on every day and "send at least two winks a night" to men who she thought might be suitable.

Jane hadn't been that successful at dating either. Josie made a mental note to catch up with Jane soon to see how it was all going. But for now it was all about her own profile. There were questions to answer like "aspirations" "favourite place" "ideal date". Josie put on one profile picture but kept the answers as brief as possible, as she wanted to see what was out there and to see if it was worth putting a bit more effort into her own profile. Quite quickly the messages began to trickle in "Hey beautiful" "hey sexy" "what you looking for".

Some were far more blunt and Josie quickly learnt how to block. One message came in from a "Richard" who seemed ok. 31. He was younger that Josie but seemed ok. Looks-wise he appeared normal at a glance, but it was hard to tell as he laying down on some grass and was wearing what appeared to be a large sunhat which was covering part of his face. He lived in Outer London which was about an hour's drive away. However it quickly transpired that he didn't drive and would be relying on public transport to make any dates. He also was a student and living in lodgings so perhaps would be short of funds to travel or indeed go on many dates too far away. Richard asked a few questions and there was a little conversation before Richard said he had to go *"I'm going to go upstairs to my room now to think about you"* he messaged. This seemed a bit odd considering they'd had just the one conversation. Josie screenshot his profile and the conversation, and then sent it to Aimii for her opinion.

*"He doesn't drive babe"* replied Aimii *"and London is too far. And why is he going upstairs to think about you when you've only been talking for 5 minutes? Hat Richard is weird, don't let him come to our town!"*

Aimii was probably right so Josie logged out quickly before Hat Richard sent her any more messages. Aimii suggested going on one of the more mainstream sites and looking at men whose face you could actually see.

Josie made up another simple profile on a different site to see if it was any better. Josie got a message from a user called "Fannytingler2" before she decided to close the app and mute all the notifications on her phone. This was getting a bit too much already and she felt that more advice was needed. She went to bed, her mind whirling with dating apps and oddly named profiles.

Josie woke up early and decided to go into work early so that she could leave a bit earlier, which was always nice for a Friday. As she opened the heavy reception door, Josie could see that Bridie the receptionist had already arrived, and was putting on her telephone headset, ready to accidently misdirect a multitude of phone calls throughout the day. If there was any doubt where a phone call should go, Bridie always put it through to Marketing. Bridie looked up from her reception desk over the top of her glasses.

"Morning Josie" said Bridie with her Irish lilt "we've got an exciting day!"

Josie paused for a second before remembering that the Chief Executive had a new PA starting today. Mrs Wilshire was a foreboding Chief Executive who most people tried to avoid if they had any sense. She had dark hair very similar to Bridie's, but it was nearly black and was in a much firmer 'set' kind of style. Mrs Wilshire wore a thick base of make-up, favouring to team the look with red lipstick over her thin wide lips. She had broad shoulders and thin legs which were emphasised with her tight pencil skirts. If she ever smiled, it looked like it pained her. Mrs Wilshire had a very masculine look about her face, which had a strong jaw line. The company newsletter assured everyone that she had a husband of many years and that the two of them had sailed many a small yacht together in marital harmony. It was an obvious attempt to try and humanise Mrs Wilshire but the stories of their marital adventures were nonetheless amusing to the other staff.

Mrs Wilshire was a tough boss and went through PAs quite regularly. However this one was going to be different, assured Bridie to anyone who would listen.

"So what's this new PA called then?" asked Josie.

Bridie smiled "Her name's Sandy and she just has **so** much experience, she's going to love it here"

Bridie chatted away excitedly about their new colleague, not noticing that Mrs Wilshire's car had just pulled up outside the building. Both women looked up as the reception door slowly opened. Mrs Wilshire was stood there holding her black briefcase, wearing a red jacket and matching skirt, black tights and kitten heels.

She stood still for a second before striding through the reception area, her heels loudly clipping over the tiled floor. Bridie pulled off her headset quickly and walked over to push the lift button so that Mrs Wilshire could go upstairs as promptly as possible.

The lift pinged to signal its arrival. As the doors opened, Mrs Wilshire walked straight into the lift without even giving a glance to the two now silent women stood in Reception. As the lift went up, Bridie returned to her desk and placed her headset back on.

"Such a lovely woman" Bridie exclaimed before answering her first phone call of the day "Good morning! Ah yes ok, I'll put you through to marketing, please hold".

Jodie quickly went upstairs to her office floor, just as someone came out from the marketing department to deride Bridie for misdirecting yet another call.

Josie looked around at the empty open plan office and turned on her pc, before hanging up her coat and placing her bag in her desk drawer. As all was quiet, Josie decided to look at her dating inbox to see if there was anything worthwhile to look at.

She typed in her username - that had been a hard one to decide on. Aimii had said you have to think about what username would sound fun but also normal. And not too sexual. Another friend of Aimii's, Leah, had chosen the username 'Chocolatestarfish' which she thought sounded cute and because she "liked chocolate and she liked starfish". Sure enough this had generated a lot of messages from interested guys, although most had been of the suggestive variety. When Leah showed Aimii her profile Aimii had giggled so much she could hardly speak

"You know that chocolate starfish is another name for your arse, Leah? These guys must think you are offering it up" Aimii exclaimed through her laughter.

Leah had promptly changed her username in horror, but it had taken a good 2 weeks for the sexual suggestions to subside a little. Online daters clearly have long memories. Josie had decided on the username 'GlitteryJo' which seemed quite straightforward and not ambiguous.

As Josie signed in to her account, she noticed that she had a few messages waiting for her including one from Hat Richard asking if he could come and meet Josie on Saturday. He could come on the coach and do some studies as he travelled apparently. Josie remembered Aimii's words about not letting him come to the town and deleted the message. Automatically a different new message popped to the top. Nic arrived just as Josie clicked on it.

"Look at him! He seems ok" exclaimed Nic, putting on her glasses for a better look. Josie wished at this point she was looking at her account on her phone instead of bringing it up on her office computer.

"Yeah he looks ok" said Josie, reading through the profile

"Kind of normal".

Brian was from a town that was about 5 miles away.  He had what some might describe as strawberry blonde hair and his profile said he was 5 foot 6.

 Brian's profile picture was quite dark and his skin looked like he might suffer slightly from acne.  Helen arrived into the office and peered over Josie's shoulder at Brian's photo.

"Who's that?" asked Helen "it looks like he's got a face full of big spots".

Nic looked at Helen in disgust "It's just the lighting Helen, he looks perfectly nice.  I think you should go on a date with him Josie".

Josie looked again at his picture.  She wasn't sure.

"He lives locally, that's a real bonus. And a bit younger than you, well by 9 years, that's alright" continued Nic "send him a reply".

Josie sent a brief *"hi, I'm ok thank you, how are you?"* and a

reply quickly came back

*"Hey, I'm good. Thanks for your reply. I see you live nearby to me,*

*your photo is great"*

Helen was still stood behind Josie "Ask him why he has so

many spots".

Josie rolled her eyes "I can't do that, it's rude. I'll ask him why

his picture is quite dark".

Again the response came back quite quickly.

*"Haha! It was taken at the airport when I was dropping off a friend,*

*I was feeling a bit tired and run down but I liked the photo"*

explained Brian in his message.

Helen scrunched up her nose and flicked back a wave of her

curly hair "Bit weird, why choose a picture where you felt

rough. And he does have spots".

Josie decided to quickly change the subject "Have you seen

that Robert lately? You know, carpark Robert?"

Helen smiled a half smile "I have seen him already this week. He wanted to take me strawberry picking and have sex in the field".

Nic was zoning into the conversation "Well I hope you didn't do it! That's not what Pick Your Own is about young lady".

Helen laughed "I said no, because we could get caught, there were a lot of people picking strawberries and whilst I do like a bit of open air action, I don't fancy being arrested. So we had sex in the car".

Nic look horrified and took a deep breath "Really Helen, that's awful".

"I know" replied Helen "I went home with a bit of something on my face but luckily I saw it in the car mirror before I left the car park. Wasn't my finest moment".

"Something we can agree on then" said Nic. Nic's telephone was ringing which was a good time for her to leave the conversation.

Josie looked over at Helen who was trying to stuff a large bag into her desk drawer.

"What on earth is in there?" asked Josie, trying to get a better look.

"I have a date tonight" replied Helen "And these are the things I'll need for later".

"A change of clothes? Are you seeing Robert?" asked Nic who had just put down the phone.

"No and no" replied Helen "his name is Gary and I'm meeting him in his office"

"Office?  What kind of date is that?" asked Nic, ignoring the fact that her phone was ringing again.

Helen chuckled "It's a date in his office, he works in a tyre factory but is the boss.  I'm meeting him there and I'm taking a bag of tricks with me as it were.  I have a proper date with someone else tomorrow.  At this rate I might need to use some air freshener on my sheets before the end of the week!".

This time Nic was lost for words, Josie sat with her mouth slightly open and Nic's phone was still ringing. Through all this, Josie had somehow managed to agree to a date with spotty Brian.

## CHAPTER TWO

A date with Spotty Brian.  Josie wasn't sure how it had all come about, but she had indeed agreed to a first date with someone she didn't even know yet.  Panic welled up inside her body slightly at the thought of meeting someone who, to be honest, she wasn't physically attracted to, but she was nervous at just the fact she was going on a date.  So many things to think about, where to meet, what to wear etc.  Josie felt a bit out of her depth and felt slightly panicky.  She was good at giving other people advice but when it came to her own life, things didn't seem quite so clear.

Josie decided to pop into Jane's on her way home.  Jane was doing the online winks every night so must have some idea what it was about.  Josie pulled up onto Jane's gravel driveway and saw that the kitchen light was on.

Jane lived in a beautiful thatched cottage in a small village next to Josie's town and had been divorced for quite a few years.

Her ex husband had been quite well off and she was one of those rare women who had got the whole house in the divorce settlement. The gravel crunched under Josie's boots as she walked up the driveway and pressed the doorbell. There was a beautiful brass door knocker on the large wooden front door but Jane requested that people didn't use it as it took far too much effort to polish off the fingerprints. After about a minute Jane answered the door. She was in her pyjamas and wearing green Hunter wellies

"I've just been feeding the chickens" Jane said by way of explanation "fancy an egg on toast?".

Jane held up a dirty egg covered in a few feathers. Josie shook her head. She liked eggs but didn't like them actually looking like where they'd just come out from.

Josie walked in and shut the door behind her whilst Jane took off her wellies. She didn't work as she didn't have to.

Her ex husband was paying reasonable maintenance and the house was paid for, so Jane had plenty to time to do gardening and to look after her animals whilst dabbling in the dating world.

"Tea and peanut butter on toast?" asked Jane.

Josie nodded. Such comfort food indeed! Jane always liked giving advice over her pine kitchen table with food. Wine would also have been involved if Josie wasn't driving.

"So how's things?" asked Jane, cutting up some freshly made bread.

"I think I may have a date" explained Josie.

Jane stopped cutting the bread for a second "Who with?"

"spot.. Brian, his name's Brian" replied Josie, looking down at the floor.

"You bloody joined a dating site at last didn't you? Ha, good for you! I'm still winking twice a night but no damn luck.

All I seem to get are messages from men with the number '69' in their user names, and even if that's their birth year, for god's sake it's not a good idea. Jim69Reading keeps messaging me and I keep telling him to fuck off".

"Maybe he is 69 though?" offered Josie.

"Sounds about my fucking luck" said Jane "But actually he's 62. Still too fucking old".

Jane was only a couple of years older than Josie and was what might be called middle class. She was incredibly sweary but in a posh kind of way.

"Anyway" continued Jane "I have a date Sunday, when's yours?"

"Saturday. Who's your date with?" asked Josie.

Jane pressed the bread into the toaster "His name's George. He's a professor, very academic, looks a bit like David Essex actually. Must be better than my last date, who forgot his bloody wallet!"

Josie opened her mouth to ask Jane some questions just as the toast popped up noisily and landed on the kitchen counter.

"Forgot his wallet? Seriously?" asked Josie, watching Jane spread the peanut butter thickly onto the warm doorstep toast

"Did he go home and get it?"

"Course he didn't. I had to pay for the whole date. And he never ever paid me back"

Jane took a large bite of out her toast and continued

"Honestly, it's a minefield out there. I had a tiler in here the other week, was a friend of a friend, redoing my bathroom tiles. Had a lovely chat then afterwards he told my friend I was desperate for him. All we did was discuss tiles and drank tea, for fuck's sake! Thought that just because I am a divorcee. Bloody outrageous. Should of told him where to stick his grouting".

Josie started wondering if it was all worth it, all this hassle. Seemed like the dating world was full of a lot of strange people and she wasn't sure if she was ready. Jane smiled at Josie's concerned face.

"It'll be fine, at least you are not getting hit on by very old men!" laughed Jane "repeatedly!"

As the evening got late, Josie finished her now lukewarm tea and gave Jane a hug.

"Thanks for the advice, let me know how your date goes" said Josie as she walked to her car. Jane stood in her doorway and waved to Josie as she drove away.

The date with Brian came about much quicker than Josie had anticipated. She hadn't decided what to wear at all. She had decided where they should meet though - it was a pub just about within walking distance for Josie, and one she felt comfortable in, though she wasn't sure if a local-ish venue was a good thing or not.

She opened her curtains that morning and saw the black clouds looming in the sky and sighed. She really didn't want to drive to the date but if it was pouring with rain, it might be her only choice. Josie's phone bleeped. It was Aimii.

*"OMG! It's your first date today! Best of luck babes xx"*

Josie smiled. Aimii was good at remembering stuff that was important to Josie. A lot of the time they were busy with their own lives but there was always time to share the good, bad and stressful times. This was a stressful time and Josie wasn't sure yet if it was good or bad. She looked at Brian's photo again. Still didn't fancy him but she felt she should meet him anyway.

They had spoken a couple of times on the phone and he seemed ok. He had sent Josie the odd message in the week, albeit not very exciting ones that spoke about his bread going off too quickly and refitting a kitchen in his new job. They were meeting at 6.30pm. Not too early but not too late either Josie thought.

Josie decided on wearing a simple top, skirt and boots combination, having sent different photograph options over to

Aimii who analysed all the outfits and gave her best advice. Aimii had a very different figure to Josie, as she was very petite with a perk chest whereas Josie, although not tall, was much chestier, so advising her to wear a boob tube was never going to be an option. Having decided on where and when to meet, it was then a matter of keeping busy for the rest of the day.  As the day drew on, so did the rain. It had been dry for weeks, but today, date day, the heavens seemed to have opened.  Time was getting on so Josie grabbed her phone and called Aimii.

"It's raining and I'm meeting him in half an hour. It's windy too so an umbrella's not an option so am going to have to drive" declared Josie, feeling exasperated.

Aimii immediately stepped up "I will drive you round, you can't turn up looking all soaking wet, and you'll need a drink! Meet me outside in 5 minutes".

Josie thanked Aimii profusely and gathered all her stuff together. Phone, bag, keys. All set. Aimii knew where she would be and Josie would text her when she got back. All was on track. Josie went to the foyer in the flats and saw Aimii was already sat in her car waiting. She tooted her horn, so Josie threw her coat over her head and ran to the car door. Aimii smiled.

"Oh you look so nice!" Aimii looked Josie up and down "you are hot! I will drive you now to meet Brain" said Aimii in all seriousness.

"Brian" corrected Josie, putting her seatbelt on. As they drove down the road, the car slowly steamed up and Aimii passed Josie a tea towel that had been on the edge of Josie's seat.

"We are steaming up babes, quickly wipe so I can see" said Aimii.

Josie wiped the condensation off the windows of the old car, until they pulled up in the car park of the pub.

There was no sign of spotty Brian. Aimii got out her vape and then wiped the window with her sleeve and peered through the clear part of the glass.

"He's coming babes, I know it", Aimii took a long puff of her vape then let out a high squeal "It's him!"

A black volvo pulled into the car park and passed their car, at which point Josie could see it was a woman in her 60s.

"Well I've either been catfished or he's not here" said Josie, watching the woman drive by.

Josie let out a nervous laugh then realised she felt a bit moist and cold on the car seat.

"Aimii is it wet in here?" asked Josie feeling her skirt.

Aimii let out a horrified shriek "ahhh babes, the car roof leaks sometimes, and so much rain! That tea towel we used for the windows was to keep the seat dry, I forgot".

Aimii grabbed a pack of tissues and began plugging a small hole near the car window, just near to Josie's head. It was too late to keep completely dry but it was worth an attempt to stop getting even wetter. As they sat there, the grey sky began turning much brighter, and glimpses of blue began to peak through the clouds.

"It's a good sign" said Aimii, wiping the windows off again. She paused and saw a guy walking across the car park and towards the path of the pub. Aimii stared at him hard, and rearranged her fringe with her fingers before taking another puff of her vape.

"That's him, you'd better get out! This car park spying was so much fun!" Aimii started the engine as Josie got out the car "Call me when you get home".

Josie nodded as she closed the car door and felt the back of her skirt. It was a little damp but too late to worry about that now. Aimii seriously needed to get another car that didn't leak! Josie walked up the path to the pub. It had a garden in front which was covered with picnic benches and a small play area to try and attract families.  As Josie walked up the path

she looked towards the doorway and saw the man that had

walked across the path.  It had been hard to see through

Aimii's car windows very much of his physical appearance

but now it had become very clear that it was Brian.  His profile

had said he was 5'6 but as Josie approached she realised that

he had not been very truthful.  Josie wasn't tall at just over 5'2

but she could definitely look him in the eye. And he appeared

to be wearing a heeled boot.

Brian stood smiling with his hands on his hips.  He wore a

beige shirt, with what looked like 2 embroidered panels down

the front and his 'blonde' hair was much more red than Josie

had thought.

Josie braced herself and carried on walking towards him with

a fixed smile on her face.  Brian smiled back and gestured with

his hand towards the pub door in a 'ladies first' type manner.

As Josie walked past, Brian put his arm around Josie's waist so she quickly distanced herself physically to avoid any further physical contact. Josie wondered if all men were this tactile upon meeting, but tried to keep an open mind as they approached the bar. As they walked across the pub, Josie wondered again if it was really such a good idea to meet somewhere quite so local. She made a mental note to not come here on a date ever again. Brian bought the first round of drinks and made his way towards a table near the window. As he sat down, Josie took a seat opposite, rather than next to, Brian. As she sipped her coke, Brian opened the conversation. "Do you like cherry coke?" he asked.

Josie didn't know quite what to say "Umm no not really, not sure flavoured coke should be a thing".

There was a pause as they looked at each other. The more she looked at him the less appealing she found him, and it had started at a low level appeal in the first place but somehow people had convinced her that meeting Brian was a good thing.

"Do you like firemen?" Brian asked, smiling over his pint glass.

Josie didn't reply as she didn't know quite what to say again. She found the conversation a bit of a struggle.

"I've got a fireman's outfit at home" offered Brian, sipping his pint, and leering slightly over the table.  He gave a wink as he placed his pint back on the table, maintaining eye contact the whole time.

Josie resisted saying "aged 7-8 fireman's outfit??"  and just gave a weak smile. She felt the dig at his height might be missed.   This was awful, just so awful.  He wasn't attractive, he was a bit of an octopus and he thought that dressing up clothes were the way to a girl's heart. Or maybe her body.

Josie gave a silent shudder and tried conversations about family, maybe that would help if she changed the subject.

Brian offered that he had one sister and his parents lived

about an hour's drive away. Josie spoke a little about her mum and sister, but didn't want to offer up too much information. As there was a pause in conversation, Brian leaned forward and gave Josie an odd look.

"Are you ok?" asked Josie feeling slightly concerned.

Brian smirked and leaned forward a bit more "I was thinking of kissing you".

What?? They had been in the pub for all of 15 minutes, and he had touched her around her waist, talked about a fireman's dress up like he was every girl's short guy fantasy, and now he was suggesting a kiss. Josie immediately lent back and pulled a face.

"I don't think that's a good idea" she replied, holding onto her glass of coke rather too firmly.

Brian took the hint briefly and changed the subject himself.

"You've talked about your mum, but haven't mentioned your dad?" said Brian.

Josie explained that her dad had died when she was very young so didn't talk about him very much. Brian quickly moved round onto the window seat next to Josie and quickly embraced her, not giving her any option to say no.

"Aww you need a hug" he said whilst hugging her in a tight embrace. She could smell the beer on his breath and a slightly stale odour on his clothes.

Josie pulled away from him as quickly as she could and just wished the date could be over. She stared at the adverts on the pub table, suggesting bookings for different times of the year including Fathers' Day. Josie felt a sense of sadness and fought hard to keep it together in the whole situation.

"So" said Brian "As your dad isn't around, I'm guessing you're free when it comes round Fathers' day then? I'll have to remember that" he smirked and continued "So do you spend much time away from your family??".

At this point it was all way too much and Josie excused herself to go to the toilet and have a think and a calm down. Before she reacted, she needed to quickly assess if she was being oversensitive, which she sometimes had a tendency to be. She closed the cubicle door and stared at the wall which was covered in some mildly offensive graffiti that said "Joe is a wanker". Josie was tempted to scrawl over the name Joe and write 'Brian' instead. She shook her head and brought her thoughts back on track. Ok, she thought, he's been overly tactile, tried to kiss you within 5 minutes and on hearing on your dad's dead, acted with rejoice on knowing she wouldn't be otherwise engaged on father's day when it came about. Josie gained her composure and went back out into the pub and walked up to the table where Brian was looking completely unaware of how completely horrible the date had been.

"I think it's time I went home" Josie stared at Brian who looked back at her in complete bemusement at what had happened to make her leave quite so abruptly. How could he seriously have no idea about what a bad evening this had been. The best part of it had been in the car park, getting wet in Aimii's car.

"Can I walk you home?" offered Brian, quickly finishing up his pint, some froth sticking to his thin upper lip.

"No you fucking can't" said Josie, and turned and walked away. She tried to look dignified but began stumbling slightly as her heel hit an uneven floor tile. She continued to walk out the pub and back down through the pub garden and didn't turn to look back. She couldn't hear Brian's heels coming after her so she knew it was ok to keep walking.

Josie walked home as the rain began to fall again. It made her perfectly blow dried hair hang in what her nan used to call "rat tails" as the rain landed and dripped off the ends of her hair.

By the time she got home she was tired. Fed up and tired. It was late but she texted Aimii to see if she was still awake. The message was left on one tick so she must of gone to bed thought Josie. What a terrible disaster for a first date. Surely they couldn't all be this bad. Josie picked up her phone and went onto the dating app to have a scroll through and check her inbox. A few messages were sat there, including one from a guy who claimed to be 55 but looked about 78 and was squeezed into a waistcoat which was barely holding his stomach in, at what looked like a wedding as he was sat next to a woman in a white long dress. Probably his daughter's, who looked exactly the same age as Josie. That'll be a nope then. As Josie held her phone, a message pinged through. It was a text from Spotty Brian.

*"Hey, I had a good time this evening but I really don't think you gave me a chance! I don't know what I did wrong but I really like you and you're just not giving us a chance. I came home and I had a*

*cherry coke in the fridge but I couldn't drink it because it reminded*

*me of you!! I invested so much time and energy into you and for*

*nothing!! I don't know why I do it any more".*

Josie reread it and the "you're not giving us a chance" bit.

What us?? Bloody weirdo. Maybe this was just bad luck

though, thought Josie, surely they can't all be like this?? She

looked at the app again and with horror noticed a familiar

face. Her ex's profile was sat there right in front of her. He

had no top on in his profile picture, which definitely wasn't a

good look, and he had a weird lecherous smile. Josie was

mortified that he had even appeared in her selected criteria.

Why had he appeared??

She wanted to look on his profile but couldn't bring herself to

do it.

She knew that he would get a notification that she had seen it.

But she really wanted to know why on earth he had been

selected as a possible match ffs! Jane might have the answer.

She'd ask Jane. Jane had a profile on that site and was a night owl. Josie quickly texted and quickly got a reply back.

*"Sign out of the app, search his username on a search engine and you should be able to see his profile without him knowing it was you"*.

Impressive! Thought Josie, she'd clearly done this before. Josie typed in the username and sure enough in the search results you could click and go onto his profile anonymously. The first reason why he had come up into her matches became obvious. He had shaved a good ten years off his age and made himself slightly younger than Josie was. She scrolled down to look at his profile further. Age range preferred 25-40. He wanted a 'girl with natural beauty but not too large'. It said he was adventurous and liked going out into the wild. Josie frowned. The most adventurous he had ever been was a family Christmas shop at Lidl. Going out into the wild meant going into the pub on a Saturday when the football was on.

The photos. Josie clicked on the photos. She scrolled past the bare chested one and came across one of him running through the woods with a big silly grin on his face. He was wearing a tight fitting t-shirt which outlined his large tummy and man breasts, and he had utility type shorts on which highlighted his pale, hairy legs and on his feet were some odd looking sandals with white socks. Classy. Josie closed his profile and felt a bit violated even though she had been the one looking at his profile. Josie texted Jane to say she'd found his profile and asked if it was common to put down a younger age.

Jane replied "Yes! *They all do it, my cousin is 52 but puts down that he's 45. He says the big 5-0 is off-putting and he gets loads more women with the 45 age*".

Sounds charming thought Josie sarcastically. Josie had thought briefly about lying about her own age, but truly what was the point?? She was what she was and it wasn't a good start to begin with a lie. Josie put down her phone and looked in the mirror at her damp hair from the walk home from the pub. She looked tired. It had been an odd evening that also ended oddly. She took off her wet clothes and had a nice hot shower to warm herself up then got under the duvet and made sure the alarm was still turned off, as it was Sunday tomorrow - a day of rest but not for her friend Jane who had her hot date with George! Josie drifted off to sleep, and began dreaming about weird dating profiles and running away from men in the rain.

CHAPTER THREE

Josie loved Sundays. It was a chance to lay in bed, eat toast, drink tea and catch up on social media. There was a good chance it would be 11am before Josie even thought about getting dressed. Josie grabbed her phone and saw a message from Jane who was panicking about what to wear for her date with George.

*"I was going to wear a black top for lunch but can see in the sunlight that it's a bit see-thru. Do you think a white top would be any better??"*

Josie advised her to avoid the see-thru top for now and just to test the white one. Without seeing it she had no idea. Jane had chosen to meet George at a pub that was largely frequented by students and was literally on the river bank. No parking nearby, so Jane said she would cycle through the countryside to get there. George was walking, she said.

Sounded lovely.  It was an unusually warm Autumn day, and a drink by the river sounded perfect.  Jane said she would be back by 3pm and said to Josie to sound the alarm if she wasn't home by 4pm.  Josie agreed that sounded sensible and put the alarm on her phone so that she wouldn't forget.

Josie's plans for the rest of the day was to pop over to the mum's for lunch and then maybe chill before Sunday turned into "Smunday" and she had to start thinking about work. Josie got in the car and drove to her mum's.  Her mum Rebecca lived in a tower block and dreamt of a little house with a garden "when I win the lottery I will get one" she always said "And I'll buy you a house too".  The lift was broken, so Josie climbed the three floors up to her mum's flat, slightly out of breath and breaking a sweat as she reached the third landing.

"Must go to the gym" thought Josie, who suddenly thought of an admin temp at work who had said she was going to exercise more to find a man *"As noone is going to buy a house with the front door kicked in"*. It was an odd but funny analogy. An alternative was to start wearing those stretch suck in pants that they were always trying to sell on those online shopping channels, which did suck you in but always seemed to make the models appear smoother, but twice as wide. Josie decided to stick to her lumps and bumps as surely the right man would love her as she was. Josie knocked on the flat door which had been made to look welcoming with flowering plant pots and painted stones placed on the doorstep. Occasionally the door number stone would get stolen but Josie's mum would duly replace it as "Otherwise what those postmen will do?"

Josie's mum Rebecca answered the door with a smile. She had beautiful twinkling brown eyes, greying blonde hair and always seemed to have a slight tan no matter what the time of year. Her silver bracelets jangled as she gave Josie a hug and a kiss.

"Hello love, how are you?" said Rebecca with a big smile.

Josie smiled back at her lovely mum. She was always kind and generous and had a lovely way with words, she was always someone who would make you feel better no matter what. If Josie ever said she'd put on weight her mum would reply "Oh it's probably just fluid love" or "it'll probably be all gone by tomorrow".

Josie sat at her mum's kitchen table whilst the kettle went on. "I'm doing the online dating thing" said Josie.

Her mum turned around and smiled "Oh I don't blame you love, just be careful of them sending you pictures of their cucumbers".

"Wait, what??" asked Josie "Have you been online dating? And what cucumbers? Sent to you??"

Her mum laughed "I did try it for a while, it was called Senior Daters but it was full of gnarly old men and then 28 year olds started messaging me". Rebecca was in her late 60s. "Yes, pictures of their cucumbers, they just pop up when you least expect it. You'll be talking to someone about how bad the weather is lately and then a willy will pop up in your inbox".

Josie didn't quite know quite what to say, surely there was some warning?  Maybe it wasn't a good idea to sign in at work if penises were going to suddenly pop up, but then perhaps her mum was exaggerating.  As they were sat drinking their tea, some loud music started next door which seemed to vibrate the walls in a loud pulsating rhythm.  Rebecca rolled her eyes and looked at her daughter in exasperation.

"They've been doing this for hours! It stopped just before you came over but I've had enough now , I'm going to go round and have a word!"

Rebecca put down her mug of tea, walked down the hallway and out the front door, before standing outside the neighbours door where the music was still blaring out.  Rebecca hammered strongly on the door with her fist. She looked like a genteel lady but had been known to knock a fella off a barstool with one punch if things got out of hand. The music continued but Rebecca could see a shadow moving towards the door which then slowly opened. For a few seconds Rebecca seemed a bit taken aback at the sight of the woman stood in the doorway. Her eyes went to the floor and slowly worked their way up the figure stood in front of her: black patent leather thigh high boots, fishnet stockings, suspenders and a black leather basque which matched the boots. In the woman's hand was a whip.

"Can you turn the music down please??" asked Rebecca "It's too loud"

"WHAT??" asked the woman, struggling to hear over the sound system that was continuing to pulsate through the walls.

"TOO NOISY, TURN IT DOWN!" shouted Rebecca.

The woman pursed her lips and put her hands on her lips.

Rebecca expected a full argument but the woman then just nodded and shut the door, shortly after which the noise did indeed reduce in volume.  Rebecca returned to her own flat and sat down with her daughter to resume their chat.

"Everything ok?" asked Josie "It seems to of gone quiet now".

Rebecca took a sip of tea "Yes it was alright, but there was a lady of the night next door!"

Josie recalled the time that her mum had broken a light bulb and replaced it with the only bulb she could find in the cupboard, which was a red bulb.  It gave her hallway a bit too much of a Red District type glow into the corridor and she was subsequently advised to take it down by a man from the council as the flats "weren't for business use".

After that unfortunate incident, one of Rebecca's friends had got her a more normal light bulb from the supermarket.

"A lady of the night? Why do you think that?" asked Josie.

Her mum described the woman's attire, which at any time of day was a bit suspect but especially at 4pm in the afternoon.

"The music had probably been turned up to hide the sexual noises. And she didn't even put her whip down before answering the door" said Rebecca indignantly "very rude".

Josie didn't think that there was probably an etiquette for that kind of thing, but who was she to argue. The alarm on Josie's phone suddenly went off, meaning that it was time to check that Jane had returned home safely, so sent her a quick message to see that all was ok.

"So the online dating thing, did you go on any dates?" asked Josie.

"Yes, but only a couple. One bloke came from Northampton but was really old and boring.

He said he couldn't meet me again soon, as he said his daughter was getting married, but that's a rubbish excuse and

I really wasn't bothered. The other fella was alright but said he wanted a bit of sex and I said I didn't want that so he never really messaged me again, just sends me the odd joke via email".

Josie felt a mixture of general horror and intrigue in this online world where normal barriers didn't seem to count any more. Josie looked at her phone and noticed that Jane hadn't replied, so tried ringing but after 5 rings it went straight to answer phone. Josie felt slightly concerned as to what she should do next, as there was no point in having a safety back up plan if things went slightly awry and nothing was done to follow it up. She sent Jane a second message asking if things were ok but still no reply.

"Mum, I'm going to have to go, as Jane's been on a date but hasn't got home yet so I'm going to see if she's ok".

Rebecca finished her tea and nodded "Ok love, I'm sure she's fine though"

Josie gave her mum a big hug and a kiss on the cheek "I know but I'd best check".

Rebecca gestured at the charity bag towards the front door "Would you drop that off for me on your way home, by the charity shop? They are open til 5pm today".

Josie looked at the charity bag which was full of a multitude of garments but seemed to have a deflated white plastic item on the top.

"What's that?" asked Josie "Is it a beach ball or something?"

Rebecca shook her head "Haha no. Do you remember that dressing up party I had and that man turned up dressed as a shepherd? That's his inflatable sheep that he came with".

Josie looked at her mum and raised her eyebrows "Mum, you can't give an inflatable sheep to a charity shop.  Some poor woman called Mavis will pull it out the bag, blow it up and put it in the shop window. It even has a hole at the back!"

Rebecca's mum grabbed the bag and stuffed the inflatable sheep to the bottom, underneath all the clothes.

"It's called recycling love, they won't mind" said Rebecca, tying up the bag and giving it to Josie.

Josie gave her mum a wave as she made her way out the flat and back down the flights of stairs to where she was parked outside and put the clothes bag into the clothes recycling bin along with the inflatable sheep. Still no message from Jane.

Josie got into her car and started driving. The plan was to drive home and if still no reply then to go to Jane's house to see if she was actually there. Just as Josie arrived home, her phone began buzzing with a message from Jane. Thank god for that.

*"Where have you been? Are you ok??* typed Josie. Josie could see that Jane was typing.

*"Yes I'm fine, I am home now, been home ages but next door popped in for some wine then I forgot to message you".*

Josie felt annoyed but slightly relieved.

*"Did the date go ok?"* typed Josie.

"*Yes was ok thanks*" replied Jane "*He was walking so he walked with me with my bike for a bit then messaged me when he got home. He just told me that he got yellow stains all over his trousers haha*".

Yellow stains?? So many questions! Could he not hold his bladder until he got home?? Did something else happen in his pants??

"*What were the yellow stains?*" typed Josie.

"*Oh it was from the rapeseed plants that were in the fields he walked through*" replied Jane.

Oh thank god for that, thought Josie as she put her phone down. Aimii was also going on a date but hers was later tonight. She had been out with him once before but still wanted to do the safety plan just in case. Her plan was to be back by 11pm as it was work tomorrow, and she was to message Josie by 11.30pm to let her know she was back ok.

Josie spent the evening having a nice hot bath, and looking through her dating profile messages. Still no one had caught her eye which was rather disappointing, as she was keen to have a successful date after her first disaster.  Josie got ready for bed then realised that it was nearly midnight and no message from Aimii.   This was getting ridiculous. Her friends' dating was getting as stressful as her own.  Josie sent Aimii a message but it didn't go through then she checked her social media which said she hadn't been online since 7pm. Josie decided to go and knock on Aimii's door to check she was ok, so grabbed a cardigan and some slippers and went and knocked on the door.  No answer, ffs!

Josie kept knocking and buzzing until eventually she could hear moving about from inside the flat.  A voice came from inside.

"Who is it?"

"It's Josie, are you ok??"

There was a slight pause.

"Oh my god baaaaaabe I'm so drunk. So drunk".

Josie was happy with the fact that at least Aimii was home safe, whether she was alone or not was another question but Aimii was refusing to open the door due to nakedness she said. Fine. Josie went back to her own flat, took off her cardigan and got into bed. Just as she turned the light off her phone buzzed again. She wanted to ignore it but then changed her mind as it might be Aimii needing help after all. It was Jane.

*"What does phlegmatic mean?"* messaged Jane.

Apparently internet searches weren't working for Jane at midnight.

*"I have no idea, why do you ask?"* replied Josie.

*"George has messaged me saying he's in bed feeling phlegmatic"*

Josie had a quick think.

*"Does he have a cold after getting his trousers wet and yellow after his field walking?"* asked Josie.

Josie searched the meaning of the word as felt it would be quicker at this time of night. Apparently it meant "having an unemotional and stolidly calm disposition". Josie didn't think

that being unemotional and calm was necessarily a good thing

to be after a date. Josie typed in the definition to Jane who

was already typing a reply.

*"He's just written that he thought our town was sleepy and boring*

*but then he had just had some spotted dick"* typed Jane.

*"So he's feeling unemotional and calm whilst being rude about our*

*town and blaming it on an old fashioned pudding..?"* replied Josie

in disbelief.

He sounded posh but a bit weird. And Jane paid for a lot of

her online dating but the quality didn't seem to be any better,

thought Josie. Jane had kept quoting another friend of hers

who was on a paid site and apparently had 3 eligible men on

the go, whereas everyone else only wanted one. Bit greedy, if

it was true. Where were these eligible, nice men? Maybe they

didn't exist.

Josie felt awake again so looked at her messages on her dating app. There was a message from an overly handsome blonde man called Steve. The message was simple. *"Hey, how are you?"*. Not much effort in that message but out of curiosity, Josie looked at his profile. He lived in a town about 12 miles away so was reasonably close.

He was 35. Bit younger than Josie but she had already decided that younger was better than the older, gnarlier men who had already been messaging her. Occupation - property developer.

His blurb said "I've been really successful in my business life and have already achieved so much, that I am financially stable. Now I want to find someone to settle down with. The time is right to find Miss Right". Hmm sounds a bit too good to be true. Josie decided to message back to see what he had to say.

He sounded quite chatty but then Josie noticed that he had misspelt the name of a local town. Josie became more suspicious and looked at all his pictures in which he appeared tanned, blonde and muscular with incredibly white teeth. He looked like an extra from Baywatch. Josie had an idea. Only the other day she had read about this girl whose pictures had been stolen and a different girl had created a whole new persona based on these stolen images. Apparently it was a thing that people created fake profiles, called Catfishing, and one way to check it out was to reverse Google image search their pictures to see what came up.

Josie screenshot some of the pictures and followed the instructions before putting it into the search. Sure enough she got a hit. A guy called Phillippe Constantine's Instagram profile came up. He lived in California, was a fitness guru and had over 100,000 followers. And clearly had a girlfriend. So this definitely wasn't a guy called Steve who lived in a local town 12 miles away. Josie hit the block button. A catfish. That hadn't taken long at all. It was rather disconcerting to think that people who you were talking to online might not be the real thing. It was something you think happens to children and teenagers who are not streetwise enough to realise, not on dating sites where you hope that most people are genuine. Josie shook her head and deleted the message thread then looked again at her inbox. A new message from a guy called Andy.

The message said *"Boo! Answer back if you can. A xx"*.

It sounded juvenile and Josie was immediately put off by the fact that he signed himself off with an initial rather than his name in his first message. And what was all this "Message back if you can" business?? Josie clicked on his profile which had no picture attached. No wonder - his status said Married. Not single, not divorced, not even separated. Great, the internet was full of them tonight.

Josie felt annoyed and messaged back *"can you send a photo*

*please?"* if she knew him then she was going to out him! Quite

quickly a reply from Andy came back *"Yes of course"*.  A photo

was attached which Josie clicked on to reveal a random guy

who thought he was hot shit, but very clearly wasn't.

He was in his late 40s, and had dark hair styled like a Ken

doll, with a bulbous nose.  He was wearing golfing gear and

holding some kind of trophy whilst perched on a barstool.

Another message came through *"Do you like what you see....?"*

Josie laughed out loud.  This was becoming a little more

desperate each time.  Josie replied *"No"* and pressed 'send'

then allowed the message to be delivered before blocking

Married Andy for good.  Tool.

## CHAPTER FOUR

The weather was getting cooler and was suitably damp and dreary for a Monday morning. Josie pulled up into her normal car space and made her way into the reception area. Josie was greeted by Bridie, who was wearing her headset slightly off centre this morning, but it suited her quirky manner. Just as Josie was about to say hello, someone else came through the reception door. A rather tall leggy figure walked across towards the lift. She was in her mid 50s and had platinum blonde, slightly curly hair which was cropped in a 1920s flapper hairstyle. Her face was heavily made up and was matched with thick black mascara and red lipstick. She wore a red jacket and an incredibly short skirt which barely covered her underwear. Josie was a bit taken aback but Bridie beamed widely.

"Good morning Sandy" said Bridie, greeting the woman enthusiastically. Sandy smiled and carried on walking to the lift, before quickly turning back around to face the reception desk.

"Oh Bridie, can you make sure we have our coffee this morning, we have a meeting and Mrs Wilshire doesn't like to be kept waiting".

Bridie nodded and wrote it down on her notepad.

"Is that the new PA?" whispered Josie "I thought the PA usually made the coffee for Mrs Wilshire?"

Bridie nodded "Yes it is. Lovely woman. She used to be a model you know. I make the coffee now because Sandy says it's not her job".

Josie pulled a face. Seems like Sandy well and truly had her feet under the table and Bridie under her thumb. She decided it really wasn't her place to say anything, and besides if Bridie really wanted to be the coffee maker for the meetings then that was up to her.

Another bonus was that no one would ask Josie to do it either. The last time she made it, she had opened a packet of filter coffee and it had exploded everywhere, including into the cutlery drawer which Josie had left open to try and find a pair of scissors. The cleaners had been cursing and had to use a handheld vacuum cleaner to clean it all up.

Josie went upstairs to the office, and Nic was already there. As Josie sat at her desk, Helen arrived and took off her coat to reveal a beautiful soft looking jumper with a peacock design on the front. Nic had a great interest in clothes, especially of the designer variety, and looked at the jumper admiringly.

"What a beautiful jumper" said Nic.

"Thanks" said Helen "It's my favourite, because I love peas.....and I love cocks haha!"

Nic looked most disgusted.

"I had a two hander over the weekend" continued Helen whilst switching on her computer "It was amazing".

"What on earth is a two hander?" asked Nic.

"Well", said Helen, quite willing to explain "his cock was so big that I could hold it with two hands, one on top of the other and it was poking out of my top hand.  But the guy I'm seeing tonight has a really small one" Helen held up her little finger and put it just inside her cheek "you can't deep throat him at all, it barely goes past my cheek".

Nic rolled her eyes "No doubt the air freshener will be out on those sheets again by the end of the week Helen!"

Nic didn't wait for a response but turned to Josie instead  "Did you have a nice weekend my lovely?"

Changing the subject seemed like a good idea before it got worse.

"Well the date with Brian was awful" explained Josie "He was short, insensitive and creepy and then I got a ranty text message saying how I hadn't given him or indeed 'us', a chance".

Nic suggested that Josie choose someone nearer her own age but Josie wasn't convinced that being older would of solved any of Brian's issues.

Josie decided to get on and answer some emails and book some meetings. As lunch time approached, Josie decided to have hers a bit earlier to avoid the staff room rush. The staff room was an open plan area, with a kitchen area consisting of L shaped worktops and bright sofas for seating.

The offices were around a 15 minute drive from the nearest shops which was one lunch option, or there was a little sandwich van that used to visit around midday and was affectionately called The Bun Man by staff.

Josie always chose to take her own lunch as she had often seen the bun man climb out of the driver's seat to serve staff without a stop for a hand wash in between. Helen always used to joke that he probably scratched his crotch between every other roundabout on the drive there.

Helen used to occasionally buy her lunch from him with the question of "What have you got that's large?" with a wink and handful of change. He always gave her a filled roll but no one knew if he'd ever given Helen anything else.

Josie sat down in the staff room, avoiding sitting next to Mike from marketing.  He was extremely short at below 5 feet, a balding head, nearly 60, and quite creepy looking with bizarrely large ears.  Instead she chose to sit next to Marvin who worked in Human Resources and had his own colourful love life.

Last Josie had heard, he was seeing a guy called Rich who was a drag queen from London.  As they were sat there chatting, Josie noticed Sandy walk into the staff room.  Sandy walked over to the fridge and took out a calorie counted meal to put into the oven.

"I'm so fat" declared Sandy holding her lunch in one hand, whilst pinching some nonexistent fat around her middle with the other hand.

No one responded so Sandy continued to sort out her lunch. As she opened the oven door to put her lunch in, Sandy bent over in her short skirt, revealing a red thong as she did so.

Mike from marketing grinned whilst Marvin nearly gagged on his sandwich.

Marvin placed his hand to his chest in mock horror "Oh my days Josie, as soon as I was born out of the sunroof I knew that I didn't want to be near a vagina, and now look! I can see one in all its non glory".

"Sunroof?" asked Josie, whilst trying to look away from the flashing incident that was occurring near the kitchen area.

"Caesarean section" explained Marvin, as he watched Mike approach Sandy with a pot of tea to try and get a closer look. Josie put down her prawn sandwich, suddenly not feeling so hungry any more. Sandy walked over to where Marvin and Josie were sitting and sat opposite them, stretching her legs out onto the coffee table and taking a picture for her Instagram under the hashtag #tiredworklegs.

"My feet are aching" said Sandy whilst uploading the picture "It reminds me of when I used to run marathons, I was a professional athlete you know".

Josie thought she'd previously said that she'd been a model but maybe she'd had a varied career. Sandy seemed keen to chat today.

"I can't wait until the weekend" Sandy said, holding her hand out to admire her newly painted red nails "I get to see my fella. He's coming out of prison".

Sandy was quite well spoken but liked to throw in the odd word such as 'Fella' and 'bloke' which often sounded out of place with her well spoken, albeit often shrill, tone.

Josie and Marvin glanced sideways at each other with raised eyebrows.

"Prison?" asked Josie, curious as to why on earth Sandy would be with someone like that. Josie also knew that Sandy had a crush on Jonathon, the Finance Director who she'd deemed 'a silver fox' on her first day in the office.

"Yes for tax fraud and theft" said Sandy "He didn't do it of course, he's in touch with a solicitor to get all the charges lifted. He's quite famous in the world of animal rescue. He's been in prison for well over a year. I think I'll wear a denim

miniskirt, something casual this weekend".

Marvin's face contorted "Darling, denim mini skirts are so 90s,

and perhaps you should choose something, you know, that is

a bit longer. Don't want to overexcite the chap with your

beauty after all those months locked up".

 Marvin winked at Josie at the last sentence, to acknowledge

the sarcasm, that was of course completely missed by Sandy.

Sandy laughed and tossed her blonde hair back.

"Hahahaha! Oh I'm hardly beautiful, am I..?" Sandy was well

known for fishing for compliments, most of which were

ignored, except by Mike from Marketing who took any

opportunity for a leer.

Sandy scrolled through her phone and showed Josie 'her

man's' social media page. Sandy's 'man' was called BobbyB,

but it looked like his page had been quiet for a while so there wasn't really anything much to look at. There were a few people posting to his page about animals rescues but nothing personal.

"Hes always helping animals" sighed Sandy "Just can't wait to see him".

Just as Sandy finished her sentence, the Finance Director walked in, so Sandy took the opportunity to get up and remove her lunch from the oven in the same bent over method as before. Jonathon glanced over as Sandy stood back up. He was a very tall, slender gentleman with short layered grey hair, and always wore a suit with designer ties.

"Hello Sandy" he smiled as she stood holding her lasagne. It wasn't the sexist thing to be holding in front of her office crush, but Sandy tried to make the most of it, and smiled at him sweetly.

"I need some help with my figures, can you come and see me later? I know that you used to work in the London financial district" asked Jonathon.

Model, athlete, financial adviser, was there nothing this woman hadn't done? thought Josie.  It was time to get back to work, which was kind of a relief after the heavy flirting that had been surrounding Sandy.  It seemed Sandy's 'fella' getting out of prison wasn't going to stop her flirtation with Jonathon, although whether or not it was reciprocated was really hard to tell.

When Josie got home she signed into her dating app to see what other messages she had received.  One profile caught her eye.  His name was Joe, and he sounded funny and quite jokey so Josie decided to reply to his message.  The conversation started quite normally with "Hi, how are you" etc but then things started to turn a little odd.

*"Did you know about the people with cloaks?"* he typed

Cloaks? What cloaks?? Josie thought she had missed something but just replied *"No?"*

*"There are people who live amongst us, and they wear cloaks to hide themselves.  There is also a big tunnel under the sea where people*

*live between America and the UK. A whole underground city. It's kept very secret"* typed Joe.

*"Are you winding me up?"* typed Josie *"And if not, how do you know all about this if it's so secret then??"*

*"I researched it all on the internet, it's all real"* replied Joe.

Josie liked a conspiracy theory as much as the next person but she had had enough at that point and just pressed the block button. That was all a bit too weird and this Joe seemed fairly convinced that what he was saying was true. That was a different kind of weird. She looked at the next message down to see if that was any better.

The profile looked very conservative. The main profile photo showed a guy in a chunky knit cardigan, but he was holding a garden gnome like it was some kind of weird trophy. He was 50 with short greying hair and very ordinary looking. The 2nd picture in his profile caught Josie's eye and not in a good way. It looked like a stock photo of a man and a woman in their underwear and said "Doms and subs rule". The 3rd picture was of a pair of handcuffs and the 4th picture was of the grey haired man wearing a fake policeman's hat with a bare chest. It was all very bizarre and very unattractive. Not what Josie was into at all. She opened the message out of pure curiosity.

*"Hi beautiful lady, can we talk?"*

Josie typed a polite reply *"no thank you, I'm really not into the things that you are!"*

Very quickly Dom guy typed a response *"Maybe you don't understand.... let's go for a walk in the park and open your mind...we can talk about it!"*

The park?? Bloody cheapskate, thought Josie. No she didn't really understand the whole Domination/Submissive thing, but she really didn't want her mind opened by some gnome loving oddball in the park. Josie decided not to reply again, in case he viewed it as some kind of encouragement.

Josie deleted the messages and went to the next one in her inbox.

The message read *"Hello lovely lady, I'm looking for a very special person to be with. I'm looking for something quite special and wonder if that could be you. I'm an ex Olympic athlete hence why my picture is not on here, but if you private message me then I can send you one. The reason I need someone special is because I'm into something very different. It's called Pegging. If you don't know what it is then look it up on the internet. If you are interested then do reply. I look forward to hearing from you!"*

Very strange thought Josie. Pegging was something that she hadn't heard of before but just before she could look it up, Josie's phone suddenly buzzed. It was the girls' group chat.

*"Anyone up for a girls' night out?"* typed Jo *"I really need a fun night out"*.

*"Yes! I've missed you all"* typed Katie.

Melanie and Aimii quickly typed a yes too as did Josie. Felt like ages since they'd last met up, and Josie wanted to catch up all on all their dating stuff too. She was hoping that they'd had more success than her and with less weirdos!

Josie closed the group chat and looked down at the next message in her dating inbox. It was from a normal-ish looking guy, whose profile picture was of him lying down on his bed, but fully clothed which was a relief. He lived nearby, worked as a teacher he said, and was 38. Josie clicked on his profile picture which opened up to reveal a woman laying on the bed next to him. Josie looked in his profile description to see if there was a reason why there was another woman in his profile picture. Josie's phone buzzed again. It was Aimii.

*"Omg a really nice guy just messaged me! He lives nearby and is a teacher babes, a good profession"* said Aimii.

This couldn't be the same guy could it? Josie went and knocked on Aimii's door and held up her phone showing teacher guy's profile photo.

"Did this guy just message you??" asked Josie.

Aimii looked carefully at the photo "oh my god yeah, he just messaged me now, the one I just told you about!".

The two women compared the messages from him which were exactly the same. Aimii was decidedly not impressed and looked at Josie in disgust.

"He makes no effort!" she said in her strong Japanese accent and straightening her fringe.

"And what about that woman on the bed??" added Josie

Aimii stopped mid puff of her vape "What fucking woman??"

Josie showed her the profile photo on her phone which appeared to show more than it did on Aimii's phone.

"He's such a lair" said Aimii.

"Liar" corrected Josie.

"We should both reply!" said Aimii "And say exactly the same" she giggled.

Josie agreed, and they both typed the same reply to his question which was 'where would you go if you could choose a holiday anywhere?' Both typed "*The Maldives*".

Josie laughed as she typed her reply.

"You know what? I'm going to ask him who that woman is in his profile photo. Maybe it's just his sister or something. We should probably just check before hanging him out to dry?" suggested Josie.

Aimii rolled her eyes. She wanted to go straight for the kill but agreed to try and find out who the woman was.

"*I just wanted to ask you..*" typed Josie "*Who is that woman in your profile picture?*"

Josie sent it and about 20 seconds later, Aimii got a message from him in her inbox.

"*Strange question*" he put "*but can you see a woman in my profile picture??*"

"Type yes and see what he says" instructed Josie.

A reply then came into Josie's inbox *"It's my mate's wife"* he replied *"we're good friends"*

Josie showed Aimii the reply, who immediately lost her temper.

"Oh my god he such a lair. I'm going to tell him I know he's been messaging you too and if that is his mate's wife, he fucking disgusting anyway!"

As soon as the message was sent, both friends pressed the block button. What an evening of very strange messages. Josie couldn't wait until their girls' night out finally arrived. It was going to be a fun night.

# CHAPTER FIVE

The girls met at Jo's flat and each of them had brought some alcohol along to save money on buying drinks out later. Jo's flat was very neat and tidy and she always had her crystals, tarot cards and Disney ornaments on display in neat rows. Jo always did her housework three times a week and liked everything in its place. Last New Year's Eve had been spent at Jo's flat with the girls and someone had the mad idea of letting off party poppers at the chime of midnight - before they'd even hit the floor Jo had whipped out her hand held vacuum cleaner to clean up the paper strands and handed others a brush, bin and plastic bag to help with the mess.

Jo was fun though and good hearted. Her token greeting was to give her friends 'booby rubs' which involved pressing her rather large chest against everyone and wiggling herself from side to side.

It was especially impressive considering she had a double EE sized chest although was probably wasted on her female acquaintances. Josie opened the prosecco and poured everyone a glass.

"I had a really odd message on the dating site last night" explained Josie "It was from an odd guy who said he was an ex Olympic athlete who said he was into pegging".

"So did I" said Katie.

"Me too" added Jo.

"And me!" chipped in Mel.

"What?? So he messaged all of us? He's clearly playing the odds game isn't he? What is pegging anyway?" asked Josie.

Jo quickly piped up with the answer "It's when a woman wears a strap on with a man".

Bit too quick with that answer, thought Josie, but kept that opinion to herself just in case Jo decided to impart any more knowledge of such things.

"I was speaking to a bloke who really liked mermaids" said Jo, looking around the kitchen cupboards for her last bottle of gin.

"Mermaids? What as in The Little Mermaid?" asked Melanie nodding over to Jo's Disney display.

"Haha no, he just said he liked mermaids. Then he asked me to send him a photo of me in the bath with my hair under the water" said Jo, finding the bottle of gin.

Mel laughed "I went out with a guy who liked me to call him Sir in the bedroom, that was a bit weird.  His willy was a bit too big for my minky moo though".

Josie shook her head.  Were there no normal guys around anymore?? Why were they all into this different kind of stuff which Josie had never heard of.  It was all rather disconcerting to think that this may actually be the norm these days.

Aimii broke the silence "I'm talking to a guy, you want to see? His name's Garth".

Aimii showed the girls his photo from his dating profile. He didn't look her usual type at all. Garth had blonde, unkempt, greasy looking hair and his profile photo appeared to of been taken in a shed, as in the background was a wooden paneled wall where each panel overlapped each other and looked a light pine colour. He looked slightly unwashed and was wearing a high-viz jacket, but Aimii seemed quite taken with him.

"I have a date with him next week" said Aimii, taking back her phone "He's well nice I think".

The friends smiled, pleased that Aimii had found someone she liked. Josie explained to the girls about Dom guy and his weird profile that she had come across.

"Did you meet him?" asked Katie, whilst trying to take a pouting selfie with Mel. The filter was always on for such pictures, which were then selectively uploaded onto social media the next day.

"No I didn't" replied Josie indignantly "He asked me to open my mind. And in the park of all places. So he was a cheapskate as well as a pervert!"

"A cheapskate pervert is never a good thing" laughed Jo.

"Oooh do you think he read that book that everyone's been talking about? With the bondage and stuff?" asked Katie.

"I started to read that book the other day" said Aimii, laying back on the sofa "Everyone said it was soooo good, and I thought it'd be like this..." Aimii mimicked rubbing her crotch whilst pretending to read a book "But I was disappointed babes, I was not really into it all".

The girls laughed. Aimii was always very funny, always to the point and always mixing up her words.

Jo got a mint out of her pocket "Right ladies, does anyone want a mint before we hit the town?"

"Has it got mint in it?" asked Aimii seriously.

Jo laughed and rolled her eyes "What are you like?? Of course its bloody got mint in it. Right, time to hit the town!"

The five women made their way out of the flats and into the town to the first pub of their choosing. It was an 18th century old coach house conversion, with beams and grey stone walls inside. The friends got a drink then chose to sit outside in the stone walled courtyard so that Jo and Aimii could smoke. Outside were three men who Aimii and Jo knew and always seemed to be drinking in there, no matter what the day of the week. One was called Paul who had always had a crush on Jo, and everyone seemed to recognise it except Jo.

Jo had always joked that if her and Paul were still single when they reached 38 then they would get married but they were both in their 40s now and Jo was running out of excuses. It wasn't long before Aimii didn't look particularly well and was shivering in the corner, despite lots of cuddles and rubs from Jo and her usually olive complexion turned very grey. Josie asked the others if they thought they should take Aimii home as she really didn't look well.

Before they could answer Aimii threw up in an ice bucket that had been left on the table, which kind of answered Josie's question. So Josie and Jo decided to take Aimii home whilst Katie and Mel stayed in the pub.

Jo walked back to the flat in large strides which Josie did her best to keep up with, and each had one of Aimii's arms around their shoulders. Aimii's legs were so short and Jo's strides were so quick that Aimii's feet began lifting off the floor so that she was just dangling between her friends.

"Oh my god you are going so fast!" exclaimed Aimii "I need a bush, I need to be sick!"

Josie and Jo almost stopped dead in their tracks and looked at each other, deciding on what to do next.

"Let's keep going" said Jo, eyeing up the flats in the near distance "We're nearly there babe, then you can go to bed and feel better".

They reached the flats without Aimii being ill, and Jo used her spare key to let themselves into Aimii's flat. Aimii sat on the floor of her bedroom and Jo quickly looked around for a container in case Aimii was sick again, and found an empty waste paper bin.

"This'll do" said Jo, placing the bin next to the bed "You grab her legs and I'll hold her top half and we'll sort of swing her onto the bed"

Luckily Aimii decided to flop onto the bed herself fully clothed and appeared to quickly go to sleep.

"YOUR SICK BOWL'S THERE BABE" said Jo loudly tapping on the bin, and then placed Aimii's phone on the bedside table. As they left, they locked the flat door and made their way back to the pub which was much fuller than when they left. The girls carried on drinking and chatting about their week. Katie looked at her phone with a slightly concerned look on her face.

"When you left Aimii, what was she doing?" asked Katie.

"She was asleep on her bed, why what's up??" asked Jo.

Katie showed the others Aimii's latest status on her social media page which said 'OH MY GOD. MY FUCKING BUSH IS ON FIRE".

Mel looked at the status and looked at Jo and Josie "Jesus you two, has she been messing about with her waxing kit again?? Or maybe she dropped a candle on the bed?? You were supposed to leave her in a safe place!"

"We did!" replied Josie indignantly finishing off her drink "Anyway, whilst we're here arguing, Aimii's fooff is on fire so maybe we should go and help?? It's not my plan to be calling an ambulance on a Saturday night so let's hope she's got a bag of peas in her freezer."

Katie looked at her phone again and started laughing "No, no it's ok, the fire brigade are there".

"Fucking hell how big was her bush??" asked Jo looking shocked.

Katie laughed more "No, she meant the garden bush outside her window! Someone threw a fag in it and it caught fire, luckily she'd got up to get a drink of water and noticed the smoke outside".

"Thank god for that" replied Josie "Maybe now we can go to the next pub without any more drama".

Everyone finished their drink and they moved on to the next pub where they always had a quick shot of tequila rose before moving to the next pub on the list. It had a small bar area with low beamed ceilings and usually contained just the regular drinkers until the weekends, when it filled up more on the pub crawl trade. The next pub was a larger affair, full of a younger crowd, loud music and cheap drinks. In the daytime it made its money on cheap breakfasts and meals and at night-time filled up with people wanting cheap drinks and a good time. None of the girls were particularly keen but it was a cheap round and the toilets were large and reasonably clean which always helped.

Josie paid for the drinks this time and as she stood at the bar to put her change away she looked up to see a very tall, confident looking man staring at her.

"You want to check that change you know" he said with a wink "you can never be too careful in these kind of places".

He had two or three friends with him, one of which Jo seemed to take a liking to.

"My name's Charlie" he said to Josie offering out one hand whilst moving his blonde hair off his face with his other hand "Can I buy you a drink?"

Convenient question seeing as I've just bought one thought Josie. She took a closer look at Charlie, who seemed to be quite young despite his height.

"How old are you?" asked Josie.

"I'm 28" replied Charlie leaning on the bar "I'm the goalie for the football team in the city".

It wasn't a sport that Josie knew well, so he could very well be the goalkeeper for all she knew.

"What's your name?" asked Josie suspiciously. Charlie spelt out his full name as well as his phone number on a receipt that he had pulled out of his pocket.

"There you go, give me a call tomorrow and we can go out sometime".

Josie looked at the piece of paper and back at Charlie.

"Umm ok" replied Josie putting the piece of paper inside her phone case, making a mental note to do an internet search on him the next day.

The final bar was one which opened until 2am in the morning, and had a DJ with two bouncers on the door on Fridays and Saturdays. People outside were always kept waiting to make it seem busier than what it actually was, as this usually caused a queue to form outside. Jo knew the owner, so this usually got them in quite quickly.

The girls laughed and drank until about 1am when Katie declared she wanted to get some food from the van in the square before going home.

As they left the bar, Jo noticed a guy stood on the corner and randomly shouted "Toot toot" at him before marching on to the food van.

"What did you say that for?" laughed Mel.

Jo shrugged "I dunno, but he looked quite nice!"

As the women waited for their turn to order some food, a row broke out between the food seller and some blonde woman who was wearing large hoop earrings, short leopard skin skirt and a pink leather jacket.

"What's going on there?" asked Mel trying to concentrate on what to have with her kebab.

Katie pulled a face "She's drunk. She said he called her a gypsy bitch but he actually asked her if she wanted cheesy chips. This is Saturday night in the town for you!".

Josie burst out laughing and turned around to see the man who had been standing on the corner right next to her. Mel looked over at him and smiled.

"Hello how are you?" he asked Josie with a smile.

Josie really wasn't interested and moved slightly closer to Mel.

"Have you met my friend Melanie...?" asked Josie, hoping that he would be interested in Mel and vice versa.

Mel gave him a beautiful smile which revealed her perfect white teeth but the guy carried on talking to Josie. He really wasn't taking the hint, so she decided to be more forthright.

"I'm not interested to be honest" said Josie awkwardly.

The man looked slightly disgruntled as it he clearly wasn't used to being turned down.

"Which team do you play for?" he asked.

Josie was confused. What team? Was he talking about football? she thought. Maybe as the men's team was out tonight, so was the women's league?

"I'm not into football" replied Josie, trying to think on her feet.

The man looked confused before wandering off and getting a taxi away from the square.

"What was all that about?" asked Katie, holding her bag of fried chicken.

"Wish I knew" replied Josie, feeling not so hungry "I said I wasn't interested so he asked me what team I played for and I said I wasn't into football, then he walked off".

Katie laughed "Aww I think he was asking you if you were a lesbian, cos you turned him down haha!"

Josie shook her head. The men she was meeting online really didn't seem a better option than ones she was bumping into on nights out. The friends made their way home and Josie was relieved to finally take off her shoes. She liked wearing her heeled boots but after a while they made her toes ache, but it was a small price to pay for adding a few inches of height just for a night.

Josie didn't sleep very well and woke up at her normal weekday time, despite it being Sunday. After it turned 8am Josie gave up trying to sleep and picked up her phone. A small piece of paper dropped out which Josie vaguely remembered putting in there. She unfolded it and saw a name and a number. Ah yes, the mystery goalkeeper! Time to do an internet search! Josie typed in his name along with the city's football club and sure enough, got a result. She clicked on the club's website and found Charlie on there but then she realised that she wasn't looking at the main team players, but the Under 21s. Under his picture it stated that Charlie was indeed a goalkeeper but he played for the Under 21 side and was 18 not 28. Her instinct was right that he was much younger than he had said. Cheeky git.

Josie chucked the piece of paper in the bin, and texted her mum to make sure that it was still ok to go round.

Sunday was always a good day for a visit to mum's, so later on that afternoon she drove over to the familiar tower block where her mum had lived for over 30 years.

As usual Rebecca greeted her daughter with a hug and a kiss.

"You alright love? Come in and have a cuppa. I'm a bit tired as the neighbours were noisy again last night, so I banged on the wall with one of my hand weights"

"Mum!" exclaimed Josie "if you break the plaster, the council will make you pay for that".

Rebecca smiled with her twinkly eyes as she walked into the kitchen "Don't worry love, I would tell them it just dropped off, about time they spruced this place up".

Josie looked at the 70s geometric wallpaper in the spare room next to the kitchen. Her mum had decorated a lot of the rooms of the flat but had left the spare room as it was.

"There was a bit of trouble round here last night" said Rebecca turning on the plastic white kettle "And someone wee'd on my carpet! Bloody disgusting"

Josie pulled a disgusted face "Wait, what? How on earth did that happen?"

Rebecca made the tea and brought it over to the table.

"I woke up and it smelled of wee and the carpet near the front door was wet, so he must of done it through the letterbox".

"That's disgusting" said Josie drinking her tea out of a Christmas mug that her mum used all year round.

"It's ok" replied Rebecca "I've left a wooden spoon next to the inside of the door, so if anything pokes through, I can whack it! Then they won't come back".

Josie winced at the thought, but decided the perpetrator would deserve it if they did dare to do it again. Josie explained to her mum what had happened to Aimii's bush the night before.

Rebecca laughed "I nearly caught my bush on fire once".

Josie knew that her mum wasn't talking of the garden variety.

Rebecca continued with her story "You see I had a put some essential oils in the bath and lit some candles because, you know, everyone says how relaxing it is."

Rebecca paused and adjusted the silver bracelets on her hand, her tanned skin highlighting the turquoise gems of the bracelets that she had bought in Greece.

"So I had my oils and my candle and then I had a lovely bath. But as I stood up and swung my leg over to get out, I knocked a candle into the bath onto the essential oil which caused a bit of a flame to go up just as I was getting out. I nearly had a singed growler!"

Josie raised her eyebrows "Seriously mum, where do you pick up this kind of language?"

Rebecca giggled "My friend Jean calls it her growler. She's about 76 and doesn't wear any underwear you know, so if she's wearing a skirt, it's best not to sit opposite her".

Josie rolled her eyes and explained to her mum what had happened last night.

"I really didn't expect to be rolling my drunk friends into bed in my forties" explained Josie

"I'm still doing that in my seventies love" laughed Rebecca.

Josie shook her head and laughed at her mum's young at heart nature. She picked up her phone and noticed a message from Aimii. Greasy Garth had stood her up. Josie quickly finished her tea and gave her mum a kiss on the cheek.

"I've got to go, there's a friend I have to see" explained Josie grabbing her bag. Aimii had been looking forward to her date with Garth and it was going to be interesting as to what his excuse was for letting her down. Josie made her way back down the stairs of the flats as the lift was still broken and noticed that one of the stairwells had a strong urine smell. Well if the culprit used her mum's letterbox again then they were going to have a violent introduction to that wooden spoon thought Josie.

As Josie pulled up in her car outside her small block of flats, she noticed Aimii stood outside the communal doorway having a proper cigarette instead of a vape which meant she was very annoyed. Josie walked up to Aimii with a big smile.

"How's your burnt bush?" laughed Josie.

Aimii inhaled her cigarette again before blowing out a big slow puff of smoke.

"Oh my god I couldn't believe my bush caught on fire! I rang 999 and I explained my bush was on fire and they thought it was a prank but my bush really was on fire! And now Garth never showed up".

Aimii began pulling brown leaves off the burnt hedge and scowled.

"Why didn't he come to see you?" asked Josie.

Aimii took her phone out of her back pocket and showed Josie a photo of a car at the roadside.

"His car broke down.  Such bad luck. He better not be a lair" said Aimii.

"Liar" corrected Josie "but it must be true if he sent you a photo, and if it matches his car when you do see him then you know it's real".

Aimii shrugged.  She tried not to appear bothered but she was.  The dating scenario took an awful lot of effort just to get to the point of arranging a date, so it was disappointing to be let down last minute.  Aimii read a message from Garth asking for it to be rearranged for the middle of the week which she agreed to.  And this time he had better show up.

# CHAPTER SIX

The working week came around a bit too quickly and winter
was slowly settling in with dark but cold and crisp mornings.
Bridie the receptionist was looking her usual perky self as she
greeted Josie on the way in.

"Sandy's looking for you" chirped Bridie in her beautiful Irish
lilt.  Her hair looked more bouffant than usual thought Josie.

"If you go into her office upstairs you'll find her, use the lift
it'll be quicker" suggested Bridie.

Josie starting walking into the lift just as Helen arrived into
reception.

"Oooh Josie look at you going up in the world" said Helen, her
long false eyelashes fluttering.  Helen was wearing a shorter
length flowery dress with black leggings underneath which
was flattering to her curvy figure.  She looked semi demure on
the surface of her appearance which belied her many dating
adventures.

"Let me get in with you" said Helen, quickening her step to enter the lift before the doors started to close. The two women stood side by side as the lift doors closed. Helen eyed up the inside of the lift and started rubbing her hand up and down the lift wall which had carpet like material on the two side walls and a big mirror at the back of the lift, and a handrail that went all the way around the three walls.

"I got a carpet burn once" said Helen as they waited for the lift to go up "I did it on the stairs which was really uncomfortable".

Josie stayed silent as Helen moved closer to the carpet material.

"This carpet stuff on the walls is weird but if you forgot to brush your teeth you could give them a rub on it" declared Helen moving her face from side to side on the wall as if to test the theory. As she moved her face away, she looked in the mirror behind her and noticed a red mark on her forehead.

"Carpet burn!" declared Josie.

"Bloody hell!" said Helen, examining the red mark on her forehead "And I've got a date tonight too."

The lift doors opened which revealed the balcony that overlooked the reception area and a glass barrier. To the right was the door that lead to Sandy's office which you had to go through in order to get to Mrs Wilshire's office. Very few people actually went in there apart from Sandy and visitors from outside. To the left was the open plan office in which Josie worked. Josie wasn't quite sure what Sandy wanted as nothing was booked but she was sure it could wait, so decided to turn to the left and went in the office with Helen. Nic was already there as usual.

"What on earth is that red mark on your head Helen?" asked Nic.

"Carpet burn" said Helen taking off her coat "I was in the lift with Josie when it happened".

Nic looked over to Josie with raised eyebrows

"Nothing to do with me" said Josie quickly, before any rumours were started.

Josie started looking through her emails whilst Helen started telling everyone about her latest dating adventure.

"So I've met this guy, Darren, he's so lovely" explained Helen, playing with a strand of her curly black hair that had fallen out of her bun that was tied on top of her head in a very messy up-do "I was so attracted to his profile because he had a gimp mask on it".

Josie silently typed 'gimp mask' into a search engine under images, which quickly displayed a variety of leather masks on her screen.

"Was he also holding a gnome?" asked Josie.

Both Nic and Helen looked over at Josie quizzically "What?" they both asked together.

"Nothing, random question, just ignore me" said Josie, not wanting to explain about weird Dom guy who had wanted to open her mind.

"Anyway" continued Helen "Darren is into similar stuff to me. He's even bought me a PVC dress. It's about as thin as my arm" Helen held up her pale, plump freckled arm to demonstrate the thinness of the odd sounding dress "I'm not sure how to get it on as PVC kind of sticks to your skin doesn't it".

"Could you put washing up liquid in it?" suggested Nic "That would make it slippery enough to put on".

"I want to look sexy, not like a washing up bowl" said Helen.

"Talcum powder" suggested Josie as she continued to type her email. Helen looked surprised at this sensible suggestion from someone who didn't appear to own any PVC gear.

"The only reason I suggested that is because when I was little I had a Sindy doll, and to put her rubber boots on her plastic legs, the instructions said to sprinkle with talcum powder" explained Josie "No pervy knowledge, sorry!"

Nic and Helen seemed rather disappointed at the reason for the suggestion but both agreed it would probably work. Just as Helen was going to divulge some more of Darren's purchases, Sandy appeared from round the corner.

"Josie!" shrilled Sandy, sashaying over to Josie's desk before sitting on it and crossing her legs right next to Josie's computer screen "Darling I need to see you, did Bridie not say?"

Sandy rolled her eyes in an exaggerated fashion to display her exasperation at Bridie's apparent ineptness.

Josie didn't answer, and rolled her chair back away from her desk slightly so that she could stand rather than sit right next to Sandy's legs which today were adorning shiny flesh coloured tights and a red leather wrap around mini skirt which as usual left little to the imagination.

"Come with me" said Sandy who was already walking away "We need a chat".

Josie followed Sandy back through the door and across the balcony towards the Chief Executive offices which were much plusher than the open plan offices that the rest of the staff worked in. The directors of the company also had separate offices scattered around but none had the same finish as Mrs Wilshire's. The carpet was a very dark grey, and Sandy's desk was a beautiful curved white desk that faced the door. In the room next door was Mrs Wilshire's office that contained a large meeting desk and an individual desk made of mahogany. It was very traditional looking and highly polished and on the left hand side was a paperweight made of granite in the shape of a skull.

Sandy gestured for Josie to sit on the dark brown leather sofa to the side of the office as she sat on the edge of her desk. Sandy much preferred sitting on the edge of desks, as she felt it showed off her legs to their best advantage.

"So Josie, I've been thinking about the Christmas party, do you have any ideas for this year?"

Before Josie could answer, Sandy continued talking.

"I was thinking we could go somewhere that does meals and then dancing afterwards. I just love dancing so maybe that would be the best idea?" Sandy smiled as she stood up from the edge of the desk, her leather skirt creaking slightly as she walked.

It felt like more of a rhetorical question so Josie felt it best to just nod at Sandy's suggestion.

"Well that's decided then" said Sandy, her red lipstick creasing as she pouted into her small hand held mirror that she kept on the desk, using her finger to take away a tiny smudge at the edge of her mouth "Can you let Sarah know that's what we'll be doing. There's a hotel I know that hold dinners and dancing, I'll email you the details for you to book it for everyone".

The 'Sarah' who Sandy referred to was the Human Resources Director.

Sarah was a tall attractive brunette who was a straight talking woman in her 30s and who Sandy had seemed to develop a liking for. Marvin had referred to it as a crush but Josie wasn't so sure as she had heard Sandy talk about BobbyB, her fresh out of prison boyfriend. Josie also knew that Sandy liked Jonathon the Finance Director, so her crushes seemed too man heavy for anything else. There seemed to be a lot of crushes going on at the moment from Sandy's direction.

"How's BobbyB?" asked Josie, taking an opportunity to change the subject from work. Sandy sat back down at her desk, her leather skirt making a loud creak as she did so.

"Well I haven't got to see him yet" said Sandy looking disappointed "He said he was busy getting a new car and phone. When he was in prison he told me to stop writing to him as I made him depressed, can you imagine that?"

Sandy was quite self centred so Josie could quite imagine that receiving letters all about Sandy's life whilst being behind bars was probably incredibly difficult to be fair.

"He has apologised now though" continued Sandy, tapping down the page of the large, heavy diary on the desk with her heavily polished nails "anyway, speak to Sarah to get a date booked in for the Christmas party, the company might even stretch to an overnight stay".

Josie left Sandy's office and back into the open plan area to make her way to the Personnel Director's office which was at the opposite side of the building to Mrs Wilshire's office. Sarah's door, like the other Director's doors, had a wooden plaque on it with a metal name plate on it. Josie knocked firmly until she heard Sarah's voice asking her to come in. Sarah had a far less intimidating desk than Mrs Wilshire but she had managed to bag a corner office, giving her some impressive views of the countryside and of the police headquarters next door. As Josie came in, Sarah looked up from her computer and smiled "You alright Josie?"

"Sandy sent me here to speak to you about the Christmas party, she wants a date so that I can book it" said Josie, feeling a bit awkward that she had been sent as the messenger.

"Bloody woman" said Sarah looking at her online diary "Just tell her to fucking book it, I really don't care. Last week I was trying to talk to her about needing a new meeting room for the directors, with some nice wooden furniture in it and she tells me she used to be a carpenter. A carpenter?? I mean for fucks sake Josie, there's only one thing that woman can screw and it doesn't involve DIY".

Josie tried not to laugh. Some staff didn't like Sarah's straight talking, but Josie felt at least you knew where you stood with her unlike some of the other staff. And by return, Sarah liked people to be honest with her.

"Can you sort out the interview room Josie?" asked Sarah, pouring herself a coffee out of the machine she had set up in her office so that she could avoid speaking to as many people as possible during the day, including Sandy it would seem.

"Yes of course" said Josie, making a note on her pad "Who are you interviewing today?"

Sarah sighed before taking a big gulp of coffee "It's for an assistant for Jonathon in Finance. He can't interview him as he knows him from uni. Bit of a stud apparently and hung like horse. I'm going to shake him by the hand and look him in the eye to let him know I'm not afraid of that big dick".

Josie laughed out loud then quickly went back into professional mode "Ok, I'll get Bridie to give you a call when he arrives then".

Sarah nodded, put her coffee down on her desk and went back to work on her computer before quickly looking up again.

"I've got another meeting later in the week, can you come and take the minutes? I've got so much to do that I won't have time myself" explained Sarah.

Josie made a mental note to herself before making her way out of the office and shutting the door behind her. She made her way back to her desk where another pile of paperwork had been left for her by Sandy. Josie wasn't quite sure what Sandy did all day but it certainly wasn't taking care of Mrs Wilshire's filing.

Helen and Nic were having another in depth conversation about purchases. The raciest thing that Nic had ever bought was a pair of lacy panties from M&S whereas Helen's purchases were a whole new world.

"You ever bought any sex furniture Josie??" asked Helen, biting into a jaffa cake to go with her latest cup of tea.

Helen stopped eating as Jonathon the Finance director walked by in a very smart looking tailored grey suit. Her long black eyelashes fluttered as she crossed her legs and tried to look seductively at him over her mug. Jonathon shot a quick glance over to Helen and smiled before quickening his step towards the Human Resources department.

"He fancies me" giggled Helen, tossing back her curly black hair, unaware that a piece of chocolate from her biscuit was stuck to her chin.

"Helen you've got something stuck on your face" said Nic, offering over a wet wipe.

"Story of my life hahaha!" replied Helen grabbing a wipe to try and clean her face without removing too much make up "anyway what you been up to Josie? What did madam Sandy have you in the office for?"

"Christmas party" said Josie, making various notes in the diary so she didn't forget anything.  Josie's phone buzzed.  It was an old school friend of Josie's called Karen.

*"It's my 40th birthday, am planning a night away, bit of dancing and overnight stay, do you fancy it?"*

Josie had been friends with Karen since they were 10 years' old and had been at school together.

It never seemed to matter how long they had not seen each other, they could just pick up the conversation again like it was yesterday. It sounded like fun. The venue was a large Georgian mansion house that had been transformed into a hotel with spa facilities. They were putting on various themed nights with overnight stays at very reasonable prices. Josie didn't really know anyone else who was going but thought she would throw caution to the wind. It was the coming weekend but Josie didn't have any other plans so quickly typed *"I'd love to"*, before she changed her mind.

Just as she looked at her phone Josie had a quick look at her online messages to see if anything exciting was in her inbox. There was a message from a guy called Steve. He'd messaged her a couple of times and seemed ok, nothing amazing but who knows until you meet someone thought Josie.

*"Fancy a drink tonight?"* asked Steve in his latest message.

Nic looked over Josie's shoulder to see Steve's profile picture. He had tousled mousy brown hair and was wearing a leather jacket. Josie wasn't really sure that he was her type.

"Well he looks ok, nice teeth" said Nic "you could do worse my love".

Thing was, Josie didn't want 'could do worse' she wanted fireworks and butterflies and a heart that skipped a beat when she thought of her special someone. Steve looked a bit like a skinny version of George Michael in the 80s with a leather jacket and torn jeans, whilst trying to look mysteriously into the distance in his profile pic. It wasn't a great look but Nic persuaded Josie to agree to the date.

"Dating should be fun! Go out and enjoy yourself!" smiled Nic, rubbing Josie's arm "What could go wrong??"

What indeed. Josie arranged to meet Steve in a bar that evening, which was about a 10 minute drive from the flats. She decided to wear boots and jeans rather than dress up too much, especially as Steve looked a much more casual dresser.

Once Josie was ready she decided to pop in to see Aimii to catch up on what had been happening with her and Garth. Aimii was already in her PJs and boot slippers, watching TV.

"Are you not watching Netflix?" asked Josie.

"Nah, he changed the password. After 9 months! And I still had half a box set to watch. Bastard! You look nice babe, you going out?" Aimii looked Josie up and down in approval at what she was wearing.

"Yeah just meeting a guy called Steve" Josie showed Aimii all the details of her date and told her when to expect her back as a safety measure "Did you meet Garth?"

Aimii nodded "Yeah he was ok, we are meeting again tomorrow".

"Cool" replied Josie "Right I need to go otherwise I'll be late". Josie gave Aimii a hug before leaving the flat. As she walked along the street to get to the bar, she started wishing that she hadn't worn her new boots.

They were a leather pair of long brown boots with a slightly higher heel than she was used to, which made her feel like she was walking heavy footed. The bar where she was meeting Steve used to be a large, old fashioned looking pub with flocked wallpaper and chunky white radiators on the walls which always seemed to feel cold. In recent years it had been completely revamped into a very classy looking venue with clean white walls and dark polished wooden floors. Wide glassed doors allowed a beautiful view over the river and the passing boats. Outside was a decked area and permanent gazebo which in the summer housed an outdoor bar area and occasional open air cinema. The cold winter evening seemed a far cry from those warm summer months of wearing summer dresses and drinking cold ciders outside.

Josie took a deep breath before going inside the bar.

Steve had already messaged her to say that he was already there, but there was nothing worse than walking into a crowded bar on your own, and not be able to see who it was you were supposed to be meeting.

Josie opened the bar door and immediately saw Steve. He was standing opposite the main door with his back to the wall, and had one leg bent up so that one foot was resting against the wall in a pose. He was wearing a white shirt with the top two buttons undone, 80s faded jeans and a shoelace type choker. He was a man in his 40s who obviously hadn't updated his own style for a couple of decades as he was still very much set in the era of his teenage years. Steve was also very clearly chewing gum in an open mouth type fashion. He smiled as he noticed Josie walk in.

"Hey chick, let me buy you a drink" Steven put his hands on Josie's shoulders and gave her a quick peck on the cheek before moving to the bar "What would you like?"

Josie decided that whilst it was tempting to have an alcoholic drink to get her through the evening, the thought of her high heeled boots made her stick with an orange juice. Steve picked up both their drinks and walked over to a table that had a low dark brown leather sofa each side. Josie sat opposite Steve and kept telling herself to give it a chance.

"So what do you do for a living?" asked Josie, cringing at her own boring question.

"I'm a painter and decorator" replied Steve, taking a sip of his whiskey. He put his drink down and looked back at Josie, without asking a question in return.

"Ok, how did you end up doing that?" asked Josie.

Steve leaned back and put his feet up on the table, revealing camel coloured leather boots underneath his faded jeans. He scowled slightly at the question.

"What do you mean 'end up doing that'? It's a good profession" said Steve indignantly.

Josie felt slightly embarrassed that he had felt she was looking down at him which wasn't her intention at all.

"I know it is, I just wondered how you got into it that's all" explained Josie "I was just being curious".

There was an awkward silence for a moment which Steve finally broke.

"My ex used to be a hairdresser and used to cut my hair. What could you bring to a relationship?"

He looked at Josie intently, making her feel slightly awkward again. This really wasn't going well. She decided on a boring reply to suit the rather rude question.

"Nothing" said Josie "I have no skills at all. Just typing, I can type".

Steve smiled "What programmes do you like to watch then?"

"I don't really watch much TV, I prefer films" replied Josie.

She quickly glanced at her watch and realised only 15 minutes had passed since she had first walked into the bar.

"So what do you watch the films on then if you don't watch the TV at all??" smirked Steve. Josie sighed.

"What do you like to do in your spare time then?" enquired Josie politely, thinking that her cheesy questions were coming thick and fast that evening.

Steve had barely touched his drink whilst she was trying to finish hers as reasonably quickly as possible. Steve leaned forward and looked Josie intently in the eye. He had unusually deep blue eyes but any hint at a decent facial feature was distracted by his loud, constant chewing of gum.

"I like quantum physics, do you know what that is? I watch videos on quantum physics on the internet".

Josie shook her head. She had taken mixed science as a subject at school but physics wasn't her strong point.

"Well" said Steve, tapping on the wooden table between them "Do you really think that this is a wooden table? And the tree outside, do you really think that's a tree?"

Josie was a bit lost at this point "Umm yes because that's what they are?"

Steve laughed "Bless you" he said condescendingly. Josie decided to make her excuses and go the toilets to try and eat up some of the time. She hoped that Steve would use that time to actually drink some of his drink. The toilets were located up a slightly incline away from where they had been sitting and through a set of double wooden doors with glass panels. Josie looked at herself in the toilet mirror. Seriously, what was she doing sat in a bar listening to this pompous man who really thought he was hot shit and rude with it. Josie slowly washed her hands over the white enameled sink but realised she couldn't delay it for too long so made her way back to the main bar seating area. As Josie returned to the table, she walked back down the slope. Josie felt it hard to stop her new high heeled boots from clomping down on the wooden floor as she walked along it.

"Steady girl" laughed Steve "What are you wearing on your feet, wooden skis??"

Rude. Just rude, thought Josie who had had quite enough at this point.

"I really should be going" said Josie standing up and putting on her coat. Steve looked startled and looked at his watch.

"Early night eh? Ok well nice to meet you" said Steve, as he followed Josie out the bar. Josie quickly shook his hand before making her way down the street the opposite way to which Steve was walking. Josie hurried back to the flats and knocked on Aimii's door.

Aimii let Josie in and put on the kettle for a cup of well deserved tea. Josie slumped on the sofa and looked despairingly at Aimii.

"He asked me if I thought the table was a table and a tree was a tree. Something to do with quantum physics?" asked Josie.

Aimii shrugged as she tucked her legs underneath her on the sofa as she cupped her tea between both her hands to keep warm "No idea what he's on about but it sounds boring babe".

Josie's phone buzzed. It was a message from Steve.

*"I had a really good evening, let me know if you want to meet up again".*

Josie showed Aimii the message on her phone.

"For fuck's sake, was he on the same date??" Josie shook her head in exasperation and placed her phone on the coffee table "I'll answer that tomorrow, I can't bear to do it tonight".

The dating game was definitely not fun, it was in fact exhausting.

## CHAPTER SEVEN

Josie woke up early, realising that she still needed to think about what she was going to take to Karen's 40th birthday 'do' that weekend at the spa hotel.

Josie wondered if she even had a swimming costume that fit her any more, as the one she had worn the last time she went swimming had completely worn through around her bottom area and she hadn't even realised until she'd finished her swim and caught site of her rear in the changing room mirror.

It had gone completely transparent and had resembled a piece of gauze where the elastic had worn out, and given the whole swimming pool a shocking view of both her bottom cheeks in all their glory.

She looked on the internet for a replacement, it didn't need to be a proper swimming costume, just a simple, reasonably priced one that she would take for the weekend.

Josie found one that was dark navy with a stripe down each side and seemed like a reasonably flattering shape around the bust area, so ordered it straight away in a medium/large size to accommodate her large chest.

Whilst she was browsing on the internet, she also thought about something Helen had said to her yesterday about 'sex furniture'.

She hadn't had the opportunity to question what it was as Helen had become distracted by Jonathon, but Josie's curiosity got the better of her. She typed in 'sex furniture' in the search bar and looked at the results. Top of the list was a website called 'LoveBunny' which seemed to sell a variety of lingerie, toys and the aforementioned sex furniture. In fact when clicking on the site, Josie discovered that there was a whole section dedicated to sex furniture. She clicked on the tab and filtered the results from most expensive to see what on earth people could purchase from these sites. Forewarned might be forearmed after all.

The most expensive product came in at £275 and was called

'The Power Machine'. Josie clicked on the product and up

came a large photo of a man dressed in his briefs, holding

what looked like a large black box under his arm with a hose-

like extension coming out the front and standing in front of

him was a woman in lingerie, bending over and smiling. On

closer inspection, attached to the black box was not a hose but

a penis shaped extension piece. Josie pulled a face. What the

heck was this?? She read the description *'Does your woman*

*need a little extra excitement? Well the Power Machine can help! It*

*runs from the mains, so no batteries required. It's back and forth*

*movement pulsates faster than any man, satisfaction guaranteed'.*

So basically it's a massive, plug-in vibrator attached to a box,

thought Josie feeling quite puzzled looking. The man in the

photo was holding up the machine to the woman as if he was

going to fill a car up with it rather than satisfy anyone. It also

sounded a bit dangerous if it was mains powered and you

either had to back onto the thing blindly or rely on someone to put it in the right place.  Hardly sexy at all thought Josie.

What was wrong with good old fashioned naked togetherness

without any of these extraordinary gizmos?

This was hardly 'furniture' anyway.  She clicked to re-sort the

products and up came more furniture-like items.  Sex swing.

It looked like some straps hanging from a frame, and looked

exhausting rather than exciting.  Next on the list was sex

cushions and sex chairs/stools.  Up came pictures of cushions

with penis shapes rising out of them and sex stools, one of

which had 4 short legs, a rectangular seat and a pole coming

out at an angle of one end of the stool, giving it an almost

horse like appearance.  In fact Josie was pretty sure she had

seen one in Jane's front room but Jane had always said it was a

footstool she called "Keith".  Maybe she should tell Jane what

it was, or maybe Jane knew already so best to leave it unsaid.

Whichever way, Josie made a mental note to not put her feet

on it again in Jane's house just in case.

Josie's phone buzzed. It was another message from Steve, the quantum leap guy from last night's date.

*"Just a heads up Josie, it's very rude to ignore people's messages. You are so ignorant not to reply straight away. Remember it's nice to be nice"*

Josie felt a bit annoyed. He had been quite rude to her on the date and very self absorbed but she had bitten her tongue the whole night. He was clearly not used to women not replying to his messages straight away. Josie wrote a quick reply back.

*"I'm so sorry that I didn't reply to your message within your timescale. Just a heads up, it is nice to be nice, so why don't you try it sometime?"*

Josie pressed send then blocked Steve's number. The block function had come in very handy, it was just a pity that there wasn't such a thing in real life.

Josie hurriedly got ready for work, as the internet searching and the message from quantum leap Steve had got her a bit behind her normal schedule, despite waking up earlier than normal. She hadn't had a chance to check her online dating messages but hadn't really been in the mood. Josie got to her desk, hoping that no one would notice that she was about 15 minutes late. Nic hurried over to Josie's desk, ignoring her phone that was ringing loudly on her desk.

"Sarah's looking for you, something about minute taking?" said Nic in a whisper.

"Oh bloody hell is that today?? She said later in the week, didn't say it was today" said Josie feeling slightly panicked. Josie quickly grabbed her notebook out of her desk drawer and hurried to the meeting room. No one was there yet, so she quickly went to the kitchen area to top up the filter coffee machine with a jug of water, as the filter and coffee already being in place.

It was hard to see in the top of the coffee machine's water tank as it was tall and black inside, but Josie carefully measured a jug full of water to pour in, then switched the machine on.

The tray next to the coffee machine was already stocked with sachets of sugar, wooden stirrers, clean cups and tea bags for anyone who wanted to use the hot water urn next to the coffee machine to make tea as an alternative.

Josie heard footsteps outside in the corridor and then could hear Sarah's voice.

The visitors were from Italy and were interested in making an investment so that some more offices could be opened in their country too. Josie opened the door to see Sarah, Mrs Wilshire, Jonathon the finance director, two male Italian delegates and Sandy who was dressed in a black mini dress and high heels for the occasion.

The meeting room had a large oval table, with a screen situated at one end of the room which was used for presentations when needed. Mrs Wilshire, who was power dressed for the occasion in a bright red suit and matching lipstick, stood up once everyone had taken a seat to begin her presentation.

Josie took a seat just behind Sarah, away from the table, so that she could take notes if needed but not be too intrusive. Sarah opened up her laptop, as did Jonathon who was sat opposite them. Mrs Wilshire went through some facts and figures and referred to some complicated graphs about profits and investments, which Josie struggled to focus upon, given that Sandy was wildly flirting with Jonathon directly opposite. She was giggling and tossing her head back with every word he said, touching his arm whenever she could. Josie took some notes then heard Sarah tap her pen on Josie's chair arm to get her attention. Josie looked up to see Sarah pointing at her screen and looking at Josie with a very straight face.

"Make sure you note that" said Sarah, pointing at some words she had typed in the search bar on her screen.

Josie looked up from her notepad and leaned forward to read the words "*Sandy is being such an old slapper with Jonathon and I can see her pants*" said the words on Sarah's screen.

Josie tried not to laugh. Sarah was well known for pulling these type of stunts in meetings, yet always appeared to know exactly what was going on at the same time. Josie looked again at Sarah's screen and noticed that nothing on the screen was related to the meeting at all. Sarah's daughter's 2nd birthday was coming up and she was doing some online shopping on her laptop in the meeting. She had two tabs open and was comparing prices of two talking baby dolls on two different sites. As Sarah emptied her shopping basket on one site and checked out her items on the other site, Mrs Wilshire turned to Sarah to ask a question.

"Sarah, how do you see an Italian office impacting our business?" asked Mrs Wilshire, her make-up creasing on her cheeks slightly as she forced a rare smile from her thin lips. Sarah completed her online purchase then looked up at Mrs Wilshire "As we saw from the financial presentation, our profits are increasing each quarter especially from the Italian region so it makes sense to have a physical office there to explore that side of the business even further. This investment would support that aim, and I can deal with recruitment from our side of things, so that's not a problem".

Everyone nodded their heads to Sarah's brief statement and Jonathon stood up and handed out some financial paperwork. As he did so, Josie could hear a slight bubbling and hissing sound but couldn't quite work out where it was coming from.

As Jonathon took his seat again, Josie looked around to see that the coffee pot had filled up and was now overflowing.

Someone must of already put some water in the coffee machine before Josie had got there this morning, and it was now steadily overflowing and hitting the hotplate, making an impressive hissing and bubbling sound, before dripping off onto the table and then onto the floor.

Josie froze in horror at the coffee pot disaster that was happening and didn't quite know what to do. Then to Josie's amazement, Sandy shrieked and stood up, before heading quickly towards the overflowing coffee pot.

This really wasn't like Sandy to get stuck into anything that involved hard work or indeed cleaning up.

As all these thoughts went through Josie's head, Sandy grabbed a nearby tea towel and knelt on all fours to start mopping the floor giving the two male Italian delegates a good eyeful of her thong.

Both men raised their eyebrows and looked at each other as Sarah typed on her screen in large letters "WE'RE FUCKED" for Josie to see.

Mrs Wilshire quickly stepped in "Well I think this is a good time to wrap up this meeting, thank you everyone. We can break for lunch, I have a table booked at a local restaurant and we can perhaps continue our discussions there".

Sarah closed her laptop and rolled her eyes, as Jonathon helped Sandy up from the floor. She held onto his suited arm, looking rather flustered.

"Oh thank you, what a mess! Hopefully the carpet will clean up properly" simpered Sandy, still holding onto Jonathon's arm unnecessarily tightly. Once the room was empty, Josie breathed a sigh of relief. For once she was thankful that Sandy's thong had distracted everyone from the coffee pot that seemed to have its own mind today. She left a message with Bridie to pass on to the cleaners about the carpet, then went and got her bag out of her office drawer. Now seemed a good time to have her own lunch break, so she messaged her mum, Rebecca, to see if she was free to meet up for 45 minutes.

Rebecca answered her message *"Yes love, that would be great. I'm down town now, so I'll meet you in that coffee shop by the museum"*.

Josie walked out to her car and drove into town, managing to find a parking space in a side street. It was another rainy day, so the town wasn't too busy. As Josie walked towards the museum she could see her mum Rebecca sitting at a table at the window drinking a cup of tea, the glass steaming up from the warmth that was generated inside by the coffee machines and grills which were constantly on the go at this time of day. Josie got herself a hot chocolate with cream and marshmallows before taking a seat opposite Rebecca.

"Hello love, you okay? I hardly slept last night, that woman next door was making a right racket again, but business is obviously going well!"

Josie told her mum about the coffee and thong incident, as both women drank their hot drinks, looking at the near empty streets outside due to the heavy rain.

The leaves on the trees were turning a beautiful burnt orange and red and made reflective patterns in the puddles on the ground below.

"I need to get a new bra" said Rebecca, finishing up her tea "There's a new shop in town called Love Bunny and it's got some good discounts on its bras at the moment".

Josie hesitated.  Surely it couldn't be similar to that website she had been looking at? She didn't say anything but nodded her head and drank the last creamy remnants of her hot chocolate before putting her coat on.  The shop was situated in a large shopping centre, and new units had been recently opening.  They found the Love Bunny store situated at the top of the escalator and Josie went in first.  The first part of the store was rails full of beautiful lingerie including bras, which Josie tried to steer her mum towards.  As they made their way over, Rebecca became distracted by a display of smaller pieces.

"Oh look at those earrings, they look nice" said Rebecca pointing at the packet containing 2 flower shaped objects with tassels hanging down.

Josie took a closer look. "Mum they are nipple clamps, you can't buy them, come this way".

Josie grabbed her mum's arm and quickly made their way to the back of the shop, hoping that they would find something more suitable and also to try and keep out of sight of anyone passing by who might recognise them.   The back of the shop seemed darker than the rest of the store and as Josie's eyes adjusted she realised that she was surrounded by sex toys of the vibrating variety.  Each toy had its own little white pocket shelf to sit in on the display.  Josie quickly turned to drag her mum back out, only to be faced with a very happy and perky looking shop assistant.  She had dark hair tied back in a pony tail, a round face with small black round glasses and wore a cardigan which would of suited someone three times her age.

"Hello ladies!" she shrilled "I'm Stephanie.  Can I help you ladies today?"

Josie shook her head "Nope, no, we only came in for a bra and we got all confused".

Stephanie chuckled "That's what they all say. Don't be shy, have a look at what we have on offer".  Stephanie held out her hand towards the imposing display.

"If you want to check how hard the vibrations are, just put them against your nose to test it".

Josie looked at her mum who was already picking up an item to push the button.  The toy vibrated wildly and Rebecca quickly went to put it back on its tiny shelf, only for Stephanie to grab it back.

"This is one of our popular models!" said Stephanie, adjusting the front of her cardigan "I have one at home and it's amazing".

Too much information, thought Josie, grabbing her mum by the arm.

"Get a bra another day" whispered Josie to her mum "We need to go".

Rebecca pulled a face and followed Josie out towards the entrance of the shop where a male promotional shop assistant was stood holding some products by the door. Just as they were leaving, they heard the words "*I'm a soldier and I wanna hold ya*" coming from the direction of the shop assistant. Rebecca hadn't noticed that it had come from the box that he was holding rather than him speaking it.

"Excuse me??" said Rebecca glaring at the shop assistant "what kind of chat up line is that young man? Come on Josie, we'll get my bra somewhere else".

Josie was relieved to get out the shop without any purchases and made their way back down the escalator. Josie's lunch was nearly up so she said her goodbyes and made her way back to the office. As she sat back down at her desk, Helen came into the room and took off her coat.

"Saw you in that new shop, Josie" said Helen with a grin "that Bunny one". Helen gave a wink.

"Are you getting a new pet?" asked Nic, eating a rice cake at her desk "That might be nice for you, take your mind off these horrid men".

Helen laughed and tossed a curly black hair as she shook her head "No Nic, it's not that kind of shop. I've had some lovely stuff from there, their shackles are really good. I went out with a bloke last week who likes to tie his partners to a chair".

Nic placed her half eaten rice cake on the desk "Really Helen, that sounds more like a kidnapping than anything sexy".

Helen laughed again "Oooh no, it is sexy. You dress up in lingerie and he ties you to a chair then he blindfolds you".

"Still sounds like a kidnapping" exclaimed Nic "Why don't you go out with a nice man who wants to take you out to dinner rather than tie you up?"

"Because that would be boring!" replied Helen, deciding to get on with her work.

Josie felt repelled at that whole idea and quickly looked at her online dating messages. There was a couple that she might reply to later, she thought, then got back to her work. The afternoon passed quite quickly and as Josie drove home in the rain she thought she'd pop into Aimii's before she settled in for the evening.

Aimii was busy cooking some noodles whilst answering some online dating messages at the same time. She was always incredibly good at multitasking in these things.

"How did you date go with Garth?" asked Josie, watching Aimii stir fry her noodles.

Aimii stopped mid stir and looked at Josie "He let me down again babe, I'm so cross".

"What was his excuse?" asked Josie, taking a seat on the stool in the kitchen.

"He dropped his phone in the bath" said Aimii, ignoring the noodles that were now sticking to the bottom of her black wok

"So he said he couldn't tell me because he didn't know my number! He such a lair".

"Liar" corrected Josie, pointing at the burning noodles in the work.

Aimii turned off the heat and sat on the stool next to Josie "I don't believe him, he could of messaged me on his online app to tell me but no, he said he lost his contacts when his phone fell in the water".

None of it seemed plausible to Josie either. For one thing, he had looked too dirty in his picture to be having any thorough kind of wash at any point, let alone a bath. Josie said nothing but gave Aimii a hug. Aimii poured Josie a glass of wine.

"Have any guys asked you to do any weird stuff?" asked Josie, taking a sip from her large glass.

"Sometimes" shrugged Aimii "When I came home the other night, one guy asked me to skype him in the shower, I was like 'oh my god you weirdo'!"

Josie looked concerned "You didn't did you?"

Aimii laughed "No! Men think we shower like this".

Aimii mimicked gently washing her long hair and slowly moving her hands down her body with a pretend satisfied look on her face.

"But really it's like this" Aimii then proceeded to pretend to roughly wash her hair, followed by vigorously rubbing her arm pits and her groin "It's not sexy! It's cleaning".

Josie laughed "I'll watch out for those requests then".

"Oh" said Aimii, recalling another odd request "one guy asked me if he could put it in there as he said it was illegal in his country" Aimii pointed to her bottom "But I said NO WAY!"

Josie laughed "Good response! Oh I'm away this weekend by the way, can you keep an eye on my flat? My old school friend Karen is having a 40th birthday weekend, and she's invited me. There's food and drinking, and some dancing entertainment. I can't wait for just a bit of a break really".

"Yeah of course, oh my god that's so exciting" Aimii smiled and clinked glasses with Josie "Maybe you'll meet someone at your weekend away".

"I don't know" smiled Josie "maybe I will".

## CHAPTER EIGHT

Josie was all ready to be picked up for her weekend away. She had a small pink case, with a handle and wheels. She had packed very carefully and her swimming costume had arrived just in time. It wasn't quite what Josie had wanted as it had some odd padding around the chest area, but it fitted and there was no time to get anything else.

Karen had sent through some information via email about the spa facilities the day before so that Josie was aware of what she needed to take. Within the spa was the normal swimming pool, sauna and steam room, but it also housed a salt water pool. The brochure said that the salt water pool enabled participants to float in the pool, as it was so salty, with a maximum of 8 people at a time, to calming 'whale' music. At the bottom of the page, in small print, it stated that the salty water could cause discomfort to cut or recently shaved skin, so Josie had made an effort to shave her legs the day before, just in case the salt water really did cause a stinging reaction.

There was a group of about 15 of Karen's friends going, only one of whom Josie really knew, so Karen said that they could share a room together and would give Josie a lift to the spa hotel. At 9am Karen's car pulled up outside the flats and beeped the horn to indicate her arrival, her car stereo blaring out a Bon Jovi track, one of her favourite bands. Josie was ready and waiting in the hallway, and walked quickly out to the car and put her bags in the boot then got in the passenger side next to Karen.

"Oh my god Josie, I haven't seen you in such a long time!" Karen kissed Josie on the cheek then nodded to the back seats. "This is Lauren and Dawn, my two besties" said Karen pointing to the two women in the back. Both women grinned at Josie. Lauren had dark brown, short hair with a floppy fringe and wore bright pink lipstick whilst Dawn was more demure looking with shoulder length mousy brown hair and no make up.

"Let's get this show on the road!" yelled Karen, pulling out onto the main road and turning up the stereo even further. The four women sang to the songs at the top of their voices as the car made their way through the country roads and they felt full of excitement, winding the windows down to let the cold autumn air blast through the car. The hotel was only an hour's drive away and as they drew closer, they could see an imposing looking mansion sitting on the side of the hill, its white walls looking even brighter in the morning sun. There was a winding driveway up to the hotel with two pillars sat proudly either side of the large wooden front door.

Karen parked the car and the 4 women unloaded their bags before making their way to the reception area to check in. The receptionist gave the women their electronic keys to their rooms and two leaflets detailing the spa facilities and the evening's entertainment.

Josie looked carefully at the leaflet in her hand *'An evening of fine dining followed by entertainment with our favourite drag artiste, then enjoy our variety of male dancers'*.

"Karen?" asked Josie "these male dancers... are they strippers??"

Karen laughed "No don't be silly. The drag artist does some jokes and then does some dancing with her male dance troupe that's all".

Josie wasn't completely convinced and put the leaflets into her bag to look at more closely later. The rest of Karen's party had already checked in and were in their rooms, so the four women decided to follow suit and meet up later. The rooms had high ceilings, with long windows and equally long heavy green velvet curtains that touched the floor. Josie looked at the beautiful view of the rolling green hills outside the window and felt relaxed at the thought of the spa day ahead. Karen carefully hung up her clothes in the wardrobe, and turned to look at Josie who was now laid back on the bed.

"Right then, let's plan our day" said Karen, picking up her leaflet "We've definitely got a session booked in for that salt water pool thingy which we must go to, because I went through three razors this morning shaving EVERYTHING so am not going to let it go to waste".

Josie shrugged "Maybe we could have a swim and sauna first?"

Karen checked the time "Nah I think we need to do the salt pool first as we need to be there for an instruction chat 20 minutes before our slot. I'll message Lauren and Dawn to meet us there".

Both women changed and put on the white towelling robes that had been left in their rooms neatly folded at the end of each bed, along with a very large white towel each. Karen grabbed the electronic key before leaving the room to make their way towards the spa where Dawn and Lauren were already waiting.

"I forgot my glasses" complained Dawn, squinting to see which sign indicated the salt pool.

"What did you want to be seeing?" asked Dawn, going through the door "You'll be floating around looking at a ceiling full of stars whilst listening to whales having a moan".

As they entered the salt pool area, they entered a changing room area and were greeted by a male spa employee wearing black shorts and a white polo shirt with the spa emblem on the top left side.

"Hello ladies, come in come in! Let's start our chat before you start your salt pool experience".

The women took a seat on the wooden bench, alongside 4 other people who were already sat there.

"My name's Matthew and I'm your salt pool host today. When you get in the pool, you'll notice that due to the salt content you will find it very easy to float, however you will also find it quite difficult to put your legs back down so try to float to the edge carefully in order to get out.  I'll also be giving you all some balm to apply to any sensitive skin before you enter the pool"

Matthew held up a large pump dispenser "The salt water can aggravate any cuts or recently shaved skin, so please use the balm wherever you have shaved recently".

Matthew dispensed a large dollop of balm to everyone to rub onto their skin for protection.

"Oh for fuck's sake" whispered Karen "I've shaved it all off now so I'll put this balm to good use".

Karen pulled out her bikini briefs, ready to employ the balm on her crutch area.

Josie raised her eyebrows "Don't rub it down there! Seriously Karen, just put it on your legs".

Karen sighed and reluctantly just rubbed it on her leg area instead.

Matthew clapped his hands "Right everyone, time to float!"

The group made their way into the salt pool room, which had very dimmed lighting and sparkling lights on the ceiling. The whale music was already on and echoed around the room as the group got in one by one via steps into the pool and began to float around. Josie wasn't keen. Within minutes someone close to her had made a splash which caused some of the salt water to go in her mouth. It tasted like the sea and other members of the group kept floating around and bumping into her which she wasn't finding calming at all. After the session was finished the lights went up and everyone got out the pool "Oooh I'm all relaxed now" declared Karen "Though it did sting a bit downstairs. Right let's go for a cold shower then a sauna".

Josie, Karen, Dawn and Lauren all made their way to the sauna which was unisex and already had a gentleman sat on one of the wooden benches which went around the side of the sauna walls.

They opened the door and Josie and Karen sat next to each other, whilst Lauren sat on the bench facing the door and Dawn sat next to the man who was already sat on the bench. It didn't take Josie long to realise that the man on the bench had no towel on and was completely naked. Dawn smiled at the man and began a conversation.

"It's nice at this hotel isn't it, have you been here before?" asked Dawn, sitting quite closely to him.

Dawn chatted away, whilst Karen began laughing and whispered to Josie "she's not got her glasses on, she has no idea she's sat next to a bare penis haha".

Dawn carried on her conversation until the sauna got too hot for everyone so they decided to move to the pool area.

"Did you see that willy?" asked Lauren laughing.

"What willy?" asked Dawn looking around in surprise "If I see a willy then it will of been worth coming here just for that haha".

Karen shook her head and laughed "Get your glasses on next time! Come on let's swim".

Josie laughed and decided to lay and relax on a lounger next to the pool rather than swim, so that she could catch up on her social media and messages. She noticed that Sandy had tagged BobbyB in her latest online status, as she had been for a meal in the pub with him and was calling him 'my dear friend'. Josie clicked on his highlighted name which took her through to his profile and as luck would have it, was completely public for anyone to see.

 BobbyB seemed quite a character. He had greying hair which sat on his shoulders and judging by his facial features, looked about in his early 60s. His profile picture was a selfie of him sitting in a nice car, wearing sunglasses and smiling widely at the camera.

The aviator mirrored sunglasses completely hid his eyes, and attached to the arms of the sunglasses was a metal chain that went around his neck, similar to that of an older librarian who wanted to keep their glasses resting on their chest via a chain, just in case they were needed to read a book at any point. None of it was very flattering, but Sandy had spoken reasonably highly of him, apart from mentioning that he'd said she had been making him depressed in prison, with her letters. His main photo behind his profile picture was a dark image which showed the outline of 6 men stood on a hill with the sun low behind them, appearing to look like soldiers in the distance. Very odd, thought Josie, making a mental note to try and enquire if he had a military background. Josie wasn't quite sure how Sandy had met him, she only had said they had been 'friends for years'. Knowing Sandy, that probably meant she'd befriended him online just before he got detained at Her Majesty's pleasure for 18 months.

Dawn got out the pool and laid on the lounger next to Josie, who put her phone back in her robe pocket.

"Karen just told me about that naked bloke, can't believe none of you told me" said Dawn in disgust.

Josie shrugged "he was sat right next to you, it was a bit difficult!"

"Yeah I guess" replied Dawn "So what you been up to lately then?"

Josie explained that she was single and had been slowly venturing into the online world of dating.

"I met a bloke online once" said Dawn whilst picking up a magazine from a nearby table "the date was alright I suppose but then afterwards he sent me a weird video".

"What kind of video?" asked Josie.

"He was in the bath, and it panned down to the bubbles and he was, well shall we say, massaging himself. I think it was supposed to be sexy but it looked like he was kneading

dough!" laughed Dawn, flicking through the magazine

"Anyway, you looking forward to the strippers tonight?"

"I bloody knew it!" said Josie feeling awkward "Karen said

they were just dancers, supporting the drag act".

"Nah, full frontal I heard" said Dawn, whilst reading the

advice column.

Josie picked up her phone out of her white robe pocket and

went into the changing room so that she could ring her mum,

Rebecca. Rebecca had been to a strip show before with some

friends, so she might have some good advice on avoiding

being approached and dragged up to take part.

Rebecca picked up quite quickly "Hiya love you alright?"

Josie got straight to the point, as she didn't have much time

before someone else might come into changing room too.

"The entertainment tonight is male strippers, and I don't know

what to do, is it best just to avoid eye contact so that they don't

come near you? You went once didn't you?"

"Yeah" replied Rebecca with a giggle "I sat at the back of the room with my drink to avoid them coming near me".

"Did it work" asked Josie quickly.

"No, the stripper made his way through the tables and came directly over to us. Then he put his willy in my drink, so that was the end of that" said Rebecca "cost me £3.50".

Josie sighed "Ok thanks mum, I'll just keep my drink out the way then!"

Josie went back to the pool area and sat quietly with a magazine, and decided to enjoy the relaxation before the evening commenced. After a very lazy afternoon, everyone made their way back up to their rooms to get ready for the evening which was to start with the meal. The function room downstairs had a very high ceiling with ornate coving and large chandeliers.

Round tables covered in pristine white table clothes were situated opposite a stage and dance floor in the middle, and the tables were already set up with plate settings and glasses.

Karen directed everyone in the group to their tables and took her seat next to Josie. As the meal drew to a close, the lights dimmed and onto the stage came a very glamorous drag artist in a perfectly styled blonde wig and a sparkly red dress looking rather like Jessica Rabbit.

"Hellooooo ladies, are you ready for tonight?? I'm your host for the evening".

A lot of the women started screaming, along with Karen, who was wearing a '40th birthday' sash over her black velvet dress. She stood up and began waving her arms to the music which was playing as one of the dancers entered, wearing a cowboy outfit, followed by a fireman, a builder and a naval officer. The cowboy fetched two chairs and got up and put one leg on each chair before pushing them apart to do the splits.

"Oh my god have you seen their thighs?" yelled Karen over the music.

"It's not their thighs I'm looking at" laughed Dawn, munching on her bread roll as she watched the 'dancers' individually undress to different song tracks to reveal tanned, muscular bodies but with very little rhythm or talent for dance.

"Their dancing is awful" said Josie, not knowing quite what to do as the dancers then proceeded to spread out in different directions in the room. Josie slid down in her chair as the cowboy made his way over to their table and Josie instinctively put her hand over her glass of wine. At £30 a bottle there was no way a penis was going to be dipped in that. Luckily the cowboy spotted Karen in her birthday sash and pulled her up out of her chair to lead her to a chair on the dance floor, where 3 other women were also sat. The men slowly stripped off and gyrated in front of the 4 women before putting body lotion all over themselves, then spun around to reveal to all the diners their full nakedness, dripping in the white lotion and swinging their penis's around.

Josie was quite relieved when the entertainment was finished and Karen came back to the table, with a big smile and covered in dots of white lotion.  It was certainly a 40th birthday that Karen wouldn't forget.  The evening finished off with lots of wine and dancing to a DJ, and as Josie climbed into bed that night in the hotel, she felt quite tired but her mind was still whirring so decided to look at her online messages.

There was a few messages, including one from a 22 year old who appeared to be a student at a nearby university, but had no photo.

*"Hi, you're very beautiful, can I send you a  photo of myself?"* said his message.

Josie didn't normally reply to someone in their 20s, but was tired, drunk and a bit fed up so decided to send a response to put him in his place.

*"You're way too young for me, and no sending weird photos or any other funny business"* she replied.

*"What do you mean by funny business?"* he asked.

*"Sending pictures of your cucumber! None of that"* replied Josie, trying to clarify the situation.

A few seconds went by then Josie noticed a photo appear in the inbox. She clicked on it and up came a photo of something made of pastry in a packet.

*"How about my sausage roll?"* he replied.

Josie laughed and shook her head. Cheeky beggar. Josie then deleted the short message thread. No point in starting something which was clearly not going to go anywhere she reasoned. Josie decided to message Aimii to see how she was, and if she had met Phoneinthebath Garth recently. Aimii was still awake and replied to Josie's message.

*"He is taking the puss"* wrote Aimii *"He stood me up two times now, then says he's sorry but does it again. He's rubbing it on my face. I'm not seeing him again."*

*"Good idea"* replied Josie with a smile, putting down her phone and pulling up the covers before going fast asleep.

# CHAPTER NINE

Josie got back home on the Sunday morning and threw her suitcase on the bed. That could be sorted much later she decided, as she had a hangover from drinking too much wine and had an ongoing thirst from the alcohol. Gone were her younger days of being able to go out and drink into the small hours and then just have a normal day the next day going about normal business. Hangovers in your 40s could last days, or maybe it was just the tiredness of a long night out. Josie looked at her dating app messages to see if there was anything interesting that had come in that didn't involve sausage rolls or cucumbers. There was one message from a guy who seemed ok. Josie clicked on his message and was horrified to read *"Fancy a fuck?"*.

Josie pressed 'report' then block rather quickly. At least he was honest in what he wanted she guessed, but it was still rather disconcerting.

Next message was from a guy who again seemed pretty normal. Josie looked at his profile. He was in his 40s, lived reasonably locally and had dark almost Mediterranean looks. Seemed like he had a job, children etc. Josie shrugged, seems ok she thought, so replied to his message. It was normal, chatty, how are you type messages, nothing too exciting but nothing weird either which was a bonus. He had an unusual name - Than- as he said he was part Greek, which fitted in with his dark looks. Than asked if he could see Josie that day. It was quick but then Josie thought why not? Sometimes too much messaging and texting leading up to date led to more disappointment if it didn't go quite to plan. Josie wasn't a fan of wasting too much of her time so agreed to the date, but not before arranging to go to Jane's for a cuppa first. Maybe it would help calm her nerves.

Josie agreed to meet Than in the same pub by the river where she had met the quantum leap guy Steve. That one obviously hadn't panned out well but maybe this one would. Josie got changed and put a little make up on before driving round to Jane's house, crunching up the familiar gravel drive. Jane opened the door holding a piece of toast with lemon curd on it.

"Hey you! Come in, come in, mind the wellies. And the trainers. Been going to the bloody gym haven't I? Might meet a nice bloke in there you never know".

Josie laughed and followed Jane through to the kitchen where the smell of baking cookies filled the air. Jane gestured to Josie to sit down on the kitchen stool, whilst she took the baking tray out of the oven and put it on a cooling rack.

"Got a text from my ex husband the other day" Jane rolled her eyes in disgust "bloody ex husbands. Giving me his fucking schedule for the next year. And it's no use hoping they die you know, because they never do.  So glad we got divorced, as well as being a tosser, he was crap in bed".

Josie nibbled on a warm cookie "In what way?" she asked hesitantly.

Jane looked up for a moment, trying to find suitable words to describe it "He was just no good at taking hints AND he couldn't multitask either. Couldn't kiss and caress you at the same time. Was like kiss, rub, kiss, rub, do the business. Bit weird really".

"Yeah doesn't sound great" agreed Josie, putting down her unfinished cookie on her white china plate.

"Well I went on a date Josie" declared Jane, changing the subject and finishing off her piece of toast "Bloody awful, what a weirdo".

Josie pulled a face "Oh my god what happened?"

Jane cupped her hand to brush off the baking crumbs from the kitchen worktop and pulled a disgusted face.

"It was on one of those paid sites. He looked ok, reasonable job and all that. Anyway we messaged for a bit and I was joking about us wearing a yellow flower for us to recognise each other, you know like people used to do before the days of the internet?"

Josie nodded as Jane placed another cookie on a plate for her and made the tea.

"So" continued Jane sitting on the stool next to Josie "We decided to meet at the coffee shop, you know the one in the high street? I got there a bit early and needed to get some money out of the cash point".

Josie was hoping that this wasn't another dating story of Jane's about her date having no money and her having to pay for it all. Josie listened intently.

"Anyway" continued Jane taking a bite out of her warm cookie "As I took my money out of the cash machine opposite the coffee shop, I turned around and saw this man waving madly at me. Then I noticed something about him".

"What??" asked Josie, taking a deep breath.

"He was wearing the biggest fucking yellow flower on his jacket that I had ever seen. Where he got it from, fuck knows, it was like a clown's flower, you know like those joke squirty ones?"

Josie screwed up her nose "Oh, so he took you seriously with the flower then. And I guess he'd seen you by that point so no going back".

"Yeah hence the manic waving at me" replied Jane "I thought the flower was a joke but when I went up to him he tried giving it to me!"

"But how was the actual date?" asked Josie, sipping her tea.

"He had a weird lump thing under his tongue" replied Jane "so he was quite hard to understand but to be honest, the massive flower thing already put me off, I mean who does that??"

Josie shook her head "I don't know. So any more dates lined up? I've got one a bit, I'm meeting a guy called Than."

"Oh that's good, but as for me" Jane shook her head and paused to take another cookie off the cooling tray before putting it back again "I can't be bothered. Hey let me show you the plank position I've been doing in the gym, I'm bloody amazing".

Jane laid down on the kitchen floor ready to show off her new found skills. Josie hopped off her stool and got down on the floor with Jane to try and hold a plank position as long as possible. Jane set her phone timer for a minute and both got in the plank position on the floor. Josie felt the strain on her core almost immediately and tried to hold focus as long as possible. After about 30 seconds she looked over at Jane who looked suspiciously comfortable.

"Hey you've got your tummy on the floor" laughed Josie, collapsing on the floor.

"It's my jumper hanging down" laughed Jane getting up quickly "anyway you'd better be off in a minute, for your date with Than the man."

Josie looked at her watch and quickly finished her tea. She had already let Aimii know where she was going and who with, so was all set.

"See you later, I'll message you soon" said Josie walking out to her car. Jane waved her off from inside her porch whilst holding another cookie in her hand.

The pub was quite busy as Josie walked in and she spotted Than straight away. He looked friendly and he gave her a warm smile as she walked over to him.

"Let me buy you a drink, what would you like?" he asked. He was about 5'8 with jet black hair and dark brown eyes and Mediterranean looking complexion like in his photo. He was wearing jeans and a white tshirt with a casual jacket over the top.

Josie stuck to a soft drink as she was driving, then they made their way over to a table which overlooked the river. The conversation was quite normal and whilst Than did look like his picture, he was hairier than she expected him to be.

In one of his profile pictures, he was walking out of the sea in swimming shorts and his tanned skin had looked smooth in the sunlight. Whilst sat in front of him Josie could see lots of curly black hair poking out of the top of his shirt at the back.

*"Maybe he shaves it"* thought Josie, trying hard not to stare.

Than took a sip of his wine and smiled at Josie "Do you like fucking behind trees?".

Josie stopped mid-sip "Excuse me?! What kind of question is that??"

Than immediately stopped smiling and looked at Josie's angry face, realising he had made a huge mistake.

"Sorry sorry" he said, trying to paper over the situation "I was just being flirtatious".

Josie picked up her coat as she felt so uncomfortable "I'm going to leave now, I think it's for the best".

Josie walked out of the pub and left Than at the table finishing his drink. What a short and nightmarish date.

Unfortunately she had remembered giving him her telephone number before they'd met, so she made a mental note to block him to avoid any more contact. Bloody pervert. What was wrong with these people? Josie drove back home and sat on her bed. She wanted to cry. She also wanted a decent kind man who would be fun to be with and not send her weird pictures, didn't seem too much to ask but finding someone like that was proving to be much harder than she'd initially thought.

Josie decided to have a bath and a nap. The weekend had been exhausting for different reasons, so she just wanted to chill out and relax in a hot bath with some bubbles. The hot bath was lovely to sink into and made Josie feel relaxed and tired. When she got out she put on her dressing gown and laid on her bed as her eyes felt heavy, so quickly went to sleep. Josie had been asleep for about half an hour when she heard her phone buzzing which had woken her up. She felt annoyed she hadn't silenced it but picked it up in case it was important.

It was a message from Aimii *"Ring me now babes!"*

Josie rang Aimii who picked up straight away.

"Oh my god babes" shrieked Aimii excitedly "Me and Katie are in the pub and we were talking to some people and there's this really nice man here called Todd. He's single and thinks you are pretty".

"Wait" said Josie suspiciously "How come he thinks I'm pretty when he hasn't even seen me?" Josie sat up, rubbing her eyes, trying to take in what Aimii was trying to tell her.

Aimii let out a little giggle "I showed him your profile pic babe. What do you think?"

Josie felt a very small glimmer of positivity. Maybe she would meet someone in real life and not online after all, and through friends too.

"How do I know what he looks like though?" asked Josie.

Aimii paused before replying "I will send you a picture".

Aimii hung up.

Josie stared at her phone, wondering how on earth Aimii was going to find a photo of Todd to send. Maybe she was going to find one on social media. About 10 minutes later, Josie's phone buzzed with a photo of Todd. Josie opened the picture and looked at it carefully, suddenly realising that Aimii had dragged Todd outside the pub to take a picture of him to send to her. It felt horribly embarrassing. What was even worse was that Josie didn't find Todd in the least bit attractive. He was in his mid forties and had totally white hair which was unstyled and he seemed to have no distinction between his chin and his neck which led her eyes down to a very old 90s looking green polo shirt and cheap looking jeans. Josie's phone rang again. It was Aimii.

"What do you think babe? Do you want a date??"

Josie felt disappointed and angry in equal measure. Todd was far from the man of her dreams, standing in a pub car park, ready to have his photo sent to some random woman who he'd never met.

"I don't fancy him at all!" cried Josie indignantly "What were you thinking?? Would you or Katie go out with him?? No! So why should I??" Josie felt the tears coming down her face.

"Aww come on babe it's not that bad" said Aimii "I'd go on a date with him".

"No you wouldn't!" said Josie feeling quite cross "I'm really not interested".

"Ok" said Aimii sounding disheartened "I will just tell him that you are no longer single babes".

"Yeah good idea" replied Josie, hanging up. Josie's phone buzzed almost immediately and she felt even more annoyed when she realised it was a message from Than, except it wasn't a message, it was a photo. Of his penis.

Josie stared hard at the image that was on her phone screen, and which looked like a two toned brown mushroom, not the most flattering of comparisons.

Before she could press the block button some more photos from Than appeared, only this time it was photos of two bowls of batter mix with the words "*making pancakes with my kids*" followed by a selfie of him shirtless, in front of a hob with a frying pan. How can you go from dick pics to pancake pics with his children, thought Josie. This time she remember to press the block button before anything else popped up in her inbox.

Josie felt a bit relieved to be going back to work the next day to get away from the weekend of unexpected male nakedness being thrust upon her. Why was this online dating so hard?? Everyone said dating should be fun, but it really wasn't, not in Josie's world anyway. It seemed to be full of weirdos and creeps who only wanted one thing and men who initially seemed to be nice then would either not turn up or just ghost you. Not fun at all.

The next day dawned slightly damp and cold and Josie felt a nice sense of normality as she drove to work. As Josie walked into the reception, she saw Sarah the Human Resources Director standing in reception talking to Bridie about setting up the training room. She remembered that Sarah was doing a training session that morning which Mrs Wilshire was also going to be sitting in on. It was a team building exercise which Sarah was officially calling "Building positive relationships" in her powerpoint presentation, but that Sarah had also privately called "How to suffer working with shit people who you don't really care about".

"Morning Josie" chirped Bridie in her forever perky manner "How are you?"

"I'm fine" lied Josie, just ready to get through the working week without any further disasters "What time is the presentation?"

"10 o clock!" replied Bridie "Can you tell Sandy that she needs to be there too please Josie, I think she thinks she doesn't have to go as she said she's already positive, but Sarah says" Bridie paused for a few seconds before continuing "Sarah says she needs to stop swanning about and get her lazy arse out of that office for five minutes."

Bridie went slightly red at repeating Sarah's words but also clearly thought it was funny. Josie thought that Bridie's initial admiration for Sandy was now wearing off, judging by the smirk on Bridie's face.

Josie smiled "Yes I'll tell her, but I might leave out the bit about her lazy arse".

Josie gave Bridie a wink before getting into the lift to make her way towards the chief executive's office straight away before she forgot.

As she rounded the corner she noticed Sandy was stood at the photocopier with Mike from marketing who was getting a good eyeful of Sandy's legs due to the fact that part of Sandy's wrap around skirt had fallen down, revealing part of her underwear for good measure. Sandy seemed oblivious and was chatting and flicking her hair back whilst Mike continued to stare at Sandy's wardrobe malfunction.

"Umm Sandy, your skirt needs doing up properly" said Josie, pointing at the flapping material.

"Oh" giggled Sandy, grabbing the loose part of her skirt and rebuttoning it up "Mike, why did you not tell me my darling?" Mike laughed and walked back to his office with his cup of tea, before Mrs Wilshire caught him loitering again.

"I need to pass on a message" explained Josie to Sandy. Sandy smiled and began walking away whilst gesturing for Josie to follow her. They walked into Sandy's office and Sandy took her usual perch at the edge of her desk.

"So what can I do for you Josie? I'm so busy today and my fella is just so busy he's hardly seen me at all since he came out of prison".

Sandy looked at her long, manicured nails whilst she was talking.

"He knows so many famous people you know, he's selling properties in very desirable locations whilst rescuing these poor defenceless dogs in Eastern Europe with his friends. So brave."

"Sounds.... interesting" said Josie, wanting to ask a lot more questions but wasn't always the best at being subtle.

Sandy nodded in approval "Just so interesting".

"Anyway, Sarah says you need to be at her training session this morning, the Building Positive Relationships thing. 10am it starts and Mrs Wilshire will be there too."

Sandy sighed "I'm not sure why I have to go, Jonathon in Finance says I have very good interpersonal skills".

Josie shrugged "Mrs Wilshire is going to be there and you are her PA".

Sandy smiled "Yes of course, what was I thinking, I need to be there for her. I'll see you at 10".

Josie then made her way to her desk where both Nic and Helen were already at their desks and each were on the phone.

"Good weekend?" mouthed Josie at them both as she hung up her coat and put her bag away.

Nic nodded and carried on her telephone conversation. Helen looked over at Josie from her desk and nodded too, whilst holding the telephone receiver in one hand to continue her phone call whilst at the same time miming a blow job with her spare hand. Some things don't change, thought Josie, sitting at her desk and turning on her computer.

Helen put down the phone "So what time is this 'why can't we all be friends' bollocks that Sarah's doing this morning?

I'll be friends with Jonathon if he gives me half a chance. Or that new fella that Sarah just hired. Hung like a donkey I heard".

Nic ended her phone conversation and just caught the end of Helen's sentence

"Really Helen! Who's hung like a donkey?" asked Nic, not being able to help herself.

"Haha wouldn't you like to know" laughed Helen, getting up to go to the toilet.

Nic smiled and looked at Josie "Such a terrible girl!  How was your weekend away, any good?"

"Well" said Josie, trying to type at the same time "The dancers turned out to be strippers, the sauna had a naked man in it and I got sent a photo of a penis that looked like a mushroom".

"Oh" said Nic, looking slightly startled "Did Helen go with you? Sounds like her kind of trip"

"No" laughed Josie "She can get into enough trouble on her own".

Both woman started laughing, just as Marvin came around the corner to join the conversation.

"Have you heard about Helen's latest troubles.... downstairs?" asked Nic in a semi whisper, looking around to check that no one else was listening in.

Marvin gasped, placing his hand to his chest to try and look dramatic "Oh my god what's happened?"

"Downstairs?" asked Josie, puzzled.

Nic, looked around before Helen came back "You know, *downstairs*" Nic gestured towards her groin area with both hands in a large circular motion.

"Ewww no, why what's happened?" asked Josie.

Nic began speaking in hushed tones "Well a couple of times she's had a bit of a, you know, bleed after having 'relations' recently. One fella came up from her *downstairs* looking like he'd been in a warzone, had it all over his chin apparently. Anyway the doctor said that she's got an erosion".

"A fucking what?" asked Marvin "You mean like a cliff face gets eroded??"

"Yes" said Nic "too many big willies I reckon".

"Lucky bitch" added Marvin, crossing his legs.

Nic looked around again to check again that the coast was clear to carry on talking "Anyway the doctor had to paint it with some special stuff".

"Hope he painted 'fucking keep out' on it" said Marvin, wrinkling up his nose "There's one good reason right there why I stay away from fannies".

As Helen returned to her desk, Marvin smiled over at Helen "You been to the coast lately" he asked and winked over at Josie.

Oblivious to what was being said, Helen laughed nervously "Haha no, but I've just been into the toilet and had an incident".

"Oh jeez" said Nic "What have you done??"

Helen pulled a face "I just went into the ladies, and was sat on the toilet when all of a sudden there was a gruff, manly voice that came from the next stall".

"Was it Jonathon??" asked Nic, with a random suggestion.

Marvin and Josie both looked confused. "Why would Jonathon be in the ladies toilet??" asked Josie.

"Just listen" said Helen "So I was in there and I heard this gruff voice say 'I've run out of toilet paper, can you pass me some please?'"

"Did you pass it under the cubicle?" asked Marvin.

Helen giggled nervously "No I just chucked it over the top and then the same voice said 'ouch that was my head'".

"Wait, not one of those massive toilet rolls that goes inside the dispensers on the wall?" asked Josie.

"Yeah that was all there was" said Helen, shrugging and flicking her curly hair back behind her shoulders.

"Oh well mistakes happen" chirped Nic "Wonder who that was then".

Helen shrugged "I'm not sure, all I could see under the stall were some black shoes and purple trousers".

Marvin gasped "Oh my god, you know who you just hit on the head with a full fucking massive industrial toilet roll??"

Josie and Nic looked at each other then at Marvin.

"You don't mean...?" began Josie hesitantly.

Marvin nodded "Yep.  Mrs. Fucking, Wilshire."

## CHAPTER TEN

Helen giggled as the others looked in horror at what had just occurred in the ladies toilets.

"She won't know it's me" shrugged Helen "Anyway look, it's nearly 10am and we've got to go to this team building thing. Bagsy I partner up with Jonathon!"

"We'll all fight you for that one" pouted Marvin, uncrossing his legs to stand up "Right let's do this nonsense".

Everyone in the department slowly made their way to the conference room which had been set up with tables and chairs, large writing pads and marker pens of different colours.  The coffee machine was full and the tea urn was boiled and ready to go when needed.

Mrs Wilshire and Sarah the Human Resources Director stood at the end of the room whilst staff chatted and got themselves a drink whilst choosing carefully where they were going to sit.

It was hard to know where best to sit in case they wanted volunteers, so Josie sat roughly in the middle near Nic and Marvin, whilst Helen tried to sit next to Jonathon only to find that Sandy had got their first.

"Helen why don't you sit next to Mike?" suggested Sandy, whilst pulling up her chair next to Jonathon.

Helen ignored Sandy and pulled a chair up next to the other side of Jonathon "Am fine here thanks Sandy!" replied Helen smiling.

Sandy gave a false smile in return and averted her gaze towards the two women at the top of the room who were ready to start.

"Right everyone" said Sarah "sorry we're a bit late to start but Mrs Wilshire had an accident and had to receive some first aid this morning, but am happy to say that she's ok".

Marvin caught Helen's eye and pointed towards her and put his finger across his throat before mouthing "you're in trouble!"

Helen rolled her eyes and pulled her chair closer to Jonathon, much to Sandy's continued annoyance.

Sarah continued "So you need to partner up, and everyone should have a large piece of paper and a pen that works hopefully.  There are cards on the desk which give you an object which you don't tell the other person what it is, but describe to them so that they can draw it. No cheating! It's all about thinking about the descriptive language that you are using and your listening skills".

Everyone quickly partnered up, but neither Sandy or Helen were giving in with Jonathon much to everyone in the room's amusement.  Sarah walked over to the three of them, muttering "For fucks' sake" under her breath.

"Ok you can be in a three, no more time to waste, two of you can describe and the other one can draw".

Helen picked up the pen "I'll draw, I'm really good with my hands" she said whilst smiling at Jonathon.

Sandy let out a sigh of exasperation and sat back in her chair, clasping her hands in tight disapproval of the whole situation. Sandy had been waiting on a message from BobbyB who was supposed to be coordinating a dog rescue mission in Romania, so was anxious to know how it had gone, the last thing she wanted was to be fighting over Jonathon for flirting rights with Helen.

Jonathon picked up the card and showed it to Sandy. They object they had been given to describe was 'cannon'. Helen sat with her pen poised above the paper.

"Ready when you are my darling" Helen squeezed Jonathon's knee and gave him wink "should be fun".

"I'll start describing" interjected Sandy "ok, Helen you need to draw a squashed oval shape".

"Is it a big sausage??" asked Helen, whilst drawing.

"No" replied Jonathon "But that's a good guess".

Sandy rolled her eyes "Just keep drawing Helen, this isn't a gameshow. So once you've drawn that, you need to draw two circles either side on the end of it".

Helen paused and looked up at Sandy "Two circles? Are you sure".

"Yes!" replied Sandy "then draw one circle on the other end".

Nic glanced over at Helen's drawing and leaned over to Josie who was trying to draw Marvin's weak description of a traffic light.

"Pssst" said Nic "Why is Helen drawing a penis??"

Marvin leaned over, squinting to get a look "If it is, it's not big enough for her. Anyway Josie have you drawn my rectangle and 3 circles yet??"

Josie also looked over at Helen's increasing risqué looking drawing and pulled a face, what was she thinking??

"Draw something coming out of the circle at the end" declared Jonathon "Like something is shooting out of it with a big explosion!"

"Shhh" said Sandy "you'll give the whole game away. Helen draw a ball coming out the end of it with spark shapes and then you'll be able to see exactly what it is".

Helen finished her drawing and took a careful look at it.

 "It looks familiar ha ha ha" laughed Helen, looking over her phallic drawing which she was secretly actually quite pleased with.

"Pens down everyone!" declared Mrs Wilshire "Let's have a look at everyone's drawings and see how everyone got on".

It was very school-like as Sarah and Mrs Wilshire went around the room, looking at the different drawings compared to the actual object it was meant to represent. When they got to Helen's drawing it was the last one, and everyone was looking forward to leaving the entire experience to get on with their day. Helen grabbed her piece of paper ready to hold it up.

Sandy flicked her hair as she stood up and beamed around the room "Jonathon and I had to describe an object to Helen that, to give you all a clue, was cylindrical, has two wheels to help to manoeuvre it, is made of metal and can be part of an armoury, so am very much hoping that Helen drew a cannon!"

Helen held up the piece of paper to lots of muffled giggles. "Why's she drawn a big dick??" shouted someone at the back. Mrs Wilshire had a look on her face like thunder and everyone felt that somebody was going to die at her hands, and very soon.

Sandy blushed "It's supposed to be a cannon! Don't be so childish".

Sarah held back her laughter "Umm yes ok, I can see that's what it's meant to be. On that note I think we are all done for the day, if everyone can tidy up their tables before they leave that would be most helpful".

Sarah quickly walked out of the room, wiping the tears of laughter from her face as she went down the corridor. Helen quickly folded up the large piece of paper to take with her. "Been a pleasure as usual Jonathon!" she giggled before going out the room.

Sandy grabbed Jonathon's arm "oh gosh I'm so sorry about that Jonathon, she's such a terrible girl. I thought my description was so good and then she goes and does that. It's horrifying".

Sandy looked up at Jonathon who smiled back and gently touched Sandy's arm "Oh it wasn't your fault, I'm sure that Helen meant well, it was an easy mix up I'm sure".

Sandy pursed her red lips "Well perhaps, but she makes things very difficult sometimes with her stories and innuendos I've heard".

"Oh really?" replied Jonathon raising an eyebrow.

"Let's not worry about that" said Sandy, trying to change the subject "It's just been very upsetting, I think I need a sit down".

As everyone went back to the office, Helen took a photo of her drawing before she threw it away "I might use that as my tinder profile pic haha" chuckled Helen, saving the photo in her gallery for later "you got any more dates Josie?"

Josie shook her head "I'll have a look at my dating app now".

Josie clicked on the app and had a look at her inbox "oh actually a really nice looking guy has message me, is local too."

Josie held up her phone and showed Helen and Nic his picture.

"Very nice!" said Nic

"I would" added Helen, eyeing up the black and white profile pic "He is like, really good looking though, almost model-like, do you reckon he's a catfish?"

"What's a catfish" asked Nic whilst typing up a report "Never heard of it".

"It's when people go on the internet and pretend to be someone that they're not" explained Helen eating a mint "it's quite common".

Josie looked at the black and white picture more closely "I don't know, it looks ok to me but what do I know?"

Helen shrugged "Chat to him for a bit, what's his name?"

"Dylan" replied Josie "no harm in chatting I guess".

As Josie was looking at her phone a group message popped up from Aimii *"hey girls, get together at mine Friday night? Miss you all!"*

Even though Josie and her friends lived close, sometimes it was a struggle to get together with their busy lives, but Josie was really looking forward to a chat and replied yes immediately. Jo and Melanie replied quite quickly, leaving only Katie to reply, who was notoriously slow at replying to messages at times.

Josie looked again at Dylan's profile picture which did seem too good to be true, so when she got home she did an image search on the internet but nothing came up. As she was searching, a message from Dylan popped up *"fancy a chat on the phone, this is my number"*.

Josie was bored so she picked up the phone and dialled Dylan's number. He had a much deeper voice than she expected and with a slight Welsh tone.

"Hey" Dylan answered "good to hear from you. How are you doing?"

"I'm ok thanks. That's some nice photos you have on your profile, very professional looking. You look like a model".

Dylan gave a deep laugh "Yeah they look ok don't they. It is me. My sister is a professional photographer so she took them for me, glad you are impressed. You're really beautiful in your photos".

Josie found it hard to accept compliments and blushed "Thank you, that's very kind".

The line went silent for a moment until Dylan spoke again "Do you fancy video chatting? Prove to you I am who I say I am?" Josie wasn't sure but agreed to do a video chat to put her mind at rest. Almost immediately the video call notification lit up on her phone and Josie swiped to answer it. Sat behind a desk on an office chair was Dylan, looking very much like his pictures and was indeed very handsome. He was wearing cycling shorts, with no top on which revealed a muscular torso and was wearing black leather cycling gloves.

"Hardly dressed for the occasion are you" commented Josie. Dylan swung back and forth in his chair slightly and gave a throaty laugh "I've just been cycling obviously, and got a bit hot. You are such a suspicious person!"

"Well I've had my fair share of weirdos contact me I'm afraid" replied Josie screwing up her nose "It's not good".

Dylan shook his head "There are a lot of arseholes out there, but I'm not one of them".

Josie smiled but wasn't quite sure whether to believe him or not. Or maybe she was just too suspicious and should just take things as they come.

"Anyway I've gotta go" said Dylan "I'll give you a call tomorrow if that's ok?".

Josie smiled and agreed "Ok why not".

Dylan smiled back before ending the call. He seemed quite nice, thought Josie, and quite fit and handsome which always helps.

The next day dawned cold and bright, leaving a hard frost on Josie's car. As she turned on the engine to warm up, Josie's phone began ringing. It was Dylan.

"Hey babe how are you?" he asked in his dulcet tones "I've been thinking about you. Why don't you come over to my flat this morning?"

Josie turned down the radio in the car "Excuse me?"

"Come over to my flat" repeated Dylan "I've got a doctor's appointment at 11 but am free before that".

"I can't, I've got to go to work" said Josie turning up the windscreen blower "Anyway I don't know you do I. Doesn't sound sensible".

Dylan laughed "I'm hardly likely to do anything untoward am I? Just thought it would be nice to meet up".

"Yes for a coffee or something" said Josie indignantly "not your flat".

"I've got coffee here, it'll be fine" replied Dylan "or we could meet in a nearby park and come back to mine".

Josie sighed. It hadn't taken Dylan long to show his true colours, and she should of realised when he appeared shirtless when video chatting he had more on his mind than getting to know her.

"No really, I have work today and it doesn't sound like a good idea anyway" insisted Josie.

"Ok, your choice" said Dylan. The phone went dead and Josie felt disappointed yet again. Where were the normal, decent men who actually wanted relationships rather than a quick shag?? Nowhere to be found. Josie had discovered that one of Jane's friends was on a paid site and was currently dating three men. Three men!! And actually dating them. Josie and Jane had both agreed that that was exceptionally greedy, especially as the 'friend' had declined to even divulge which site it was from.

Josie drove to work and as she pulled up, her phone went off again but this time it was a message from Aimii.

*"I found a new dating site, you need to try it! It seems good fun and am getting lots of messages".*

That didn't surprise Josie at all. Aimii was very beautiful and attracted many a man's attention without even trying, whereas Josie felt she had to try that little bit harder with what she felt was mediocre looks.  Josie took a mental note to sign up for it later and walked into work to be greeted by the ever cheerful Bridie.

"Good morning Josie, how are you?" asked Bridie.

Josie gave a weak smile and shrugged "I'm ok, hope you are too".

Bridie nodded enthusiastically, making her headset wobble slightly as she continued to answer calls on reception.

Helen was already sat at her desk when Josie arrived, seeming keen to divulge something to Josie as quickly as possible.

"You'll never guess what??" whispered Helen, flicking back her curly back hair "I reckon Sandy and Jonathon are doing it!"

Helen's eyes widened as she spoke, her long false eye lashes fluttering in excitement of the latest gossip.

Helen paused to reach for a nearby jaffa cake, even though it was only 8am in the morning, she always had room for snacks.

Whenever there was a birthday in the office, Helen was always the first to reach for a slice of cake in the kitchen and was usually the one to eat the last piece.

Slimming clubs had been her life for the past ten years, but nothing stopped getting in the way of a good piece of cake. Helen bit into the jaffa cake, not pausing for a breath.

"She was seen with a man in the pub last night, and it sounded like Jonathon. Get on her social media Josie! It's bound to be on there somewhere".

Josie was on Sandy's social media but it wasn't something that she particularly broadcast to everyone. Josie was also on Helen's social media which had turned out to be a bit of minefield as she was constantly tagging Josie and others into pictures of willy shaped soap, slippers, vegetables, decorated cupcakes, it was never ending. Josie had somehow managed to put her settings so that tagged pictures didn't automatically show up to her own friends which had been a relief after the latest tag had involved a video of a penis shaped soap dispenser that you had to rub up and down to get the soap out.

Josie opened her social media and clicked on Sandy's name. No photo but there was a post that had tagged her in a nearby wine bar with someone else.  Helen gasped, spitting out crumbs of her cake as she did so.  She flapped her hand at the screen.

"Click on the tag, quick Josie".

Josie rolled her eyes and sighed.  She clicked and they saw the name BobbyB.  It wasn't Jonathon after all, it was her 'boyfriend'.

At this point Marvin walked up behind the two women and clapped his hands, making them both jump, including Helen who stood up and spun around to see who it was.

"For fucks sake Marv, I nearly had heart failure" said Helen sitting back down next to Josie.

Marvin squinted at the screen "who are you two darlings spying on then?"

"Sandy" replied Josie, much to Helen's annoyance "Helen thinks she was out with Jonathon last night so we're just having a look".

Jonathon looked at the screen "Isn't that the fella who was recently sewing mail bags at Her Majesty's pleasure?"

Josie and Helen both looked at Marvin quizzically.

"I thought he was some sort of rescuer" said Josie.

"A puppy rescuer" laughed Helen.

"I meant he's been in a prison you pair of spanners" laughed Marvin, shaking his head and sitting down to join them "So what have you found out then?" Marvin sat on the edge of the desk and crossed his legs, his hands grasped around his knee.

Josie clicked on the BobbyB name to go onto his social media page. The post that Sandy had put on didn't appear on his own page at all. She then clicked on his profile picture to show them what it was that Sandy was attracted to.

"Medallion man with old lady glasses" commented Marvin

"How hideous is he?? Bet even you wouldn't have a go Helen".

"Oi!" replied Helen, though quite realising it was the truth.

 Josie scrolled further down the profile to see statuses about properties in Sandbanks, daring animal rescues in the UK and abroad and a couple of statuses about famous people who he claimed to have known.

"Have a look at that status about George Michael" laughed Marvin.  Josie and Helen read down the page.

*It was on this day in 1986 that I first met George Michael.  It was in a restaurant in London and neither of our dates had shown up so he asked me to join him.  We both had his favourite Greek salad and it was something I'll never forget".*

"Bloody liar" said Marvin "like George Michael, the most private person ever, would of invited that criminal to join him for lunch. Neither of their dates turned up?? Yeah ok ha ha".

Helen stood up and pulled her short flowery skirt back down over her leggings in an unladylike fashion.

"Ok so it's wasn't Jonathon but I still reckon something will happen" said Helen walking back to her own desk. Josie's phone suddenly pinged.  It was a message from Dylan.  Or it was  a video to be more precise. Josie debated whether to click on it just as Nic walked in.

"Morning, you ok everyone?"  asked Nic taking off her coat and hanging it on the back of her chair.  Nic had very expensive, boutique type clothes yet always paired her outfits with plastic type jewellery.

"I've got a video from a guy who asked me round his flat this morning" said Josie, clasping her phone in her hand "Wonder what that's about?".

Helen got back up from her desk and stood next to Josie, followed by Marvin then Nic.

"It's probably just a funny video, open it" encouraged Marvin.

Josie clicked on the video. The camera panned around what looked like a small bedroom. The end of the bed could be seen, along with a couple of clothes airers which were full of washing that was untidily hung all over them.

"What on earth is he sending you a video of his laundry for?" asked Nic in disgust.

"Wait look" gasped Marvin, pointing at Josie's phone screen which was continuing to play the video.

The camera was now clearly pointing down at Dylan's crotch, which revealed his cock held in his hand which was moving up and down to stimulate it.

"Ewww!" shrieked Nic, cupping her mouth with her hand. She had only seen her husband's penis in the last few decades, and had definitely not been prepared to see this.

"Pause it!" shouted Helen, stumbling over slightly in the excitement "How big is it??"

"Fucking hell, can you send me that?" exclaimed Marvin, not quite believing his eyes.

Josie just froze and continued to watch the video in horror. Within about 5 seconds, the penis had shrunk back down to a much smaller size. Helen's stumble had made the video go out of sight for her so she had missed the ending.

"Did he do it in the sink??" asked Helen, trying to lean over to get a better look.

"What are you talking about Helen?" said Nic, in absolute horror "That was disgusting. And what sink??".

"Whenever I get videos they usually do it in the sink" she shrugged, clearly being experienced in these matters. Helen walked back to her desk yet again and logged in to the system "That's my excitement for the day haha!"

"It was disgusting" agreed Marvin "It couldn't stay up for 10 seconds, and no one wants that, let alone a sad video of the shrinkage!"

Josie shut her phone down just as Sandy walked around the corner. She appeared particularly bright and breezy, wearing a black polo necked dress with bat winged sleeves, dark tights and exceptionally high heels.  The dress would of been nice had it of been a bit longer, but as it was, it barely covered Sandy's bottom, but that was mostly how she liked to wear her skirts and dresses.  She flicked her blonde and pursed her lips which today were coated in shiny pillar box red lipstick.

"You'll never guess my news" said Sandy to no one in particular "I'm in charge of organising a ball!"

"It's not even Christmas yet" said Nic, playing with her plastic necklace.

"I know" said Sandy curtly "I'm doing it on behalf of my friend BobbyB.  He wants to raise money for charity by doing a ball and auctioning off pieces of jewellery that he's made himself.  Me and his other friend Maureen are dealing with the bookings and the tickets".

"Why is he not organising it himself?" asked Marvin equally curtly.

Sandy glared at Marvin who simply glared back.

"Because of his recent troubles, he can't be involved in charity things himself" said Sandy tapping her newly manicured fingers on top of the nearby filing cabinet. Marvin flicked his fringe to the side and put his hands in the pockets of his straight, skinny trousers and shrugged "Prison you mean darling? Anyway I must go and do some work. Ciao".

Marvin sauntered down the corridor in his tight trousers, whilst receiving admiring looks from Colin in computing. Sandy's heavily made up eyes widened in annoyance "How very rude, he's innocent you know and now he's just trying to raise money for those poor homeless people".

Josie looked up from her computer. Sandy was leaning with her elbows on the top of the filing cabinet, her head in her hands in a rather dramatic fashion.

"Err you ok Sandy?" ventured Josie whilst still typing. She felt she should be polite and show some interest in Sandy's drama "I thought he liked helping animals".

Sandy looked up and put her fingers through her slightly dishevelled hair "He helps everyone, animals, homeless people. His team even have a van where they dish out food to homeless people each week".

"Where does he get the money for all this?" asked Josie.

Sandy shrugged "Donations I think. He has all his money wrapped up in property so has asked me to loan him some until he sells one of them".

Josie and Nic glanced at each other, and raised their eyebrows in unison, clearly thinking the same thing. That this pretend ageing rock star of a man was unlikely to have honourable intentions.

## CHAPTER ELEVEN

Josie loved her evenings in with her girly friends and that evening was no different. They had all met around Aimii's flat, the pizza was already cooking in the oven and two bottles of prosecco were cooling in the fridge.

Jo reached out her heavily tattooed arm and took a puff on her vape "Are we staying in tonight or did you want to venture out later?"

Aimii shook her head whilst leaning down and checking on the pizzas in the oven "I have no money until pay day babes".

Mel laughed and pointed to her hair and clothing. She had literally got out the bath and towel dried her hair before putting on her pjs and slipper boots before coming round to Aimii's "Not sure I'm suitably dressed to go out out!"

"Ha ha I never noticed what you were wearing Mel. Yeah no money is crap" agreed Jo "I can read cards tonight if anyone fancies it?"

Everyone shook their head.  None of them had had a particular successful week,  Katie had fallen out with someone at her work, Mel had met a soldier who turned out to be married and Aimii was receiving weird messages from Phoneinthebath Garth.

"So what's this new website or app that you've just joined?" asked Josie.

Aimii picked up her phone and pointed it towards Josie to show her "It's called Iloveyoo2.  Have a look at mine".

Josie took Aimii's phone and scrolled through the profiles.  It was a very odd set up as you could see lots of comments that men had made against ladies' profile pictures.  Usually on the main sites you could just see the male profiles if you were a straight woman.

Josie scrolled down until she saw a man had put a comment under a woman's photo.  He'd simply put *"You look nice"*.

The thumbnail picture showed a woman sat in a leather arm chair in lingerie, with one of her legs draped over one of the chair arms to reveal that she was wearing no pants at all.

"Umm Aimii" said Josie "Are you sure what this site is?? What kind of messages have you been getting?"

"A bit sexual actually" replied Aimii, placing the pizza onto large plates "Like, do you want to come right over and that, no proper chatting".

"Well" said Josie dramatically, holding out the phone for everyone to see "I'm not surprised if the women have pictures like this on!".

Katie leaned in to get a closer look "Oh my god, it's a good job that chair's leather! And someone must of taken that picture of her, either that or it's on a timer.  Let's hope for the latter eh??".

Jo and Mel hurried over to also have a look "Give me that phone" said Jo "oh my god I can see her fanjita".

"Oh my god what is on my phone" cried Aimii, hurrying over to grab it "What have you clicked on??"

"It's that site you told me to go on" said Josie "We can see someone's fanjita on it for everyone to see".

"And gnarly looking Bob from Bristol thinks she looks 'nice'! Bet he does" added Katie.

Josie searched the site name on the internet and it came up with a review that said *"great hook up app for casual meet ups"*.

Josie showed the review to Aimii "I think you need to come off there, love! It's a hook up site".

Aimii laughed, looking slightly embarrassed "Well that's one I won't be using again! No wonder they were all straight to the point!"

Jo poured everyone a glass of wine as they sat down on Aimii's comfy corner sofa. As they started drinking, they could hear a thudding noise on the wall outside the flats. Local children regularly came to play football on the concrete slabs in communal area outside near the car park, but unfortunately it also involved them kicking the ball against the wall of the flats which made horrible reverberations inside.

"Bloody kids" said Jo scowling "I told them the other day not to do it. I'm gonna shout at them to stop".

"Don't bother" said Mel, curling up her legs on the sofa "They are little ratbags who just swear at you if you say anything. Even called the police the other week and they did nothing, so what's the point".

As Mel finished her sentence, the banging got louder. Jo stood up looking cross, and went to the living room window and opened it.

"Oi, stop that bloody banging, it's giving us a headache" yelled Jo at the boys playing football outside.

There were three boys stood outside who looked about 14. They stopped kicking the ball and one of them put their foot on top of the football to stop it rolling away before they spoke. He had spiky gelled hair, extensive acne and a skinny body which his tracksuit didn't cling to at all.

"Who's gonna stop us??" he shouted towards Jo, pointed and laughing.  The other two boys laughed and began gesticulating towards Jo in a rude fashion "Yeah who's gonna stop us??".

"Right that's it" said Jo opening the window a bit wider "I'm coming out to get your ball!"

The boys looked in shock as Jo cocked her leg up to get it through the window and began to pull herself through it "And I'm coming to get you!"

"Haha you paedo" yelled one of the boys.

By this point Jo was completely through the window "I think you mean psycho!!" she yelled as she ran towards them in her slippers.

"Fuck, Jo's lost it" said Aimii drinking her prosecco looking out the window and seeing Jo disappearing down the alleyway, but not seemingly overly concerned.

"Do you think we should help her?" asked Josie, not knowing quite what to do.

Katie laughed "This is Jo you are talking about. She once hit a fella who cheated on her, so I think she can handle a couple of skinny teenagers. If she's not back in 5 minutes we could call the police I suppose".

Within minutes Jo had returned, but this time through the front door and not the window. She was a bit out of breath and was walking slightly bent over and had her hand on her back, the other arm was holding a football.

"I've hurt me back" said Jo "On the plus side I've got their fucking football, and it's a good one!"

Jo massaged herself in the small of her back to help ease the pain "Last time I hurt this much was when I did that bloody good cartwheel but I landed funny".

Aimii nodded in approval whilst exhaling smoke from her vape "Oh my god babes, yeah, that cartwheel was amazing".

"Didn't help that I had to get my legs so wide apart to get out your window just now" said Jo trying to stretch herself out.

"Her legs haven't been that far apart in years" joked Josie. Jo laughed, she was forever hurting herself one way or another, everyone always said she should cover herself in bubble wrap.

"So dating" said Josie, picking up her glass of wine "Where's everyone at?  You heard from Phoneinthebath Garth lately?"

Aimii scowled whilst straightening her perfect fringe.  She really wasn't one to suffer fools gladly and Garth had managed to push her further than she would normally let a man push  his luck.

"You know I said he was sending me weird messages?  Well I told him he was taking the puss and I wasn't going to see him again and he didn't really take it that well."

The girls all looked at each other.  They all knew that there were plenty of oddballs online but it was different to of met one in person and then have to deal with it. Especially if they knew where you lived, and Garth did know where Aimii lived as he had picked her up the one time for a date.

"What's he been doing then?" asked Jo, looking concerned.

Jo was always protective of Aimii and would look  anyway she could.  It was a long standing joke that she  referred to Aimii as 'wifey' as Jo was always doing stuff like  fixing her car, her vape or indeed anything else that she had  broken.

Aimii picked up her phone to look up the messages  Phoneinthebath Garth had been sending her and read out his  last message......

*"Hi Aimii, I'm just so disappointed that you don't want to meet up  again, but I want you to know that I will do anything for you to  change your mind.  I really like you so much. You can run me over  in your car and kick me in the balls for free.  I will wear a bow tie  and sing a song from Frozen, naked, outside your window until you  decide to see me again"*.

Aimii looked up from her phone to see a row of confused and  horrified looks on her friends' faces.  No one knew quite what  to make of that message, or even if it was a joke.

...'or free??" said Katie "Does he usually

after her

...id Josie, finishing her glass of

...g it on the wooden coffee table "He better

not turn up here, bloody weirdo!"

"If he does" added Jo "I'm going to be kicking some balls and it

won't be a fucking football either! If he turns up I'll be out of

the window even quicker this time to sort him out!"

Aimii laughed nervously and placed her phone on the table

"I'm sure he won't turn up but he is very odd, wish I'd never

been out with him in the first place especially when he let me

down so much".

Josie shrugged "Hindsight is a wonderful thing!  Anyway I've

had a weirdo called Dylan message me. Well sent me a video

actually" Josie screwed up her nose at the recent memory of it.

"I was talking to someone called Dylan" chipped in Jo "Was he

a nice looking chap? Let's see".

Josie found Dylan's profile picture and showed it to Jo "Yeah that's him. He never sent me a video though. What did he send you?"

Josie brought the video up on her phone and passed it over to the other girls, and they watched the video panning over the room before focusing on the erect penis, just like when she had shown the others in her office.

Mel nearly spit out her wine "Fucking hell, you could of warned me" she laughed, grabbing a tissue to mop her cleavage "What the fuck is that, it looks like a pointy rocket and it shrivels, why on earth did he send you that?"

Josie shrugged. It didn't really take much to get a dick pic from these online dating sites. Sometimes there was barely time to exchange numbers before photos were being sent of their 'members'. Maybe men thought that was attractive and women would fall at their feet. The truth was, it was a massive turn off to be sent an unsolicited dick pic from someone you didn't even know, but that didn't seem to ever stop them from doing it.  But now dick videos seemed to be more the thing, so you could 'see it in motion' as it were. Still not great.

"How's things with you Katie?" asked Josie "you been up to much?"

Katie smiled "Yeah there's only one bloke I've spoken to online and he was the first one I started messaging actually.  He's broken his leg and is at home all day so has plenty of time to message me haha!"

Josie was pleased that at least one of them seemed to be talking to someone decent.  Everyone said that dating should be fun.  Except it was turning out not to be so, at least not for Josie.  Too often men seemed to be after just one thing or were just very weird and sometimes very hard to get rid of.  The ones that she did like either ghosted her or just didn't respond, but she had only ever made the first move of messaging first twice and as that hadn't gone well, Josie decided to stick to her original idea that men should make the first move.

"I'll tell you what you need Josie" said Jo, reaching inside her bra.

Josie looked up at Jo "Jeez I know I'm having no luck with men but I don't want to resort to your boobs quite yet".

Jo laughed "Nah! I'm not talking about my boobs, this is where I keep my crystals. I cleanse it regularly but keep it close to me so that it works better".

"Cleanse? What with soap?" asked Mel, peering over at the crystal.

"No! You cleanse them by either running them under clean water or put in sunlight. Different crystals do different things, you should all try it" explained Jo, popping the crystal back inside her bra and tapping it "They can help with allsorts. Rose crystal is the best for love".

The others looked doubtful but took a mental note just in case they wanted to try it one day. Josie looked down at her phone and noticed a message from a guy who lived about an hour away.  His name was Devon.   He seemed quite normal (as they usually did at first glance), had cats, had a job, not too far away.  Josie wasn't quite sure if she fancied him though.  Josie brought up his profile picture and showed it to Aimii.  Aimii was always the first one she asked, as she was quite honest and upfront if asked for her opinion.

"What do you think of him?" asked Josie, raising her eyebrows.

"Let's have a look babes" Aimii took Josie's phone and had a closer look "Yeah seems ok, do you like him".

Josie shrugged.  She didn't seem to have much luck in the dating world and was always trying to over analyse whether or not someone could be a suitable mate.... did they live close enough, were they the right age, did she fancy them, did they like similar things?  She felt all these things were important but maybe she should just meet up and see if they got on rather than over think everything.  Josie replied to his simple

"*Hi how are you*" message with a "*am good thanks, spending an evening with my friends*".

He seemed ok. Not lecherous, quite decent, maybe not overly fanciable but Josie wasn't sure how much that mattered.

"How important do you think it is, to fancy a guy that you want to date?" asked Josie, looking round at the others on the sofa. Mel was the first to chip in.

"I don't think it's too important, more important that they are nice I think". Mel had never really been into men's looks, she was more a personality type of person, though she did seem to prefer men in the forces from time to time.

"I disagree" said Katie "I think there needs to be some level of attraction otherwise what's the point? May as well just be friends".

"There is a test" said Aimii "Can you imagine kissing them?"

"Or shagging them" added Jo, taking off her jumper over her head as she was still way too warm after chasing the lads outside.

Josie looked again at Devon's profile picture. He had blonde, slightly curly hair, with a small mouth but quite sparkly eyes. She didn't know quite whether or not she fancied him but decided if the conversation was decent then she would probably meet up with him, to see if there was any of that elusive chemistry that everyone talked about.

As the evening wore on, the women chatted and a laughed whilst Josie also carried on messaging Devon who seemed to have quite a good sense of humour. Aimii's flat was always warm and cosy, it had a nice lived in feel and the living room was lit with star shaped fairy lights around the door to the kitchen, and well placed lamps around the room. Aimii was always a great hostess and that evening was no different, because as well as pizza Aimii kept the drinks flowing including hot tea for anyone who wanted one. Aimii topped up Josie's drink.

"I think you should meet Devon, he seems ok?" said Aimii "You never know you might really like him".

The others agreed that Josie should meet up with him and to see how things go, and by the end of the evening Josie had set a firm date with Devon, agreeing to meet in the main car park near the centre of town. Not very romantic but quite practical and in a public place.

Josie gave Devon her phone number, which as well as being the obvious next step, was also a test to see if any dodgy pictures came her way, as often when guys had your number that's when they started misbehaving. The conversations with Devon stayed pleasantly polite and quite funny, and Josie ended up quite looking forward to her date with him.

# CHAPTER TWELVE

The day of Josie's date with Devon dawned quite bright but cold, and when she started her car that morning she noticed that one of her headlight bulbs wasn't working. She tapped the headlight firmly with an open palm in the vain hope that it would make it come on, but to no avail. Josie had a mechanic who was very good at coming out to pick up her car for servicing or MOT etc but felt it might be pushing it to ask him to fix just one bulb. Problem is she had no idea to fix it herself. As Josie was stood looking at her car, her phone pinged. It was Devon.

*"Morning! Hope you are well, am really looking forward to seeing you later".*

Josie smiled at the thoughtful message *"I'm good thanks"* she replied *"Just a bit annoyed that one of my car headlights isn't working".*

*"I can get a bulb and fix that for you"* replied Devon *"What kind of car is it? I'll pick one up before I come over".*

Aww how lovely, thought Josie, would save such a hassle "It's a Micra" she replied.

"Not a problem" replied Devon "I'll fix it when I meet you later".

Josie thanked Devon then made her way into work, feeling much more bright and cheerful. As she walked into the reception area she saw Sandy stood talking to Bridie the receptionist.

"You really need to buy a special ticket to the ball Bridie" Sandy was explaining "If you buy a special ticket, you'll go into the raffle for an extra special piece of jewellery, it'll be £250 and an amazing experience".

Sandy looked up as she noticed Josie walk in "Morning Josie, did you want ticket to the ball? Maybe not the £250 one, but surely you could afford £50 darling for you and extra tickets each of those interesting friends of yours? Maybe you could treat them, it will be such a fun night and BobbyB will be there".

No one cared about BobbyB except Sandy, who seemed to have put him on this pedestal and could do no wrong in her eyes. Josie raised her eyebrows and looked back at Sandy, wondering why on earth Sandy thought she could afford something like that. Sandy always clearly had spare money and never could quite understand when people said they couldn't afford something. Sandy always said she earned a meagre salary, yet went abroad on holiday at least twice a year, wore designer clothes and also managed to afford fake tans and gym memberships. Sandy's idea of being 'broke' was not being able to afford a £300 designer handbag that month. Her latest ruse was to go on to a fund raising website to ask for help to pay for hypnotherapy to help her stop 'overeating', with a price tag of £600.

"No it's ok thanks" replied Josie, walking past the reception desk "I'll pass this time. Maybe you could ask Jonathon?"

Sandy pursed her red lips and shook back her hair "Yes I will darling! Shame you can't come, just look at this jewellery people could win".

Sandy held up her phone which was held in a sequin encrusted case. Sandy never did anything subtly. She showed both Josie and Bridie pictures of what looked like stock photos of very expensive looking jewellery on BobbyB's facebook page. The stones were large and gawdy looking and BobbyB was claiming they were worth thousands of pounds and he was going to make and donate them - the photos were purely for reference. Judging by the comments underneath the photos, BobbyB had quite a following of ladies who also seemed quite taken with his ageing has been rock star looks. The phone lines began lighting up and ringing rather insistently on Bridie's desk, so she readjusted her headset and motioned to Sandy that she ought to get on and do some work.

Sandy patted Bride on the shoulder and then beckoned Josie towards the lift.

"Come this way darling, so much easier than those awful stairs. I used to go the gym every day and spend so many hours in there it was like a part time job. No time at all for that these days, as I'm sure you can tell".

Sandy grabbed about half an inch of 'fat' around her midriff as if to emphasise this, then used her well manicured hands to straighten down her mini skirt and smiled at Josie, showing the crows feet around her eyes which she so much hated. It was one of the reasons she posted an awful lot of older photos on social media, or pictures of just her legs. That reason, and the fact that she simply liked a lot of compliments on a weekly basis and did indeed seem to have a lot of online admirers, albeit older lonely looking men.

As the lift doors shut, Sandy admired her reflection in the mirrors situated above waist height and sighed.

"Oh Josie look at me, who is going to love a woman such as me?" exclaimed Sandy.

Josie kept quiet as she presumed it was a rhetorical question, and besides which she had no idea how to answer. Sandy ignored the silence as the lift slowly crawled it's way to the upper floor. As the doors opened and Josie went to walk to her office, Sandy grabbed Josie's arm.

"Come with me, I want to show you something!" whispered Sandy.

"I have work to do?" replied Josie, pulling a face and not particularly wanting to listen to Sandy's latest woes.

"Oh it won't take a minute" said Sandy, hurrying ahead "come into my office".

Josie dutifully followed as Sandy turned her computer around to show Josie the most beautiful orange glowing sunset from a golden sandy beach.

"Look, Greece! It's where I'm off to very soon, isn't it gorgeous??" Sandy gazed at the screen "I want to live there one day and walk on the beach every morning!"

"Very nice" agreed Josie, having not been on a plane since her original honeymoon which was over 15 years ago "Now I really must go..".

Josie walked out of the office whilst Sandy rested her chin on one hand and continued looking dreamily at the screen and thinking of her very own paradise.

Josie walked round to her own desk and hung up her coat on the nearby coat hooks before sitting at her desk.  She caught sight of her own reflection in her computer screen which was still turned off.  Josie's long blonde hair rested on her shoulders and her green eyes stared at the reflection of a woman in her 40s who was worried that her moments in life may of passed her by.  Josie jumped as someone suddenly tapped on her desk to grab her attention.  It was Helen.

"Mornin' gorgeous" said Helen with a wink "How's things? Got any dates lined up?"

Josie nodded "Yeah I have actually. Bit younger than me, only by about 7 years. Am seeing him tonight".

"Oooh get you" replied Helen, swishing back her black hair, revealing her choice of blue sparkly eyeshadow for the day "Where are you meeting him?"

"What's this?" asked Nic, interrupting the conversation "you got a date Josie? How exciting!"

Josie shrugged. Those in relationships always seemed to think that dates were exciting but the truth was that Josie would much rather be settled down with just one person, rather than trawling through what seemed like endless profiles and dates with what turned out to be unsuitable men.

"Yes" sighed Josie "He seems ok, am meeting him down town later".

Nic smiled and nodded "Hope it goes well then".

Josie smiled back and got on with her work. This day was going to be a long one she thought.

As the end of the day eventually came, Josie logged out of her computer and checked her phone. Devon still hadn't pulled out of the date so Josie decided to make her way straight home so that she had enough time to get ready. Deciding what to wear on dates was always a challenge. You never wanted to look too dressed up in case they got the wrong idea, but being too casual brought the risk of looking like not having put in any effort. Josie decided on a green dress with capped sleeves and stopped just short of the knee. Not mini skirt like Sandy but not too frumpy looking either thought Josie as she looked back at herself in the bedroom mirror. She took a deep breath as she drove towards the car park where they had agreed to meet. Josie texted Aimii for some moral support and Aimii texted straight back.

*"OMG it's exciting babes, he will soon be there! Have a lot of fun and message me when you get back".*

Josie quickly put a thumbs up reply before noticing a very large white van circling the car park before taking parking up and taking two car parking spaces because the van was so long. Josie saw a blonde, curly haired, stocky man jump out of the van. He was wearing trousers and a checked shirt. Josie felt slightly overdressed, but got out of her car and straightened her hair. Devon noticed her and walked straight over.

"Hi there! Sorry about the works van, but my car is broken, let's fix your headlight shall we?" Devon smiled, looking Josie right in the eyes, and grinned a bit more. He was true to his picture but Josie still didn't know if she found him attractive or not. Devon had a very friendly manner and seemed very sweet, which were two good qualities to have, Josie decided. Josie followed Devon to his van as he removed some packets of sweets from his dashboard in order to reach the headlight bulb.

"Do you like jellybabies?" he asked, grabbing a packet "I got given loads, have a packet, I have such sweet tooth it's not good for me" Devon rubbed his slightly padded midriff as if to emphasise the side effects of too many sweets.

"I'm good thanks" replied Josie "How much do I owe you for the bulb?"

Devon shook his head whilst pushing up the sleeves of his shirt "Oh don't worry about that, anything for a lovely lady such as yourself. Consider it a gift".

Josie smiled and mouthed 'thank you' whilst Devon worked out how to pop the bonnet of Josie's car. Josie continued to look at Devon whilst he manoeuvred his hand into the small opening to reach the light fitting. In a matter of minutes it was all done.

"Right as rain" smiled Devon "Now let's go and get a drink".

They walked through town and Josie decided on a pub where she hadn't been into for a date before. She hadn't been on many dates but was always a bit paranoid about going into the same pub more than once in case the dates were as disastrous as her first one.

The pub had lots of oak beams and lots of nooks and crannies in which to sit and have a conversation uninterrupted.  Devon made his way to the bar and got Josie a soft drink whilst getting himself a cider.  They made their way over to a small table in a corner of the pub and began talking, where Devon turned out to be quite funny.  He was very gentlemanly and had no qualms about buying more than one drink or opening doors and being exceptionally polite.  Josie just wished that she found him more attractive as he had a very slightly effeminate quality about him which didn't appeal to her, but the conversation was very easy and he wasn't at all creepy which was always a bonus!

"So what is it you do for a living?" asked Josie "You have a very large van".

Devon took a sip of his cider and smiled "I only work 4 hours a day but I work selling my own pizzas in my town's market place. I set up about 11.30am and then go home around 3.30pm. Earns me more than enough to live on so can't complain. The van is so big because it has a mobile pizza oven in it and all my catering stuff. I love to cook, I'll have to cook you a meal".

Josie smiled. It was always a good sign when a man mentioned something he thought they might do together as it was a clearly indication that he wanted to see you again.

"Yes that would be lovely" said Josie, stirring around her ice cubes with her straw.

Devon continued to make her laugh and smile and by the end of the date, Josie was feeling slightly more comfortable. Devon didn't attempt to kiss her properly but instead planted a polite peck on her cheek.

"So lovely to meet you" smiled Devon "Hope your car light lasts on the way home haha! Can I see you again?"

It was so nice for a man to be straightforward and polite at the end of the date that Josie agreed straight away.

"Yes that would be lovely" Josie smiled. And Devon smiled straight back.

Josie drove home with both headlights working well and was pleased that she had met a normal, polite man for once. As she parked up outside the flat, Josie decided to pop into Aimii's flat to let her know what had happened and that she was back safely. Aimii opened the door sucking furiously on her vape.

"Oh my god, you will never guess what happened to me??" said Aimii, puffing out a cloud of vape "fucking Garth messaged me saying he's coming over! I mean what the fuck? I told him no but now I'm scared he will show up babes. Fucking weirdo". Aimii always swore a lot when she was mad, and this was definitely one of those times.

Josie walked into the flat and put down her bag and took off her shoes.

"I doubt he will" said Josie opening Aimii's fridge "Is it ok if I have a wine?  I had to drink a soft drink tonight as was driving".

"Oh yeah your date, how did it go?" asked Aimii grabbing two glasses "was it ok?"

Josie poured two glasses of wine and sat down on the sofa "yeah it was ok actually.  He fixed my headlight, bought me a drink, was funny.  Even wants to see me again, wonders will never cease haha!"

"Oh that's so good, maybe he is the one??" said Aimii hopefully.  Josie thought this might be a bit ambitious to think from one date but it was nice to have such positivity and someone who wanted you to have nice things.

"I don't know" said Josie "but he was very polite and funny and he fixed my car".

Aimii nodded in approval "sounds good babes.  Did I tell you about my weird date the other day??"

Josie shook her head "What do you mean weird?"

Aimii straighted her fringe and took another puff from her vape "Well" she began "He seemed ok, and we met for a date but then he started talking about weird kinds of stuff".

Josie scowled "Like what?"

"We were sat having a drink right, and then he looks at me and says "*I really like girls from Thailand*" and I thought that was rude for a start".

"Well it is considering you're Japanese babe" laughed Josie.

"Exactly" said Aimii indignantly "Anyway he says on his last holiday that there was a Thai girl who worked in the golf shop and he paid her to have sex with him. I mean what the actual fuck??"

Josie looked horrified "Why did he tell you that?? Bloody weirdo".

"Pervert more like" replied Aimii sipping on her wine "He was disgusting, so I left. But your date sounds really good".

"Was ok" agreed Josie as they both continued to drink their wine. Suddenly Aimii stopped what she was doing and gestured Josie to be quiet.

"What?" whispered Josie "What's the matter?"

Aimii turned her head round in order to listen out for what she heard was a noise.

"Josie, can you hear some singing outside?"

Aimii and Josie looked at each other then ran to the window to see where the singing was coming from. Phoneinthebath Garth had been true to his word in that he would turn up that evening. He was also true to his word in that he was stark naked except for a bow tie and was singing the song "*Let it Go*" at the top of his voice towards Aimii's window. He was of very slight build and the cold night air was doing nothing for his manly state, which was hanging limply between his legs.

Aimii looked both panicked and enraged "Oh my god, oh my god, he has come back! Where's his fucking clothes??"

"*LET IT GOOOOOOOO LET IT GOOOOOO*" continued the tuneless singing outside.

"I think he's already let it go to be fair" remarked Josie "What are we going to do?"

Josie turned round to see Aimiii texting on her phone "I'm getting Jo, she will come to help us!"

"Call the police!" replied Josie "There is a naked man singing outside your window with a small limp penis, what's Jo going to do??"

"*AIMIIIIIIIIII, I CAN'T HOLD IT BACK ANY MOOOOOOOOOOOOORE*" continued Garth outside the window.

Garth remained stood naked, singing away tunelessly as both women watched out the window in dismay.

"It's a cold night" remarked Josie "maybe he'll get cold and go away??"

Aimii shook her head "He's gone to all this trouble so I don't think so. Oh my god look, now he's dancing and shaking his thing".

At that point there was a loud knocking at Aimii's door. It was Jo.

"You alright you two? Cheese easy?" Jo always had the most amusing expressions but this really wasn't the time for banter.

"Naked man, babes!" shrieked Aimii pointing to the window "Naked man! Garth is outside with no clothes on, he's singing that song he said he would sing".

Jo looked very cross. She was always very protective of Aimii and this was more than one step too far.

"I've called the police" said Josie trying to be helpful "They'll be here soon, hopefully".

"I'm gonna hit him in the bollocks!" yelled Jo.

Aimii looked slightly panicked and moved towards her kitchen cupboard "Wait wait babes, I need to find you my cleaning gloves, don't touch it yourself".

Jo looked horrified and Josie tried not to laugh "I'm not going to touch his bollocks Aimii!" shouted Jo "Just wait here".

Jo marched to her flat and grabbed the football which she had confiscated from the lads she had chased, and ran outside with it. She then put it down on the concrete and kicked the ball with all her might towards Garth, who was obliviously still singing towards Aimii's window. The ball smacked Garth in the groin with an almighty slap, just as the police patrol car arrived.

The sound of sirens filled the air and the blues lights of the police car flashed and reflected on the flat windows. Aimii and Josie looked at each other from the safety of the flat window.

"Fucking hell" said Aimii "they never came that quick when they bang their balls against my windows".

Josie nearly spit out her wine "haha you might want to rephrase that! Anyway ball games are a bit different to a naked man outside your window! Bloody weirdo. Anyway we best go outside to help Jo in case she gets done for assault".

Josie and Aimii quickly put on some footwear and made their way outside to see Garth sat inside the back of the police car and Jo talking to a rather handsome looking policeman.

"Oh my god you ok?" asked Aimii giving Jo a hug "that was so scary".

Jo smiled "yeah yeah, I knew my ball skills would come in handy. Anyway this is Danny, I mean PC Wilkins".

Jo gestured towards the police officer stood next to her. He was wearing black combat trousers, a black protective vest and a black shirt, where you could just see peeping out some tattoos. He had dark, slightly gelled black hair, blue eyes and a very engaging smile. He looked just Jo's type.

"Evening ladies" said Danny "I'm going to have to take a statement from you all if that's ok? "

Jo nodded "Yeah me first".

Danny smiled "I think all three of you need to come, so we can get a better idea of what happened.  Can you come to the police station now and then we can hopefully charge him.  If you can make your own way then I can see you there".

Danny got into the patrol vehicle with his colleague and drove away with a sheepish looking Garth sitting in the back.

"Oh my god he was fit!" said Jo "Let's go to the police station, seems like there's been a positive side to seeing Garth's knob this evening after all!"

# CHAPTER THIRTEEN

Josie and Aimii sat in the police station feeling rather bored. They'd been sat waiting on the hard grey plastic chairs for over an hour and Aimii was losing her patience. Jo was already in with Danny giving her statement and seemed to be taking an awful long time.

"Oh my god I am so bored!" Aimii began swinging her legs, her small feet barely touching the floor.

"Yeah I know babe, but we've got to give our statements" offered Josie "Can't have Garth coming back in his birthday suit".

"But he was naked?" said Aimii, not understanding the phrase.

"Birthday suit IS naked" explained Josie, watching several police officers walk by. Josie checked her phone and saw a message from Devon asking her to stay at his for the weekend in a few weeks' time and help out at an event he was helping to cater for.

Aimii peered at the message over Josie's shoulder "Oooh you gonna go??"

Josie put her phone back in her bag "Yeah maybe, but don't you think it's a bit soon?"

Aimii shrugged "We know who he is and so why not. You don't have to sleep with him".

"Yeah that's true" said Josie "I'm free that weekend and he did say that he'd pay me for helping".

"There you go then" said Aimii "just message me his address before you go and all will be fine. And you'll get some cash too, always handy".

At that moment one of the doors swung open and Jo walked through with a big grin on her face.

"Only got his number haven't I? He bloody loves Disney too. He's lush" said Jo.

"His number?? Isn't that a bit unprofessional?" asked Aimii.

"Well he said it was for if I needed to give him any more information, and I'll certainly be doing that haha" laughed Jo "He was impressed with how accurately I kicked that football in Garth's nuts. Boom!"

"Well neither Garth nor PC Wilkins will be messing with you Jo" laughed Josie standing up "now maybe the rest of us can give our statements and we can get back home, I've had enough of this place".

Aimii turned her head towards some shouting which she could hear coming from down the long grey corridor "yeah let's try and hurry, this police stuff is not for me!"

After giving their statements, they made their way home and all went straight to bed as it was now way past midnight and it had been an exhausting evening.

Things began moving on all round. Garth was charged with one count of public indecency and harassment which Aimii had been quite pleased with and Jo had managed to arrange a date with Danny.

Josie had been on a couple of dates with Devon, including an evening at her flat where he had cooked her a meal from scratch which had been incredibly delicious. Every time Devon came to see Josie he made sure that he gave her a gift, whether it was something she needed like a new charger for her phone, or something more romantic such as a bunch of flowers. He was very gentlemanly and never offered or asked for more than a simple kiss which was quite a refreshing change from all the crass and explicit messages that Josie had received on the dating sites. Things seemed to be going well and to be on the look up.

Soon enough the weekend came around where Josie was due to stay at Devon's and help out with his catering event. It was an outdoor cinema screening which was unusual in the winter months but it had been advertised with outdoor heaters, blankets, hot chocolate and hot water bottles to keep everyone warm.

Josie had had no trouble finding Devon's house, as his large van was parked outside and his directions had been very concise.  It was a simple looking red bricked terraced house in a sleepy village, and was also inhabited by 5 very friendly cats who insisted on sleeping on the bed rather than the cat beds that Devon had supplied for each of them.  The house was small but simple and in need of a good clean and a vacuum.  His conservatory was filled with items for his catering business including boxes of food, cooking utensils and a spare fridge and freezer to keep his business food separate from his domestic items.  Josie took her bag upstairs.

"Where am I sleeping?" asked Josie looking around.

"You can share my bed" explained Devon.

Josie raised her eyebrows "Oh, I'm not sure I'm quite ready for that" explained Josie.

Devon laughed "Oh don't worry I'm not going to try it on with you, you're really quite safe".

Josie gave a weary smile not knowing whether to feel reassured or insulted by his remark, and placed her bag next to the bed and sat on the edge of it, not knowing quite what to do.

Devon sat next to her and put his arm around her and gave her a squeeze "Am so glad you're here! We've got a lot to do. Not sure if I told you but the event is tonight so if we pop out and get the food stuff for the pizzas tonight and maybe some stuff for desserts I could rustle up. Then we need to be there by about 6pm, as the screening starts at 7pm".

Josie felt like it had all turned quite business like but realised that Devon had a job to do, and weekend catering made up his yearly income quite well. Josie quickly brushed her hair and grabbed her bag before making her way outside to Devon's van.

She was quite glad to of put trousers on as it was two steps up to get into the cab of the van and there was barely enough room to sit down.

The front seat was full of bags of sweets, old coffee mugs and in the footwell was large catering tubs of mayonnaise and salad dressing.

"Just make room and plug yourself in" shouted Devon from the back of the van where was trying to make room for the shopping that they were about to get.

Josie pushed some items to one side and had to put one leg each side of one of the large tubs in order to make room to sit and put her feet down. She had been hoping for a more glamorous type of weekend rather than sitting astride an industrial tub of mayonnaise in a white van. Devon climbed in and smiled at Josie.

"Glad you got in ok! Right let's go to the supermarket and get what we need".

The van roared into action, making several coffee cups roll off the seat which Josie decided weren't worth catching and let then roll onto the floor.  Devon circled the supermarket car park several times before finding a space big enough for his van to fit.

"It's such a faff" admitted Devon shutting his door and leaving Josie to climb out herself whilst avoiding standing on any packets of sweets "But this van is my business".

Josie smiled meekly and nodded as Devon grabbed a trolley.

"You know there's a guy who comes to my pizza stall in the market place every week. Very camp!  Loves it when I offer meatballs on my pizzas!  Says I've got a great arse too" explained Devon putting things in his trolley and rolling his eyes "I mean, what do you say to that??"

Josie shrugged not knowing what to say whilst Devon continued to fill his trolley with various items needed for that evening.  At the end of one of the aisles, Devon suddenly grabbed Josie and gave her a kiss and smiled.

"You really are beautiful you know" said Devon, placing one hand on Josie's shoulder and putting his other hand through his curly blonde hair "Thank you so much for help today".

"You're welcome" said Josie, trying to focus less on the fact how unromantic it all seemed and more on that fact that she would be getting some extra money for helping Devon out as he'd promised.

Josie followed Devon back to the van and loaded it up before making their way towards the cinema screening venue. It was in a wooded area and the catering tents were being put up on the stoney ground, just before the pathway into the woods which was being lit up with lanterns to help people find their way to where the film was being screened.

Josie helped Devon carry the pizza oven up to the hard standing area which involved a steep gradient upwards and was physically hard work.

One other seller had set up their stall for selling hot dogs and burgers and the organisers of the event were selling refreshments from a nearby wooden hut. Everything seemed to be in place.

Gradually people started to arrive and ordered pizzas although the hot dog and burger stall was proving to be more popular, much to Devon's annoyance. Devon got Josie to prepare some toppings at the back of the tent and had a slight initial rush before things quietened down as the screening of the film drew near and the light began to fade even more.

"Where's the toilets?" asked Josie, realising that she wouldn't be able to hold out before the event was finished.

Devon carried on cooking pizzas without looking up "follow the lanterns and it's on the right hand side. If you reach the cinema screen then you've gone too far".

Josie followed the instructions and made her way up the stony path which was surrounded by thick woodland and grass either side of the pathway.

As she started to hear the film she came to a slight clearing and saw a small hut located precariously on a ledge, with a drop the other side. Josie took a photo and sent it to Devon.

"*Is this the loo??*" typed Josie.

"*Yes*" came back Devon's reply.

Josie sent the picture of the odd looking facilities to the group chat and almost immediately Aimii sent back a laughing emoji at the photo of the small wooden hut on the ledge.

"*What is that, a fucking hobbit toilet?? Haha!*" typed Aimii "*If you got to go you got to go!*"

Josie opened the hut door and revealed what looked like a medieval toilet facility - inside the hut was a bench with a hole in it, and no plumbing - anything deposited from the bench hit a pile of straw located a few metres on the ground below. Farms had smelt better.

Josie did what she had to do in the hut and made her way back down to the catering tents where Devon was starting to pack up and appeared to be in a mood.

"Why are we packing up?" asked Josie as Devon starting giving her things to carry "I thought we were staying on so people could have dessert later once the film was finished".

"No point" said Devon "It's not as busy as I was told it would be and I've not really made any money".

Josie made several journeys up and down the stony path with Devon's catering stuff whilst he got another man to help him carry down the pizza oven down the steep path back to the van. It had been tiring and not very fruitful it would seem. Josie thought it would be fun. Once they were back at Devon's house, he played some loud music whilst making Josie some pizza and then he poured himself a whiskey.

"Want one?" he asked.

Josie shook her head. She was tired and ready for bed and was glad when Devon finally decided to retire too - it had seemed too rude to go to bed by herself, especially when she was a guest.

Josie put her on her pyjamas as Devon got changed and into

bed but as he got changed Josie couldn't help but notice what

a very tiny penis he had. It was just a glimpse and Josie

didn't have her glasses or contacts in so couldn't be convinced,

but it did look tiny. Josie was too tired to think about it too

much and pulled the covers up over herself as the house was

cold, and arranged her legs around the cats which were

sleeping soundly on the bed. Devon slept right on the edge

the opposite side and Josie knew that there was no immediate

danger of him making any kind of move on her.

The next morning Devon seemed in a slightly better mood

than the night before and explained the day ahead.

"I think it would be nice for you to meet my mum and her

boyfriend today, we'll meet them for coffee in the village,

maybe a walk first. Then later my Gran's having a party and

I'd said we'd go".

Josie looked a bit taken aback. She had only just added Devon

to her social media which was a big step for her, but meeting his family in person seemed a bit soon.  Devon was insistent.

"My mum really wants to meet you.  She'll love you, it'll be fine".

Josie looked through the clothes that she had brought to see if anything was suitable for a first meeting with what Devon had described as  very confident and domineering woman.  Devon said she was a director in a large engineering company and had taken no prisoners on her way to get there. He said she was forthright and outspoken and had not always been approving of his choice of career in catering.

Josie had a quick shower and put on a dress that she had brought with her in case they went out, and put some make up on before drying her hair.  Devon took Josie on a long country walk to the next village and into the restaurant where his mother and her boyfriend were just having coffee after finishing their meal.  Devon greeted his mother with a stiff hug and gestured towards Josie.

"Mum, this is Josie, Josie this is my mother Margaret and her partner Robert".

Josie smiled nervously as Devon's mother dipped her head and looked at them over her glasses before gesturing for them to sit down with them at the table. Margaret had dark brown layered hair which was peppered with grey hairs and looked like it had been slightly back combed and set with an awful lot of hairspray in a style reminiscent of the 1960s.

"So Josie" began Margaret sipping her coffee "what is it you do my dear? Hopefully something more exciting than my pizza peddling son!".

"She works in an office" replied Devon dismissively, looking out the window and not even offering to get Josie a drink after their long walk.

Margaret smiled with her thin lips "Well I'm sure it's useful to someone".

Josie shifted in her chair awkwardly. She had no idea why Devon had wanted her to meet his mother, especially in these awkward conditions where it felt like they had gatecrashed the end of their meal.

Margaret stood up "Must powder my nose" she declared, before making her way towards the ladies' toilets which were nearby.

"So how did you two meet?" ventured Robert to Josie, trying to help stimulate the conversation.

"We met online" replied Josie, not giving Devon a chance to interject.

"Haha" laughed Robert "Same with me and Margaret, love at first sight eh?" Robert gave Josie a wink.

Devon stopped gazing out the window and looked towards Josie and Robert, not being aware of the conversation that had just taken place.

"Right let's go" declared Devon standing up "We've got places to be".

Josie looked at Devon quizzically.

"There's that family party in a bit, my gran will be there and a few of my family, I said we'd go, remember?".

"But your mum is still in the toilets" said Josie, grabbing her bag "shouldn't we say goodbye".

Devon shook his head  "She'll be ok, I'll message her later, she'll be in there ages".

Robert nodded in agreement "That she will young Devon, nice to see you both anyhow".

Robert gave Josie a polite peck on the cheek and shook Devon's hand, before they made their way back to Devon's house.

"Time for a quick shower before we go" declared Devon, removing his clothes.  Josie had another quick view of Devon's penis.  It was very very tiny.  More disconcerting than that was the fact that Devon hadn't really made any real 'moves' on Josie.  They had shared the odd kiss, but even sharing a bed together had not made Devon made any further moves, not that Josie was ready but she felt it was a bit odd. As Devon was showering, Josie gave Aimii a quick call.

"Hey babes! You back already?" asked Aimii cheerily.

"No" whispered Josie "This is just a quick call whilst Devon's in the shower!"

"Ah ok" replied Aimii "How did the food thing go?"

"Bloody nightmare" replied Josie "I had to lug loads of catering equipment up a slippery stony hill then he kept saying he never made any money, so I don't think he'll be giving me that £50 he promised".

"That's not on" replied Aimii, sounding annoyed "you did the work though babe, I know you are together but still".

"Yeah I know" agreed Josie reluctantly "anyway I met his mum today and later we're going to a family party".

"Oh my god, that's a bit quick innit?" said Aimii sounding surprised.

"Yeah I guess, but there's another thing. We're sharing a bed but he hasn't tried it on with me AT ALL" said Josie.

"Bit weird" agreed Aimii.

Josie decided to keep it to herself for now about his micropenis, just as she heard the shower turning off.

"Got to go, he's just finishing in the bathroom".

"Ok babes, have fun" said Aimii before hanging up "love you!".

As Devon came into the room, Josie went and had another shower and mulled things over. It all felt a bit odd. She had liked Devon and he seemed very gentlemanly, not trying anything sexual and bringing her gifts each time she saw him, but there was something almost clumsy about it all. She was also slightly annoyed about the non payment of her efforts for helping out at his pizza stall but also realised it was difficult when he hadn't made any money either. She felt awkward that she had met his mother already and even more awkward that she was being taken to a family party - she was hoping it would be a small gathering as big family occasions really weren't Josie's thing.

Once Josie was ready, they made their way outside and Josie had to clamber back into Devon's huge van. It was a short drive to a small housing development and they parked up outside a nice looking semi detached house. As they walked up the short driveway, Josie could hear lots of chattering and music coming from inside. Devon opened the front door which was unlocked and walked through the hallway and into the large kitchen/diner which was at the back of the house. The house seemed full of people, all of whom Josie didn't know and all of sudden felt quite intimidated.

"Come and meet Gran" said Devon, making his way over to a small white haired lady who was perched on a green, well upholstered sofa. She had a very kind looking face and smiled as Devon approached her.

"Hi granny, this is Josie"

Granny remained seated and gave Josie a warm smile "I live in the village you know" she said.

Josie smiled and nodded and looked around to realise that Devon was no longer next to her and was now eating food in the kitchen without her. A teenage girl approached Josie, appearing to be very excited. She had beautiful, straight brown hair, lots of make up, high waisted jeans and a cropped top.

"Hi hi! I'm Jeanie, did you come with Devon?"

"Yes I did" replied Josie, trying to catch Devon's eye to help her socialise with his family.

"Are you his..... girlfriend?" asked Jeanie, swishing back her shiny long hair and giggling.

"Umm yes I guess so" replied Josie, not knowing what else to say.

Jeanie giggled and made her way over to a similar looking

teenage girl in the living room and they began mutedly

talking to each other whilst casting the odd glance back to

Josie. Josie sat awkwardly.

"I live in the village, do you?" asked Granny, smiling at Josie

again.

"No, no I live about an hour away" replied Josie standing up

"please excuse me, I need to go to talk to Devon."

Josie spent the rest of the evening stood next to Devon whilst

he consumed different parts of the buffet in the kitchen and he

talked to various family members about how well his pizza

business was going.

It turned out that the house belonged to Devon's dad who was

very very different to Devon's mother who he had divorced

years previously. He was a builder, with very tanned rough

looking skin, greasy looking hair, a portly belly and very hairy

thick arms. He had a brief conversation with Josie about what her favourite song was before continuing to drink cans of beer and singing along to a song his new wife had put on their new stereo.

It was Josie's least favourite evening for quite some time and was relieved when it was time to go and Devon made his farewells to his family, most of whom Josie remained unintroduced to.

As Devon and Josie made their way back down the hallway, Josie noticed Jeanie giggling again from a side room, along with the other girl she had seen her talking to earlier.

"I can't believe Devon's got a girlfriend" Josie heard Jeannie saying to her friend "Who'd of thought it??"

Josie thought this was a bit of an odd comment to make but before she could think about it too much, Devon seemed rather irritated and gestured her into the van. Josie felt tired so left the comment behind and got into the van, sitting astride the tub of mayonnaise as Devon started up the van and made their way back to his house.

Josie woke up the next day surrounded by the cats and with Devon laid on the bed as far away from her as he could possibly be. She could hear the birds singing outside and the sun shone through the dirty window and onto the duvet cover where Devon cats tried to stretch into the warm spot as best they could.

Devon stirred and rolled over to see that Josie was awake. He didn't smile but gave a long groan and a stretch.

"I've got such a busy day today" said Devon, looking over at his alarm clock "I've got to get the pizza oven looked at, as I think it's playing up, then I have to get more supplies for work tomorrow".

Josie felt it was a firm hint for her to leave sooner rather than later so tested the water "Would you rather I leave this morning?"

Devon didn't hesitate "Yes that's a good idea, then I can get on with my stuff".

Josie felt let down by the whole weekend. The catering had been a tiring disaster without payment, she'd had an awkward meeting with his family and now she felt like she was being made unwelcome in someone else's home.

"Ok" replied Josie. She got changed into blue jeans, t shirt and a hoodie and didn't bother putting on any make up though did brush her hair. Even though she felt Devon had been reasonably gentlemanly at times, Josie didn't feel particularly attractive in his company and knew that wasn't a good thing. Once Josie had packed her holdall, she made her way downstairs and put on her shoes. Devon was still in his pyjamas and so it was obvious that he wasn't even going to see her out to her car.

"Bye then" said Josie, making her way out the door. As Josie got to her car she looked back to wave, but Devon's front door was already shut. It summed everything up. Josie had no idea why, but it had not been a good weekend at all, and one that Josie would rather forget.

# CHAPTER FOURTEEN

Josie got home to her flat and slumped on her sofa, feeling rather fed up. She'd had visions of spending until the Sunday evening with Devon so being at home so soon was rather an unexpected disappointment. Josie decided to catch up on some housework then sat down at her laptop to pay some bills and look at her social media. On logging in, she noticed that Devon had been tagged in an odd post from his sister who lived in America. It had a cartoon of a rainbow and stated "Happy World LGBT Day". Devon's sister had tagged Devon in it and written *"Happy LGBT Day to my Big Brother Across the Pond!"* and Devon had immediately commented underneath *"are you crazy??"*.

It was a very odd exchange, but Devon had said that his sister could be slightly random at times so put it down to that. Then Josie noticed a private message from Devon via social media which she clicked on and read rather slowly.

*"Hi Josie,*

*Thank you for coming over this weekend. It was kind of you to help out with the catering and keep me company with my family and friends. I've been suffering for a while with my mental state and I spoke to one of my friends who is a psychologist, and told him about the issues I have been having about the thought of being intimate with you. Whenever I thought about you, I just couldn't get an erection. He said that it was all your fault that I couldn't get close to you but of course I don't believe that. Anyway I think that it's best that we don't stay together and we both find someone more suitable to each other's needs.*

*All the best,*

*Devon"*

Josie re-read the message several times to take it in. How dare he?? It was he who wanted her to come over for the weekend, him who kept his distance, him who wanted her to meet his family etc.

And what on earth had he told the psychologist to make him think all this was Josie's fault??

Why was it her fault his micro penis didn't work?? Josie was

rather dumbstruck and replied sarcastically to the message

*"Does this mean it's over??"*

Devon read it but never replied, and Josie then removed him

from her social media with a press of the block button.  It was

never going to be the greatest of love stories, but it was very

odd how quickly things had progressed but then gone wrong

so suddenly.  Josie got changed into tracksuit bottoms and a

tshirt, grabbed a cardigan and went and knocked on Amii's

door  to let her know what had happened to try and make

sense of it all.

Aimii put on the kettle and puffed on her vape, whilst reading

through Devon's message.

"Oh my god, that's so weird! Why did he invite you over if he

was having troubles in his head?? Hope he paid you that

money now for helping out and having to sit on that fucking

hobbit toilet! I'd of gone in a bush babes".

Josie curled up her legs underneath her on the sofa, and wrapped her cardigan more tightly around her body "No he didn't pay me, said he never made any money. Never came near me and then at the family party he just left me with his granny".

Aimii shrieked in horror "He never paid you?? You still did the work though, so he should still pay you. That's disgusting, what a twat."

Josie couldn't help but agree with Aimii. Aimii was quite harsh at times compared to Josie, but knew that this time she was spot on. The whole weekend was a bit of a trauma and Josie was quickly getting to the point of realising the fact that it was over was a good thing. Aimii made Josie feel so much better in pointing out that micro penises were never a good thing, as was a man that never paid what he said he would. Josie finished her tea and gave Aimii a big hug before she left. "Thank you for being here for me" said Josie, squeezing her tightly. Aimii straightened her hair and smiled.

"We are here for each other!"

Josie made her way back to her own flat and rang her mum Rebecca, who was on her way back from the gym and sounded slightly out of breath.

"You alright love? I've just been to the gym with Mandy. Not sure it's doing her any good though as she reads a magazine when she walks on the treadmill, it's barely moving!"

"That doesn't sound like alot of effort being put in" agreed Josie "How's Mandy these days?"

Rebecca laughed "Yeah she's alright. She had a date from one of those sites that you've been on".

"Did she have fun" asked Josie, hoping someone would have a lovely dating story.

"No!" replied Rebecca "So they went to the pub and he asked her if she fancied a drive and she said yes. So he drove them down this country lane and got his cheesy old willy out".

"Oh my god mum" said Josie, quite horrified "Why did she go in the car with him? And cheesy?? That's bloody vile!"

Rebecca laughed "well he got it out and asked her if she wanted to do anything with it and Mandy said even if she'd wanted to she wouldn't because it smelt of cheese. Anyway Mandy had a right go at him and he drove her back to the pub".

Josie sighed. Another dating disaster story. Josie explained what had happened with Devon to her mum.

"Aww love that's a shame. I tell you what, I've been looking at some cheap holidays for just after Christmas. Only a long weekend but we could go abroad if you get time off work in January. Would cheer us up, how about it?"

Josie smiled "That's a lovely idea. I'll ask at work tomorrow to see if I can book some time off. I was planning to work over Christmas anyway, so don't see why time off in January should be a problem".

"Ooooh that's great love" giggled Rebecca "Book the time off and I'll book us a cheap break in the sun".

Josie agreed and hung up the phone. Something to look forward to sounded lovely, then Josie realised her passport had run out. She looked at her watch and decided to pop to the local supermarket which had a passport booth, and then she could send an application off in the next few days.

The passport photobooth was situated behind the tills, and when Josie got there, there was already a man sitting inside. The curtain was drawn across the top half but she could see a man's leg's perched on the seat and lot of fidgeting going on. Suddenly the curtain swished back and a rather tall, broad man with receding blonde hair stood up out of the booth.

"It's not working!" he declared to no one in particular "I've put my money in but nothing's working, I'll have to find someone to help".

The man walked off towards the customer service desk as Josie stood waiting by the photo booth. Suddenly a young boy of about 7 got into the booth and drew the curtain across and started pushing buttons.

Before Josie could say anything the photo booth whizzed into action and the flash started going off. After the fourth flash, the young boy got out and skipped off down one of the aisles. Josie stood in astonishment as the gentleman then returned with a member of staff to explain how it wasn't working. At that point the booth churned out a strip of blank photos, as the boy had been too short to reach the height of the camera in the booth without adjusting the seat.

"It's given me blank photos!" exclaimed the man before storming off "It's useless".

Josie kept quiet, not knowing quite what to say, and silently sat in the booth and carefully read the instructions. Blank background, no glasses on, hair behind ears, head in frame on screen. Josie saw her reflection in the screen and realise that she hadn't touched up her make up or brushed her hair properly but decided to go ahead anyway.

The resulting photos were not pretty. Josie had a random piece of hair sticking up and due to the lack of make up which gave her pale skin and dark bags under her eyes, she thought she looked like an 80 year old grandmother on crack. It was not the look she wanted on her passport for 10 years so ripped them up and then had them redone once she had been home and redone her hair and make up, which made her look much more presentable. What a weekend.

Monday dawned and Josie made her usual way into work. Bridie was looking her usual chipper self and Josie could hear Sandy somewhere in the vicinity still trying to flog tickets to the ball which BobbyB was desperate for her to sell tickets for. As Josie sat at her desk, Helen and Marvin approached, both holding steaming mugs of tea. Helen's long black hair cascaded down over her shoulders onto her tight fitting black top and her eyelashes seemed longer than ever.

Marvin was looking exceptionally well groomed as usual, with a tight fitting shirt and slim tight fitting trousers which showed off his muscular body. Helen always said that him being gay was such as waste and maybe one day she could tempt him. Luckily Marvin never got wind of Helen's ideas and so remained friends with her, being intrigued with her sexual stories as anyone else.

"So did ya get some Josie??" asked Helen with a wink and sipping her tea.

Marvin rolled his eyes "Nothing like subtly Helen!" then fixed his gaze to Josie whilst cupping his mug in his hands "Good weekend? I hear you spent it with your new fella".

Josie sighed "Yes I spent it with him but now it's all over".

Marvin raised his eyebrows and sat on the edge of Josie's desk and crossed his legs "What on earth happened darling? Do tell".

Josie explained everything. She needed to tell someone else about how it had all gone horrible wrong with no clear explanation. She explained about the catering fiasco, meeting his mum and then some of his family at the party, along with the comment from the girl about Devon having a girlfriend, the lack of physical contact, his sister's facebook post and finished off by showing them his final goodbye message.

Marvin pursed his lips "Oh my darling, you may as well as given him to me. Except I'm not a fan of mini penises".

Josie gave Marvin a hard stare "What do you mean?? You think he's gay?"

Marvin laughed and threw back his head "Of course he's gay! In denial mind you. Didn't you say the other week that he told you some fella kept making saucy suggestions to him on his pizza stall?? Set off that fella's gaydar didn't he?? Look at the evidence my gorgeous Josie. You are an attractive woman, even I can say that, and he spent an entire weekend with you and never touched you once? He paraded you in front of his family a bit too soon, there were comments about being shocked he had a girlfriend, then his sister tries to randomly out him. Then finally in his very strange goodbye message, he insists some random psychologist says his lack of prowess is due to you, even though you've barely known him a few weeks. Gay, gay, gay my darling. He just has to come to terms with it".

Josie placed her elbows on her desk and put her head in her hands. Of course he was gay!! Why didn't she see it? It explained everything that had happened. Whilst the whole episode had been traumatic at times, Josie felt relieved that actually it was nothing to do with her.

Marvin rubbed Josie's back to comfort her "These things happen. If he does ever come out the closet, give him my number" Marvin smiled warmly and gave Josie a wink before sauntering down the corridor.

"Even I've never had a gay one" said Helen screwing up her nose "had a threesome mind you, does that count?"

Josie shrugged, not really wanting to go into Helen's sex life at that particular point. Maybe she needed to up her game in being more choosy about the men that she chose to go on dates with in the first place. Josie wasn't quite sure how to improve her dating game. Maybe it was a case of going on even more dates, or possibly being more choosy? She wasn't sure. Nic appeared next to the desk and interrupted Josie's thoughts.

"Helen told me about what happened" Nic put on a sympathetic smile "what you need is a date with a NICE man".

Josie raised her eyebrows "I'm trying! They seem ok, but then quickly things go wrong one way or another".

"I have an idea" said Nic scrolling down her phone then holding it up for Josie to see "What about him? He's on my social media and is really nice I think. Divorce, two kids, about your age, into running and stuff too!"

Josie looked at the profile on Nic's phone. His name was Miles. Not massively handsome but not unattractive either. He had a cheeky smile, twinkling brown eyes, dark hair and laughter lines which gave his age away. His profile had several photos of him running, where it looked like he had an athletic body.

"What do you think??" asked Nic enthusiastically "I tell you what, I'll let him know that you are interested and then you can message him!"

Before Josie could answer, Nic began tapping away and pressed send.

Nic smiled "Just call me cupid! Now message him and arrange a date Josie!"

Josie wasn't sure. She was always of the ilk that men should do the messaging first but Nic seemed so keen and had already partly paved the way, so maybe it wouldn't make much difference. The morning was busy so Josie had to wait for lunchtime in order to message him. She kept the message simple.

"Hi Miles, you don't know me but we have a mutual friend in Nic. She says we should meet up and get to know each other? Let me know what works for you. Josie"

Josie pressed the 'send' button and it wasn't long before she got a reply.

"Hey Josie, Nic mentioned that one of her friends was interested in me! How about Wednesday night? I can't do Mondays as I have my running club, Tuesdays I take the kids to football, Thursdays I play football and Fridays, well Fridays are part of the weekend! I can meet you about 6pm right after work at that pub The Great Haystack?"

Josie read the message a couple of times. He seemed a busy man and it wasn't that Josie was interested in him first, but then Josie hadn't seen the message that Nic had sent him first.

She felt slightly annoyed that he'd felt she was chasing him, but considering the circumstances tried not to let it bother her. Wednesday soon came about and Josie made sure that she had finished work on time in order to get home, changed and back out the door in time. She message Aimii before she left with a screenshot of Mile's profile and the place where they were meeting. Better to be safe than sorry.

The Great Haystack was an 18th century pub, with dark oak beams, wooden floors and a thatched roof. The garden was beautifully planted with a lawn that lead down to a flowing stream. Josie pulled up into the car park and turned off the engine. She sat for just a few minutes before a black BMW came sweeping into the car park and parked up right next to her car. As Josie looked over, she recognised Miles' profile from his picture, which was true to form, and got out of the car. Miles was about 6ft tall and dressed in a shirt and tie, having clearly come straight from work.

"Hey Josie" smiled Miles, his cheeks creasing with his full grin "so nice to meet you. Let's go and get a drink".

Josie walked slightly behind Miles as he strode into the pub and ordered the drinks.

"They have a really nice patio area here, let's sit outside" declared Miles, passing Josie her drink.

The pub did have a beautiful patio area which was lit up with hanging decorative lanterns and some outdoor heaters which were turned on, although considering it was nearly December, it was a particularly mild evening.  Josie pulled her jacket tightly round her and took a seat opposite Miles at one of the wooden tables.

"Let me tell you about myself" grinned Miles, putting down his drink "So I divorced a couple of years ago and have my kids every other weekend, not this weekend though, and I'm quite a sporty fella as you can probably tell!".

Josie gave a faint smile as Miles barely took another breath to continue to talk about himself.

"I've worked as a physio but nowadays I work in a telecoms office.  Not as exciting but it pays the bills!  I did have a relationship quite recently, but it ended and we remained friends.  Let me tell you about it".

Josie carried on drinking her drink, trying to ignore all the red flags - talking about himself constantly, seeming quite full of himself etc.  Josie decided to put it down to nerves and carried on listening.

"She was a lovely girl" continued Miles, having a slightly more serious look on his face and adjusting his tie "She thought I was her soul mate but I knew that wasn't the case".

"Oh" said Josie, not knowing quite what to say at this egotistical statement.

"Lovely girl" repeated Miles "Then she had an accident and needed taking care of for a while, which I helped with, you know, because I'm that kind of guy".

Josie tried to look at the time on her phone subtly. They had only been there about 15 minutes and she was desperate to leave. Miles continued to constantly talk about himself and Josie continued to sip her drink and give the occasional comment and nod to try and show she was still listening.

"So Josie" said Miles, leaning towards the table slightly "You know I don't think this is going to work. Our schedules just won't work and I'm just so busy as you can probably tell".

Josie put down her drink and just stared at Miles as he leant in slightly further.

"I'd better go now, I have a chicken sandwich at home that I need to eat" declared Miles.

Josie had had half an hour of listening to Miles talk constantly about himself, ex girlfriends who apparently adored him and details of his busy schedule, only to be turned down by someone who barely let her get a word in edgeways. Why had he even come on a date at all if he felt he was too busy??

"Can you wait here a minute?" said Miles, getting up to leave the table "I won't be a moment".

"Sure" replied Josie, staring out over the garden and stream, wishing that she had listened to all the red flags and turned him down first. She waited a few moments and finished her drink, until Miles returned.

"Just been to the loo!" he declared "right let's go".

It was the final insult. Not only was he selfish and big headed, he had turned Josie down within half an hour and then made Josie wait at the table so he could go the toilet and then leave together. She hadn't wanted to date him at all, but this was all adding insult to injury. Josie made her way to her car first and tried not to appear too off with him in case he thought she was upset that he had turned her down.

"Bye then!" said Josie, trying to sound more positive than she really felt. Miles smiled and waved before getting into his black shiny car and driving away.

Josie knew she would rather be single than be with a guy like that. As his car disappeared down the country road, Josie sat in her car and went onto her messages on her phone and blocked him, as she never ever wanted to speak to him or hear from him again. What an absolute tool.

Josie drove home and went straight to Aimii's flat to see if she was in, to unload about her latest terrible date. As she walked in, she saw Jo sat on the sofa, displaying a new tattoo on her midriff. It was a beautifully drawn dragon that went from the bottom of her ribs to her hip.

"Beautiful tattoo" remarked Josie, sitting next to her and taking a closer look "so intricately drawn".

Jo beamed "Yeah my brother designed it, I love it".

"How's it going with Danny the policeman?" asked Josie as Aimii poured Jo a gin and tonic and Josie some wine.

"Love him!" declared Jo, pulling her top back down "He's just so funny and fit. I'm seeing him at the weekend so we can go to the Harry Potter Studio tour. It'll be wicked".

Josie was pleased that Jo had found someone she really liked. Jo had been on her own fair share of bad dates and had some bad luck in her life so it was fantastic she was finally having some fun. Josie told the girls about the latest bad date she'd had.

"Ugh he sounds awful babes" agreed Aimii "He will get noone! You need to keep trying though Josie, and you will meet someone eventually".

Josie did enjoy her work and life with her friends, and she knew that many people were happy to remain single. It was probably less complicated after all. But Josie wanted that special someone and she knew he must be out there somewhere.

"Have a look at your inbox" encouraged Aimii drinking her wine and checking her own inbox "You never know who you might find".

Josie checked her inbox and saw a message from someone called Charles.

"He looks okay babes" said Aimii taking a puff of her vape

"Maybe he's the one!"

## CHAPTER FIFTEEN

Josie was getting date weary. Was this really the way to be going, to keep having disappointments and let downs all the time? One friend had told her that this was what you had to do, almost treat it like a job and have at least 3 dates a week - it was a numbers game surely, so maybe the more dates you had, the more likely you were to meet someone?? Josie went through stages of no dates for ages then having a couple of disastrous dates before backing all off from it again.

Josie left it for a few weeks before deciding to reply to Charles' message. Again, he seemed ok. Aimii thought he looked "posh" and Jo agreed from his profile that she thought he had money, not that this was something that bothered Josie at all. His profile pictures showed him in what looked like exotic countries or in posh hotels. Josie didn't really care about the money thing, she just wanted a nice decent man who she wanted to be with forever.

Charles did seem quite normal to be fair, and Josie's initial

reply quickly turned into a few messages back and forth.

Eventually they exchanged numbers and Charles asked Josie

out to lunch in an Italian restaurant.

The Italian restaurant was situated in what used to be an old

bank, with high ceilings, marble table tops and a shiny

wooden floor. Charles was a tall man at about 6'2 and of slim

build. He was slightly older than Josie and had dark hair with

a floppy fringe, a pale complexion and very dark brown

intense eyes. He was wearing a very expensive looking grey

suit and when Josie approached him outside the entrance, he

smiled kindly and put his arm gently on her shoulder.

"So nice to meet you" said Charles enthusiastically "Please,

ladies first".

Charles held open the heavy wooden door, and gestured with

his free hand for Josie to walk through. As the waiter showed

them to their table, he also pulled out the chair in order for

Josie to sit down. It was all very gentlemanly.

Josie smiled and cast her eye briefly over the menu which was full of beautiful pastas, pizzas and breads.

"My treat" said Charles, looking over the top of his menu at Josie with his deep brown eyes "Have what you like! You have very beautiful eyes by the way" added Charles, before looking back down at his menu.

Josie accepted the offer graciously and chose some not too expensive items to eat for lunch. Charles turned out to be very charming. He did talk a lot but it was very interesting as it appeared he'd had led a very varied life so far. He was previously married with two children, albeit with what sounded like a tricky divorce due to money, and had travelled widely, as indeed his profile had suggested. Charles had a sporting background too but had laid off from this recently due injuring his knee which had given him a slight limp. He'd done various sporting activities for charities and run various successful businesses.

Charles was very gracious and asked lots of questions about Josie, like what she did for a living, how many children she had, what she liked to do in her spare time, what films she liked etc. The lunch was very pleasant and polite and although Charles was the perfect gentleman, as usual Josie wasn't sure if she fancied him or not. She was getting to the point of thinking that maybe she was just going to have to accept that her perfect man would grow on her rather than finding him drop dead gorgeous from the off.

As the meal ended, Charles smiled over at Josie.

"I'd really like to see you again" he stated, tapping his mouth gently with a napkin before placing it neatly back down on the table "I really like you".

Josie was briefly taken aback. From her and her friends' experiences this rarely happened. More often than not, the dates ended and there was either no contact ever again, a polite you're not for me type message, or a message saying let's have another date. Very rarely did they say anything on the actual date.  Apart from with that awful Miles who was just plain arrogant and rude.

Josie accepted politely  "That would be lovely".

Charles beamed and tapped his hand on the table "Excellent! I'll text you later with a plan".

Josie smiled and just before they parted, Charles gave her a brief hug before walking away.

True to his word, Charles messaged Josie later that same day with his plan for a next date which he suggested as a meal and a cinema, his treat.

Aimii was very approving when Josie told her of her first date with Charles and his plan for the second already.

"He's very generous babes" declared Aimii "Would be good to have someone to look after you!"

Josie smiled.  She wasn't looking for someone who could "look after her", she wanted a companion, someone to share things with, someone to hug when she felt down, someone to share some special memories with.

"Money comes in useful though" shrugged Aimii "Just nice to have someone to treat you".

Josie thought she was probably over thinking it, so agreed to Charles' plan for a second date. He suggested the next night and Josie could think of no reason to put it off so agreed. Charles turned up for the second date looking far more casual than he had for the first one. Josie pulled up in the cinema complex car par and could see Charles waiting outside the main entrance . He was wearing a white polo shirt and faded blue jeans, his flopping fringe falling over his face as he scouted around, looking for Josie to appear.

Josie felt slightly overdressed in a flower print dress, with boots and a jacket and wished she had worn jeans too but dressing for dates was always difficult.

"You look beautiful" declared Charles, pushing his fringe off his face and smiling broadly.

"Let's go inside, it's rather cold outside and I want to keep you warm".

Charles opened the door to the restaurant and gestured for Josie to go in first. The waitress showed them to a table near the door and gave them both a menu to browse through. After less than a minute and the door to the restaurant opening and closing several times, Charles looked slightly annoyed.

"It's way to draughty here" he said, picking up both menus "We'll move to that table over there shall we".

Without waiting for a response, Charles picked up both menus and headed towards an empty table further away from the door. Charles told the waitress as he walked by that they were moving tables, and given there seemed to be no choice, no one objected in the matter including Josie.

Charles told Josie lots more about his sporting activities and his charity work before moving on to the matter of his divorce. "She was very unfair you know" said Charles "Bloody woman. Wanted all this money and I was the one working all those years".

"Was she at home looking after the children?" ventured Josie.

Divorce was always a tricky subject and probably one to be avoided on early dates but Charles seemed keen to discuss it.

"She did, but mostly they were at boarding school" said Charles cutting up his steak vigorously "bloody lawyers cost a fortune sorting it all out".

Charles put down his cutlery and held Josie's hand over the table.

"Sorry to discuss this, how awful of me. Let's hear about you".

Josie told Charles a little bit about the type of job she did, what she liked to do in her spare time etc. It was very difficult to know how much information to share with someone who was basically a stranger.

"I bet you get asked out all the time" grinned Charles, pushing back his flopping fringe "you probably get sent flowers, the lot!"

Josie laughed and looked down feeling slightly embarrassed

"Not at all.  Can't remember the last time I got sent flowers

actually"

"Well that's very sad, we'll have to change that won't we"

smiled Charles, holding her hand over the table again

"Beautiful girl like you should get sent flowers all the time".

Charles looked at his gold Rolex watch "Gosh, look at the

time.  I'll pay the bill and then we should make our way round

to the cinema, the film starts soon".

There hadn't been a particularly good choice of films on, the

following week all the blockbusters were being released in

time for Christmas, but on this particular day the best choice

was an 'action' film about an ageing cop who wanted revenge

on for a gang for killing his partner years before.

It was a very dark and grey looking film, with very little

action, just lots of swearing and the odd punch and gun fight

between some of the characters.

When the film had finished, Josie and Charles walked outside to be greeted by some very cold air and a slight breeze.

"Let me walk you to your car" said Charles, and started walking towards the car park where he saw Josie had parked. They stopped near Josie's car and Charles looked directly into Josie's eyes. She sensed that he wanted to kiss her but didn't quite know what to do as she still wasn't sure if she fancied him at all, plus the fact he seemed rather a dominant character by all accounts.

Before Josie could even think any more, Charles grasped Josie by the shoulders and began to kiss her. Except this did not feel like a normal kiss by any stretch of the imagination. Charles placed his lips over Josie's entire mouth and began moving his lips around all over her mouth. Not on her lips but all around her mouth. She felt horrified as she felt his saliva literally on her face and felt she was being kissed by a fish.

Josie managed to pull away and wanted to find something to wipe her face with. She was very much hoping that she had a packet of tissues squirreled away in her handbag.

"Can we sit in your car?" asked Charles hopefully.

"Errm no" replied Josie, getting out her keys "I really need to go now, but thank you for this evening".

Charles looked slightly disappointed and walked away with his slight limp whilst Josie quickly got in her car and locked the doors. Josie found an old pack of baby wipes which she kept in the car for when she went to the petrol station to wipe her hands her on, as she hated the smell of fuel. She grabbed three wipes and proceeded to clean her face vigorously, taking off most of her make up too but she didn't care. She had never been kissed like that before and never ever wanted to again. How could someone kiss you without even putting their lips on yours? Josie drove home and went straight to Aimii's flat, who was already in her pyjamas.

"Hey babes, you had a nice date?" asked Aimii.

Josie shook her head and went in and sat on the sofa and shivered.

"Oh my fucking god Aimii!! So we had a meal and then watched this awful film, which I know wasn't his fault, but then he walked me to my car at his insistence and kissed me".

Aimii sat next to Josie on the sofa and raised her eyebrows before re straightening her fringe her fingers and taking a puff of her vape.

"Oh my god he kissed you! Was it good?"

Josie pulled a horrified face at the recent memory of it "No, it was awful. The most terrible kiss I've ever had".

Aimii looked confused "How can someone get kissing wrong? What did he do?"

Josie did an impression of the kiss onto her hand "Then I had to wipe my whole face with baby wipes as it was covered in spit".

"You should of pushed him away and said 'oh my god what the hell was that'!" said Aimii "I would of done that".

Josie knew that's exactly what Aimii would of done, but she was far too polite to feel able to do that herself.

"And if he kisses like that....." said Aimii slowly "What on earth is he like in bed??"

"I'm not going to find out!" said Josie feeling horrified "Seriously, that is a deal breaker, it was so awful. I'm not shallow but I can't go out with someone who eats my face off every time he wants to kiss me".

Aimii agreed wholeheartedly "He ate your face alive babes! Yeah it was nice with the meals and stuff but the kiss, you can't do it babes. You'd have to carry wipes around with you everywhere!"

Josie nodded in agreement as her phone buzzed with a message. It was from Charles.

*"Hi Josie, I had such a lovely time this evening, let's go out again. Maybe we can go for a lovely walk and a meal. I'll work something out. Charles".*

Josie showed Aimii the message.

"He's not even given you a choice" said Aimii "I think you need to tell him, do it now".

Josie agreed and typed the following message.

*"Thank you for two lovely dates but I feel that we are not compatible so will have to decline your offer, but thank you for a lovely time, it was really good to meet you".*

Josie showed Aimii the message "Is that ok?"

"Tell him he kisses like a fish" suggested Aimii "Then some other poor woman won't have to put up with a fish kiss either".

"Bit harsh, can't say that" replied Josie, pressing send "That will have to do really".

Aimii went into the kitchen and made them tea, before sitting back down to chat. Even in her pyjamas Aimii looked very beautiful with her long dark hair and beautifully made up face.

Aimii always had a full face of make up on, not that she

needed it, and went to bed with make up on. If she was with someone then she took it off when they were asleep, then before they woke, she woke up first to put make up on again. She insisted that no one saw her without make up, only her children, and when that had happened for the first time she said they cried.

Josie's phone suddenly buzzed. It was a message from Charles.

*"My dear Josie, I can't begin to tell you how disappointed I am that you think it won't work out between us. You are a beautiful girl and very charming. I trawled through hundreds of different profiles online before deciding you were the one for me, so to find out you don't feel the same is very saddening. I hope you find happiness and I will restart my search. All the best, Charles".*

Aimii looked over the message "That's a bit weird babes. He basically decided that you were the one before he had even met you and had gone on some kind of weird selection process. I guess we all do the selection bit up to a point, but he sounds a bit crazy as well as being like a fish".

Josie couldn't help but agree. Another dating disaster to chalk down to experience then. Josie wanted to hear some good news.

"How's it going with Jo and her policeman fella, Danny isn't it?" asked Josie.

"Yeah going well" said Aimii with a grin "though he's told her she can't get into trouble or get arrested now they are together cos he's a policeman, so no more chasing kids down the road or assaulting naked men haha!"

Josie laughed "She is a nutter but she's our lovely nutter. Glad it's going well for her though, she deserves it".

"As do we all" added Aimii, looking at her inbox "nothing I am interest in on here though. Maybe we need to try and meet men in real life rather than online".

Josie sipped her tea "Yeah but I'm rubbish at flirting, I think I scare men!"

Aimii laughed "It's really easy, let me show you".

Aimii stood and up walked a few paces away from the sofa.

She then put a finger to her lips, stuck out her arse, smiled and went "Oooh!" in a high pitched tone.

At that moment Jo had let herself in the flat and spied Aimii in mid flirting position.

"What the fuck's that?" laughed Jo.

"Flirting" laughed Josie, shaking back her blonde hair "This is what I need to do to get a man apparently".

Jo flopped down on the sofa to observe the technique.

"Thing is that would probably actually work for Aimii haha! Not sure about everybody else".

"What's your flirting technique then?" asked Josie, as Aimii joined them back on the sofa.

"Well before Danny, I'd of asked if they wanted their tarot cards done, or maybe grabbed their ears, love a cold pair of ears me.  What's your technique then Josie?"

"Well that's the trouble, I don't really have a technique and I have no idea when someone fancies me either. So it's all a bit rubbish" sighed Josie "Best I can do is giggle and touch their arm occasionally, which let's face it, is a really crap technique".

"Charles fancied you" suggested Aimii trying to be helpful "and anyway, a lot of blokes idea of flirting involve pointing a camera at their groin and sending it to us, so maybe you're not so bad after all Josie".

Josie shrugged. It didn't seem to matter if she flirted or not, she felt like she was never going to find "the one". Maybe hers didn't exist, or she'd had her chance and missed it. Josie felt she'd wasted years being with the wrong person, but trying to find someone who she was meant to be with was proving to be more of a struggle.

"If things are meant to be, they are meant to be" said Jo "Look at how I found Danny. If I hadn't of sent that ball flying towards Garth's nuts, then I'm sure I'd of met him some other way, maybe even by getting arrested myself at some point. What will be will be".

"Well I've got the office Christmas party coming up" said Josie "that might help take my mind off everything".

"Any fanciable guys at work?" asked Jo smiling "Maybe that's where you'll find him".

Josie knew that wouldn't be true. The office Christmas party had now been booked and paid for. It was going to be held in a local hotel and their company had two long tables booked but other businesses having their office parties would also be there. There was a meal followed by a disco and probably lots of alcohol, but Josie doubted very much that it would be full of eligible men, and besides she just wanted to go and have fun and let her hair down - if that was at all possible.

## CHAPTER SIXTEEN

Josie had decided on a little black dress for the Christmas party. Nothing too jazzy or daring but enough to look dressed up for the occasion. Josie straightened her blonde hair and added a simple necklace to complete the look. Most people had arranged lifts to get to the hotel, or were car sharing or taking taxis. Josie was sharing a taxi with Helen, Marvin and Nic and Helen was being the last one to be picked up.

Josie waited outside the flats for the black cab to turn up, her breath showing up in the cold night air as she looked out for the taxi to arrive. It was barely a minute later when the taxi pulled up and the door opened.

"Well dontcha look gorgeous" said a male voice from inside "think both of us might pull tonight".

Josie climbed into the back of the cab, and sat in a pull down seat opposite Marvin and Nic who was wearing a large print green dress and very chunky silver jewellery. Marvin was looking very well groomed with gelled back hair, well shaved, a tight fitting shirt and slender fit trousers. His shiny black shoes finished off his look.

"We've already been drinking" confessed Marvin in a hushed tone, nodding over to Nic who was already looking slightly flushed in the cheeks "anyway let's go and pick up that girl from some street corner".

"I think the taxi driver will need more precise instructions!" whispered Nic, sipping a homemade cocktail from a disposable cup.

"Of course!" said Marvin raising his voice "Driver, we need to go to 11 West Avenue to pick up the lovely Helen".

"Good job we're a bit late" said Nic, going redder in the cheeks from the alcohol "Helen messaged me to say she was running a bit late too, but didn't say why".

Marvin poured Josie a drink and began singing 'Club
Tropicana'.

"I don't know this song" said Nic

"IN CLUB TROPICANA DRINKS ARE FREE" sang Marvin.

Josie laughed and took a swig of her very strong drink.

"Loved Wham" declared Marvin "Nothing wrong with three
quarter length trousers and espadrilles on a man, except you
get some funny looks these days you if you wear them out in
public".

"How are we managing to drink in a taxi and not be told off?"
asked Josie, becoming rather flushed herself from the alcohol.

"He's my uncle" explained Marvin "wouldn't let anyone else
do it, but he loves my mum so whenever I need a taxi, here he
is".

The taxi pulled round into West Avenue, and they could see
Helen standing near the bus stop in a very short black floaty
dress which was low cut and worn with bare legs.  Helen's

black hair seemed to cascade in even more curls than usual and her blue eyeshadow seemed extra bright and glittery. Helen climbed into the cab.

"Ooooh glad you're all drinking, I've already had a couple, where's mine?"

Marvin grabbed his bag and pulled out a bottle which contained the home made cocktail and got out a container with fruit to add to it. Marvin poured out Helen's drink and handed it over.

"Cheers everyone" said Marvin holding up his cup "Now we can have a drinking game. I will give everyone a suitable animal name. You have to keep tapping your drink as we do it, and whilst keeping in rhythm you need to say your own animal name to the beat followed by the next person's animal name who you want to pass your go onto, and so on".

Josie shrugged her shoulders and agreed and Helen let out a shriek "Oh this sounds fun!"

Nic carried on getting redder in the cheeks and drinking her drink, not seeming to care what was happening next.

"So" continued Marvin "I'm stallion for obvious reasons, Josie you're pony because you wear your hair in a ponytail quite a lot, Nic you're parrot because you're always bloody talking and Helen you're rabbit, no need to explain that either".

The game started well but quickly disintegrated into Nic having no idea what her animal name was and Helen calling Marvin 'medallion' instead of 'stallion' much to his disgust.

As the taxi cab pulled up to the front of the hotel, Marvin put all the empty cups into a bag and left it in the back of the taxi whilst ushering everyone out of the car.

As the last person got out of the taxi, a black jaguar pulled up and a long pair of legs emerged from out of the rear car door. Sat on the cream leather back seat of the car was Sandy, who had clearly had a few drinks already too. She was wearing a red mini dress with capped sleeves, tan coloured tights and bright red patent shoes. Her bobbed blonde hair was carefully curled and her red lipstick as bright as ever, and heavy mascara finished off her evening look.

"Red shoes, no knickers" remarked Marvin pursing his lips and raising his eyebrows "seems someone else has come out to play this evening".

Marvin took out his mobile and turned on the camera to take a picture of Sandy.

"Woo hoo! Smile darling!" said Marvin, holding up his phone to take a picture.

Sandy laid back slightly onto the seat and put her hand behind her head before giving a beaming smile, in full pose.

"Marvin, darling!" said Sandy, getting out of the car, and standing slightly unsteadily next to him "You look gorgeous this evening".

"I know" laughed Marvin trying to steady Sandy by holding on to her arm slightly "Who drove you here?"

"My ex husband" whispered Sandy "Such a doll. Right let's go to the bar".

Sandy walked in a wobbly fashion to the hotel double doors and beckoned everyone to follow her. The hotel had a very grand entrance of sandy coloured marble flooring and a large wooden reception desk which was manned by 2 staff in dark blue jackets and fancy blouses with neck ties, finished off with shiny gold name badges over the pockets.

"Hello" shrilled Sandy "We're here for the Christmas party this evening".

"Of course" smiled the hotel receptionist "Follow the signs to the Royal Room, you'll find the bar and the event area. Have a good evening".

The group duly followed the signs to the Royal Room which was down two carpeted corridors and past two other 'event areas' which already seemed in full throe, judging by the loud music and chattering which was spilling out into the corridor. As they entered the bar area, Jonathon the Finance Director, was already stood at the bar looking rather dapper in a dark grey suit and white shirt. He smiled as they approached and gestured the barman to serve him.

"Hello, Mrs Wilshire can't make it this evening, but she has generously asked me to buy everyone a drink this evening. What are you having?"

"Large bacardi and coke" interjected Helen without pausing.

As Jonathon got everyone in the group a drink, Helen began looking rather flushed.

"Bloody hell it's hot in here, I need something to cool down" Helen picked up a napkin that was on the bar, lifted up her dress to dab her thighs with the napkin before screwing it up and placing it back on the bar. Marvin flicked it quickly off the bar with his finger and thumb.

"Keep your sweaty thighs to yourself" said Marvin "I know it's a job but really, have a go at it love".

Helen giggled "I do have sweaty thighs for a reason".

Nic's cheeks flushed even more as she sipped her wine "Helen what on earth have you been doing now? We've literally just picked you up from your house! How have you had the chance??"

Helen giggled, fluttering her long eyelashes as Jonathon walked by, flashing her a quick smile as he disappeared into the next room. Helen continued.

"Well, my ex husband came round this evening and I was a bit short of money to pay my phone bill" explained Helen.

"So your thighs got sweaty at the thought of him paying your phone bill?" laughed Josie, sipping her large glass of wine.

Helen rolled her eyes "Hardly, Josie! Well you know I've always had a thing for him. So I told him I had trouble paying my phone bill and he offered to pay it in return for something".

Marvin looked at Josie and raised his eyebrows "Pray do tell".

"He said he'd pay it if we had sex over the loo" explained Helen "Thing is my phone bill was like nearly £200 so it seemed a bargain to me!"

"Over the toilet??" exclaimed Marvin putting his hand to his chest in horror "Hope you bloody bleached it first".

"And afterwards!" said Nic nearly spitting out her wine "Honestly Helen, what were you thinking??"

Helen sighed "It's no big deal really, when we were together we had sex for years. For free. So now we're not together it shouldn't be for free should it? Besides, he's a doctor and he has a massive cock, so (a) he's a man in uniform and (b) well he has a massive cock. No brainer!"

"Why over the toilet?" whispered Josie to Marvin, not understanding that part of it.

Marvin shrugged "No idea, but I'll try and find out later. Anyway, let's go and find out where we are sitting".

The group made their way into the dining area, which had long tables for each company, and were placed around a chequered dance floor which was headed with a DJ booth for dancing later on. Nic found the company's table and noticed that Sandy had already sat next to Jonathon who was flanked on the other side by Sarah the straight talking Human Resources Director. Nic, Helen, Marvin and Josie decided to sit the opposite end of the table at a safe distance but still able to keep an eye on things. People watching was a favourite pastime at this type of event.

Helen glanced around the rest of the room whilst placing her white linen napkin on her lap.

"Bloody hell, no talent in here this evening, is there?" commented Helen.

Marvin glanced around and nodded in agreement "Glad I'm not single, this is dire".

Josie sipped her wine and looked around the room which was mainly full of women, with the odd man thrown in on the occasional table, although there did seem to be one table that had around 8 men on it in the corner. They were middle aged and wearing brightly coloured shirts whilst drinking bottles of beer in large volume with lots of "Whey heys" being shouted out for no apparent reason. Josie quickly decided that finding the man of her dreams was definitely not going to happen that evening.

Helen pulled the cracker that was next to her plate and held up a plastic frog that fell out of the cardboard inner.

"If I kiss it, will it turn into a prince?" giggled Helen.

"Let me know if it does" laughed Josie "I seriously need some help right now!"

Marvin pulled his cracker with Nic who was now way too drunk on wine and mistakenly munching on Colin from accounts bread roll. Marvin's cracker prize was a magic trick of 3 small plastic cups and a ball. The meals started to be served by a whole entourage of waiting staff and plates were quickly placed in front of everyone to begin their meal. Most people had chosen a roast turkey dinner with all the trimmings and Helen began carefully arranging two potatoes and a sausage. Meanwhile at the other end of the table, Sandy was almost constantly giggling and leaning into Jonathon's shoulder who was apparently doing his best to nod and smile through the whole thing.

"I've got a game" declared Marvin, grabbing his cracker prize, the plastic frog and a brussel sprout covered in gravy that had rolled off of Nic's plate. Marvin turned two of the cups facing down and placed the brussel sprout under one and the plastic frog under another.

"It's called frog or sprout!" said Marvin, moving the cups around on the table "I point to a cup and you have to say what's under it. Frog or sprout".

Marvin pointed to Nic, whose concentration had been fast disappearing with the ongoing consumption of wine, and she stared at the two cups. Marvin moved them round quickly and pointed to one of the cups and then to Nic.

"Frog or sprout?" asked Marvin, pursing his lips.

"Frog" replied Nic.

Marvin lifted the cup to the reveal the sprout "Nope, try again".

Marvin kept doing the game with a drunken Nic who was failing to realise that the 'sprout' cup was pretty obvious, due to the trail of gravy being left around the table as the cups were being moved around. Suddenly the music began and Marvin looked up.

"I bloody love this one, come on Josie and Helen, let's have a dance!"

Josie got up and followed Marvin to the dance floor where he began doing a very pronounced version of the Cha Cha Slide. More people joined the floor as the tracks kept coming, and

Josie decided to sit down for a while and people watch. She noticed that Sandy was stood up against the bar with Jonathon and Sarah. Sandy was laughing and touching Jonathon's chest at every opportunity whilst Sarah looked on. Sandy flicked back her blonde hair and whispered something in Jonathon's ear and he nodded before making his way out of the room, followed by Sandy a few moments later.

Marvin sat back down and poured himself a glass of water out of one of the large jugs placed on every table.

"So hot on that dance floor" said Marvin, fanning himself with a napkin "So what's going on, anything good?"

Josie nodded over to the bar "Sandy and Jonathon have just disappeared together, maybe 5 or 10 minutes ago".

Marvin grabbed his phone "Come on Josie, let's try and find them, this could be the highlight of the evening!"

Marvin grabbed Josie's hand and trotted down the corridor, looking in some of the other function rooms to see if they were in there, before making their way out into reception.

"Bugger I think we lost them" puffed Marvin feeling slightly out of breath.

Josie caught sight of a pair of red shoes just outside the hotel entrance door and pointed.

"Look, red patent shoes!"

Josie and Marvin did a quick walk whilst trying to nonchalantly make their way to the entrance. Marvin stood slightly to the side and looked out into the car park when he could see Jonathon piling Sandy into a car and lifting her legs onto the seat before climbing in himself.

"Bloody hell" declared Marvin, zooming in and taking a picture of Sandy's legs in the air "Sandy might get her own way with Jonathon after all".

Josie raised her eyebrows and pulled Marvin away from the door "Come away before you get seen. If that picture gets out, then they'll know it was you".

"Darling I'm the soul of discretion" smiled Marvin, taking

Josie's hand and leading her back to their own function room

which was now in full swing of the party. The music was

loud, cracker debris was strewn across the floor and middle

aged men were throwing shapes on the dance floor to tunes

they had never heard before.

"Can't think why you don't want an older man" smirked

Marvin, observing one particular overweight man who was

dancing and sweating with his shirt half undone at the front

and all untucked and hanging out of his trousers at the back.

"I'd rather be single than have that rolling on top of me

thanks" laughed Josie.

Laughing was all she could do, given the situation. As she sat

back down she decided to discretely check her inbox to see if

there were any new messages from potential suitors. There

was one new message from a man called Brian.

His photo was a little blurry but showed him with very dark

hair, and a white shirt which accentuated his muscular arms. He was slightly older than Josie but only by a couple of years. Josie replied back, thinking that at least another date might be something to look forward to.

Helen looked over Josie's shoulder at the picture "He doesn't seem toooo bad Josie" said Helen, screwing up her nose "Could do worse".

It wasn't encouraging words. Josie didn't want "Could do worse", she wanted someone who was going to be the love of her life. She screenshot Brian's photo and profile and sent it to Aimii for her opinion.

*"He seems ok babes"* replied Aimii *"no harm in meeting him for a drink is there?"*

Josie climbed into bed that evening feeling slightly worse for wear. She'd had too much wine which had made her thirsty and unable to sleep though luckily she was the first to be dropped off. Nic had put her head out of the taxi cab as Josie tried to find her keys to her flat before they drove away.

"I love you my darling!" shouted Nic.

Marvin pulled Nic back into the taxi and stuck out his head

"We're going to carry on partying, are you sure you don't want to come??"

Josie had declined "Nah I'm good thanks, way too much wine! You lot go and have fun though".

"Oh we will" replied Marvin with a wink as the cab drew away into the cold night air.

The Christmas party ended up being the talk of the office for the entire week. Marvin's picture of Sandy with her legs in the air had gone viral amongst the company and Sandy was insisting that it wasn't hers, whilst Jonathon was saying he had gone home early alone. Sarah was adding to the gossip by claiming that Sandy had made a pass at her before moving on to Jonathon. Mrs Wilshire was kept in the dark about the whole thing, otherwise there would never be another office party again.

# CHAPTER SEVENTEEN

Christmas itself turned out to be a pretty uneventful affair. Josie had a small family Christmas with her mum and the children who had made their way back home from universities and college, and then had a girlie night with Jo, Mel, Katie around Aimii's flat to celebrate on New Years' Eve. Aimii poured everyone a glass of prosecco about 20 minutes before midnight.

"Oh my god I really hope that next year is a good one for us all" declared Aimii holding up her glass towards her friends. Mel nodded. She'd been seeing a guy for a couple of months but it had fizzled out and no one had quite known why. Josie had met him once when he offered to fix her kitchen tap and he'd seemed quite kind.

"What happened with him?" asked Jo "Thought you two were happy?"

Mel shrugged "It was ok to start with but then he just wanted to keep going out drinking all the time, and I can't afford that. Also he rarely wanted to have sex either which was a bit weird".

"Yeah you can't do without sex babes" agreed Aimii, puffing on her vape.

"And" added Mel, brushing the crumbs from her biscuit off her chest "He used to walk around wa....."

"Wanking??" finished Katie in horror.

"Why would he walk around wanking and not have sex with you??" asked Jo, sounding quite annoyed on Mel's behalf.

"Terrible" agreed Josie.

"And who wanders around whilst wanking?" said Jo "I could get Danny to arrest him for that! Weirdo".

Mel started laughing "You never let me finish!  I was going to say that he used to walk around waving his hands and talking to himself!  Bloody hell you lot!"

Josie burst out laughing and checked her phone. She had a message from Brian wishing her a happy new year and suggesting to meet in the next few days.

"Aww that's nice" said Aimii "I think you ought to meet him. He looks quite muscular in his shirt there".

"Ah why not" said Josie, whilst typing in her reply "Can't hurt I guess. Anyway I'm going on holiday with my mum soon, just a long weekend to Malta in the sun, so could do it before that".

Jo turned on the tv just as midnight approached, to see fireworks going off around the world.

"Cheers you lovely lot" said Jo, giving them a group squeeze as they all stood up "Happy new year to you all. May you all find love and happiness and may I always be with my lovely Danny".

Everyone raised their glasses and smiled, temporarily forgetting all their troubles. Time with friends was never wasted.

Josie managed to arrange a date with Brian before she had to go back to work in the new year. Josie was clearing up the last of her Christmas decorations when he messaged to arrange the details.

*"Hey you, let's meet tonight. I'm quite busy but I can do 6.30pm tonight"* messaged Brian.

Josie replied, suggesting a nearby pub that they both knew nearby. The pub was located next to a bridge and a car park was situated about 50 metres down the road. It was another cold winter's evening and Josie pulled up in the car park exactly on time. She hated being late so was often a few minutes early, which wasn't always a good thing when going on a date as it gave extra time to overthink and be nervous. Josie got out of the car and began walking in the direction of the pub whose white building was lit up with flood lights, giving it an eerie glow in the misty night air. Josie glanced up to see a man slightly resembling Brian's appearance walking towards her. She had her contact lenses in but still struggled to make sure that it actually was him. The man grinned and walked towards her. He was of slender build, wearing faded jeans, a white t shirt and a leather jacket. The look was sealed with dyed dark hair that was heavily gelled. He looked like a 58 year old trying to look like Danny from the film Grease. "Hey Josie, I'm Brian" he grinned, revealing many more lines on his ageing face.

Josie looked at Brian as he stood before her. She knew that he was roughly the same age as her but his face looked far more wrinkled than in his profile picture and there was also no sign of his muscles like in the picture either. At a guess, the picture had probably been about 10 years old, maybe more. Brian seemed unperturbed by the fact that his physical presence did not match his profile image and indeed seemed quite confident. Josie smiled but instantly thought she didn't fancy him at all. It was one of the those dates where she wished it was acceptable to cancel the date instantly and go back home.

She knew that she was no oil painting but also knew that you had to fancy someone in order for it to go anywhere.

 Brian went into the pub first and went to the bar to order them both a drink, then they took a seat in the pub where there was two low sofas and an armchair.  Josie sat on the sofa opposite Brian and thanked him for the drink.

"You're welcome" grinned Brian "I'm going to have to keep an eye on the time though as I have my belated works' Christmas do at 7.30pm tonight and don't want to be late.  But if you're lucky we can have another date!"

Josie smiled and sipped her drink, not knowing if he was joking or not.  Considering his confident air, she felt he wasn't. On the plus side, Brian slotting her in before his Christmas party meant that she wouldn't have to spend too long with him.

"I've had such a week, I was lucky to fit you in to be honest" said Brian, placing his drink on the curled up cardboard coaster on the table "You know I had to have a colonoscopy this week!"

Josie nearly spit out her drink "Oh right, oh that's not great. Hope it all went ok though".

Unfortunately Brian took this as an invitation to go into more detail about the experience.

"You have to wear giant blue disposable pants with a flap at the back. And you have to drink pints of a disgusting solution in order to clear you out so they can have a good look. I had to spend hours and hours on the toilet but luckily I'd taken the day off from work. Thought it was never going to end".

"Oh really" replied Josie. It was a response that Josie's mum Rebecca had always taught her to say if you weren't quite sure what to say and it did cover many situations.

"Yes" said Brian nodding "Amazing what they can do. My best advice if you ever have to have one yourself is that when they are doing it, to try and recall the lyrics to an ABBA song. Really helps you concentrate and takes your mind off it all".

"Oh really" repeated Josie. This was coming up in the top 5 worse dates and it had barely started. Brian proceeded to talk a lot about himself, his work, his house and his family whilst asking Josie the odd question but not really listening to the response. Josie was relieved when he looked at his watch and declared he should go.

"Right, time for my works' Christmas party! Lovely meeting you" said Brian, adjusting his leather jacket around his neck.

"And you" lied Josie, shaking his hand in a business like fashion before walking out of the pub and back to her car. Yet another date to put down to experience. She sat in her car and gave a big sigh. Maybe it was time to be more selective about who she went on dates with, but that was easier said than done with profiles full of old pictures and fake intentions.

As usual, Josie popped into Aimii's flat before she went to her own, to tell her all about the date.

"Hi babes, I saw you on the bridge earlier when I was driving home. Was that you with Brian? He looked ok" asked Aimii.

Josie wrinkled up her nose as Aimii put the kettle on to make them both a drink.

"It was really awful" explained Josie taking off her coat "One of the worse dates ever but luckily it was only a short date as he had his works Christmas do at 7.30pm. His photo was about 10 years old. No muscles and lots of wrinkles. AND he was really full of himself too".

Josie slumped down on the sofa and read a message on her phone that had just come through from Brian.

*"Hello, I'm at my Christmas party now having lots of fun. It was good to meet you but I really didn't feel like the chemistry was there. Hope you find what you are looking for".*

Josie read the message out to Aimii as she put down the cups of tea onto the coffee table.

"So basically" said Josie in disgust "I've just been turned down by a bloke who slotted me in before his Christmas do, had a profile pic that was at least 10 years old and had a face that had more wrinkles than my nan and thought it was perfectly ok to chat in detail about his latest medical procedure. What shall I reply??"

"Tell him the feelings are fucking mutual! Bloody cheek!" replied Aimii "Anyway what medical procedure did he tell you about??"

"His fucking colonoscopy" explained Josie, debating how to reply "He told me all about the preparation, what he had to wear and how he took his mind off it by reciting ABBA songs".

Josie typed a polite version of Aimii's suggested reply "I'll leave out the word 'fucking' but I will tell him that the feelings are mutual. Thinks he's god's gift. I mean I know I'm no supermodel, but seriously??"

Aimii agreed with Josie's sentiments "At least you are going away with your mum soon, that will help take your mind off all this".

Josie agreed "Definitely. Maybe I need to stay off the dating again for a while".

Aimii shrugged "Yeah but how are you going to find anyone if you don't put yourself out there? It's a tough choice babes. Have another look at your messages to see if there's anyone else you fancy a look at".

Josie sighed and clicked on one of her dating apps and began scrolling through her inbox messages and then put her phone back down. Dating was probably off the table for a while at least.

Back at work everyone had just about recovered from the Christmas party and Sandy was talking to anyone who would listen about the evening from her point of view.

Sandy was wearing a red mini skirt and white blouse, set off with her usual red lipstick, her blonde curls hanging perfectly in a bob around her chin. Marvin and Josie were the latest recipient of her woes.

"I can't believe I wasn't well at the Christmas the party" exclaimed Sandy, tapping her red brightly varnished nails on her desk "I was overcome with a viral infection I think".

Marvin pursed his lips and straightened his silk blue tie against his perfectly ironed white shirt before sorting out the papers in his hand that he needed to pass on to Mrs Wilshire.

"Of course you were darling" said Marvin placing the papers on the desk "But what can you do?"

Josie took the rest of the papers out of Marvin's hand "Come on let's do the rest of the reports".

"Are you coming to the ball?" asked Sandy quickly changing the subject.

"I don't think so" replied Josie slowly, looking over at Marvin who was vigorously shaking his head.

"Shame" replied Sandy shaking her head "I've still got some tickets that BobbyB wants me to sell, and I've had to put down the deposit for the function room at the hotel already".

"Did he give you the money for that?" asked Josie "seems he's asking an awful lot of you".

Sandy shrugged "He's just so busy helping different people, and I'm just trying to help him. I did get a rather odd message via social media though, claiming to be an ex partner of his, saying that he was a conman".

Josie and Marvin looked at one another with raised eyebrows.

"Did you mention that to him?" asked Josie.

"Of course" said Sandy, showing them both his latest status on his social media "He said it's someone who has a grudge, and he's defended me admirably, look".

BobbyB's social media showed the following:

*"To whoever it was who sent a nasty message to a friend of mine about me, let's meet up. You and me and a nice cup of tea".*

At the end of the message was a fist/punch emoji.

"Doesn't mention you though Sandy, does it?" said Marvin.

"He's protecting my privacy" said Sandy, closing down the page on her laptop "He's just being a gentleman".

Josie and Marvin didn't comment, and filed out of the office looking at each other.

"Bloody hell he sounds like a right conman" said Josie "What's Sandy getting herself into?"

"No idea" said Marvin quickly making his way down the corridor "anyway I just remembered that I need to delete some of the photos on my phone in case Sandy finds out where the photos of her and Jonathon came from and the company starts looking into staff phones and things. Jonathon is raging or so I heard!  Toodle pips Josie!"

Josie smiled as Marvin disappeared down the corridor, then made her way back to her own desk.  Helen was sat at her own desk looking rather despondent, tapping slowing away on her computer keyboard.

"You ok?" ventured Josie, sitting on her office chair "you seem a bit down?"

"Did you not see the photos of Jonathon and Sandy that are going around?? Oh my god, that should of been me with my legs in the air!  Been flirting with him for bloody months and then Sandy has a few too many gins and ends up in a car with him.  Anyway have you heard about that new dogging site round here?"

Nic came off the phone just to hear the end of the conversation.

"Really Helen, why would we know about that?" asked Nic

"Disgusting behaviour.  Where is it anyway?"

Helen laughed, pushing her long black hair behind her back

"Why do you want to know Nic?  If you park in the right place and get lucky, you might end up with some bollocks on your windscreen".

Josie nearly spat out her coffee whilst Nic looked horrified.

"Well I pity anyone whose testicles end up on my windscreen" said Nic.

"Why" ventured Josie, putting her cup of coffee down before the reply.

"Because" continued Nic "my wipers will be put on fast wiping mode quicker than you can say 'get your gonads off my windscreen you bloody pervert'".

"Spoilsport" said Helen "I haven't been dogging but I did have sex with someone on a car roof up the country park once. The police turned up and saw us in their headlights, and we made a dent in the car roof, so I can't recommend it".

Nic tutted in disgust before answering her phone and raising her eyebrows at Josie. Josie began packing up her stuff as she had the afternoon off to start preparing for her holiday with her mum, Rebecca. It was years since they had been away together and Josie was very much looking forward to it.

Josie left work and went to pick up her mum from the flats. Rebecca was already waiting outside dressed in a jeans, a butterfly print blue jumper and a warm looking red coat. Rebecca beamed as she saw Josie approaching.

"Hiya love, how are you?" Rebecca kissed Josie on the cheek and gave her a big hug "I thought it was you that pulled up a minute ago so I got in and started chatting away only to see it was some fella with a beard sat there haha!"

Josie shook her head in despair "Really you should be more careful mum, he could of been some weirdo".

"Ah he didn't mind" said Rebecca, putting on her seatbelt "He just looked a bit shocked and I just got out again".

Josie began the drive to the beauty salon which was situated just on the outskirts of town but on a main road, and also housed a cafe area and a gym. Josie parked around the back of the building and they made their way to the front through the double glass doors. Everything looked shiny inside, the light coloured floors gleamed with cleanliness and the reception desk was very white and reflective. A very well groomed woman with blonde tied back hair, heavy make up and a white tunic manned the front desk.

"Good afternoon, can I help you?" asked the receptionist.

"Yes I rang earlier, you said that it was pretty free this afternoon, so could make our choice of beauty treatments on arrival?"

"Ah yes" smiled the receptionist, retrieving two laminated treatment lists from behind the desk "January is a bit of a quiet time so look through the list and I can tell you what we have available to you this afternoon.  Take a seat in the cafe if you like then let me know".

Josie took the lists and thanked the receptionist, before making their way through to the cafe area which was furnished with small round glass tables and metal framed chairs with wooden seats.  Josie bought herself and Rebecca a pot of tea before taking a seat.

"What are you going to have done?" asked Josie, perusing the list.

"It says here you can have your legs or your froo froo waxed" said Rebecca "You can have a full leg or half a leg.  I think I'll have the half leg option, it's a bit cheaper".

Josie nodded, thinking that she would stick to shaving any private bits rather than waxing them - her sister had tried waxing her own bikini line but reported that it had got far too painful near the middle so had stuck to a Mohican type look.

"And I'll have a fake tan done too" added Rebecca "What about you?"

Josie decided against any waxing but instead decided on a facial and a fake tan to hopefully give her a natural healthy look whilst they were away rather than the natural pasty colour that she currently had. They made their way back to the reception to book their choice of treatments.

"So can I have a fake tan please and half a leg waxing" said Rebecca pointing at the laminated list.

"Of course" said the receptionist, writing down the choices in the appointment book.

"And" added Rebecca "As I'm only having the half leg option, can it be the front of my legs please?"

Josie gave her mum a quizzical look. Rebecca shrugged.

"Well it's better to have the front half waxed because by the time you've walked by it doesn't matter".

"I think they mean the bottom half of your legs or the whole leg mum, not front or back" laughed Josie in embarrassment.

"Ah ok" said Rebecca "bottom half then, because there's hardly any hair on the top half anyway".

The receptionist smiled and carried on writing "That's booked in for you. When you're ready, make your way up the stairs and the changing rooms are on the left and the treatment rooms are on the right. If you get changed then go into the treatment room area you can wait to be called".

Josie and Rebecca made their way up the stairs and into the changing rooms where they found tall lockers in which to put their belongings and white towelling robes to wear for the duration of their treatments. First to be done was the facial and the waxing before the fake tans. Josie laid on a leather treatment bed and had her facial before being left to relax with a mask on whilst Rebecca had her waxing done next door.

Next was the fake tan which left both women with a nice healthy glow. Josie joined Rebecca in her treatment room to see how it had all gone.

"You happy with it all?" asked Josie. Rebecca switched off the light, leaving only the glow of an unused sunbed to light up the room. She took off her towelling robe and stood near the tinted window and admired her tanned body in the mirror, standing at different angles.

"Yes love, it looks really nice. I'll give myself a couple of extra minutes to dry off and then we can go and pay".

Josie got ready first and made her way down to reception to pay the remainder of the fees before waiting outside for some fresh air, where she noticed a small group of men looking at one of the windows upstairs. As they saw Josie approach, they quickly walked away, leaving Josie standing alone and looking slightly bemused until she looked up at the window.

The sun was hitting the window in such a way that she could see her mum through the tinted window, her body being highlighted even more the light from the sunbed in the room. Josie didn't know whether to laugh or be horrified and quickly went back inside.

"Your tinted windows don't work!" said Josie to the receptionist.

"Oh dear, we've had this problem before, maybe we should use curtains" said the receptionist smiling "anyway we hope you've had a lovely afternoon".

Josie decided not to tell her mum about the window incident and greeted her with a warm smile as she made her way back into the reception area.

"You were quick love" smiled Rebecca "I can't wait for our holiday now!"

"Me neither" smiled Josie, giving her mum a hug.

# CHAPTER EIGHTEEN

Josie and Rebecca's flight was an early one, so they arrived at the airport just as the sun was beginning to rise. Both women felt tired, so after checking in decided to shop for some magazines and then sit and have a cup of tea before they were called for their flight. The hours seemed to drag by until eventually their flight was called and they made their way to the correct gate. Lots of people had already taken their seats and Josie and Rebecca's seats were situated in the middle rows of the plane seats where they had to manoeuvre past one person who was already sitting down, in order to get to their seat.

"I'll get in first" said Rebecca, holding on to the headrest of the seat in front in order to be able to squeeze by.

Rebecca suddenly lurched forward and touched the bald head of a man in front to steady herself before sitting on the lap of the man she was trying to squeeze past.

"Sorry!" said Josie, apologising on Rebecca's behalf "She does this all the time!"

Rebecca and Josie made themselves as comfortable as they could before the plane took off on its journey to Malta. They had paid for a transfer to the hotel to avoid having to take taxis and found themselves on a large coach which was dropping groups of people off at different hotels around the area. After 30 minutes, the coach pulled up outside a very grey looking hotel which was around 10 storeys high. The road outside was full of stray cats and littered with overflowing bins and the odd deserted bike.

The holiday company rep stood up who was dressed in a mauve skirt and jacket with a brightly coloured blouse, her blonde hair tied firmly pack into a ponytail.

"This is the hotel Happy Days!" she chirped "If you're booked for this one, can you make your way off the coach and get your luggage please, then the hotel staff will be pleased to check you in.  Remember that I will be coming to your hotels during every morning to see if you want to go on any excursions and check that everything's ok".

She finished her words with a broad grin, keeping eye contact with the guests and avoiding looking at the very miserable hotel that they were currently parked next to.

"This is ours" said Rebecca, making her way off the coach "didn't look like this in the brochure".

About 8 people got off the coach and stood at the roadside as the coach quickly pulled away and then they made their way into the reception area.  The reception desk was very dark looking, with dark green walls and a dark oak desk with wooden pigeon holes behind it containing keys for the rooms. It was being manned by a short, hairy, leathery skinned looking man with greased back hair, wearing a short sleeved shirt where the buttons strained to contain his rather bulbous stomach.

"Hallo hallo you people!" he said, waving them forward "welcome to the Happy Days. I give you your keys to your room and then you will be happy, yes?"

Josie looked doubtful. Off the reception area was another dark looking room with round tables covered in table clothes and one large table that seemed to have a washing up bowl on top of it.

Rebecca checked in and got the keys and then they made their way upstairs to their room. It was very simple, with two single beds, one wardrobe and an en suite bathroom where the curtain rail was looking decidedly wonky and unstable. Josie went onto the balcony where she could see the pool which had a very unsavoury green look about it and an abandoned sun lounger could be seen resting at the bottom. There was a sudden heavy rain shower so Josie quickly made her way back inside and shut the sliding door onto the patio and sat on the bed.

"Mum this hotel is awful" said Josie, staring at the ceiling which was nicotine stained and in dire need of repainting. Rebecca nodded "We'll have to speak to the holiday rep tomorrow but we'll have to stay overnight until then". Rebecca opened the wardrobe to hang up her jacket, and the wardrobe pole promptly fell down with an echoing clatter onto the wardrobe floor. Josie and Rebecca decided to stay in their rooms until the dining room opened in the evening, as the local area didn't look like the kind of place to be wandering about in once it was dark. There was no sign of the sea, which turned out to be a 30 minute walk away through the town centre, according to the small hotel information guide that had been left on the small side table in their room.

The evening dining experience turned out to be an interesting affair. Bread rolls were placed directly onto the tablecloths, and the guests' dirty dishes and glasses had to be put into the washing up bowl on the table, which Josie initially thought had been left there by mistake. It was a relief when the next morning the holiday rep turned up to listen to all their woes. Everyone in the group wanted to move hotel and for a small upgrade fee, the rep agreed, with a forced smile. A small coach arrived around midday to move the group to a different hotel and they got to see a much nicer side of Malta. The coach wound its way towards a beautiful bay area which was surrounded by white stone houses, hotels and bars and seemed to be a bustling but much nicer part of the island. In the bay, small fishing boats were anchored in the bay and were gently bobbing up and down in the waves, their brightly coloured hulls shining in the sun which had decided to come out that day in all its glory.

The coach pulled out of the bay and made a short drive to a small but pleasant looking hotel called The Rockna.

Their new hotel was much more pleasant than the previous one - it had no pool but it had clean white tiled floors throughout with fresh clean rooms and the balconies that faced the street overlooked a cluster of small hotels opposite, beyond which you could see the blue glistening sea. The sun shone brightly and whilst it wasn't hot weather, it was warm enough to wear a t-shirt without getting cold and made a pleasant change from the cold English weather that they had been experiencing.

"So much better" said Josie, breathing in the air from outside, and feeling the warm sun on her face.

Rebecca smiled and agreed "Right let's get changed and go out today, maybe walk around that lovely bay area?"

Josie nodded as Rebecca took off all her clothes, ready to shower. Josie laid on the bed listening to the bustling sound of the town outside and felt relaxed and happy for once.

Rebecca came out of the bathroom with a large, fluffy white

towel wrapped around her head and another white towel surrounding her damp body. She took off both the towels and looked into her suitcase, deciding what to wear. Josie sat up on her bed and looked at the window to notice a reflective glint from one of the windows in a hotel opposite. It was a man with an old fashioned looking video camera which was panning across the area and then paused as it spied Rebecca stood there naked next to her bed.

"Mum, mum there's a man videoing across the street!" shrieked Josie, pointing over.

Rebecca made her way to the balcony doors, still completely naked, and mouthed the word "PERVERT!" before swishing the curtains closed.

"Mum, he got an even better look of you naked before you did that! Why didn't you put your towel back on. Why didn't I do something haha?" laughed Josie "What a nightmare".

"You'd best go and report him" said Rebecca, putting a towel back on around her body "go down to reception and tell them".

Josie agreed and made her way to the reception where she found a man with the name badge 'Carlos', who was a handsome looking Maltese man, with greying black hair, in his 50s, dressed in black trousers and a palm tree patterned shirt. He looked a Mediterranean version of Pierce Brosnan thought Josie.

"Hi, my mum just got out of the shower in room 19 and there was a man videoing us from across the street" explained Josie.

Carlos smiled "You want me to come see?"

"Umm no" said Josie "He's in the hotel opposite and my mum is upstairs in just a towel".

"You want me to come see?" asked Carlos again.

"No don't worry" said Josie "we'll just keep an extra eye out for him".

Josie made her way back up and walked along the corridor, to see Rebecca start to come out of the room in just her towel.

"Did you get some help love?" asked Rebecca, just as the door slammed shut behind her with the breeze from their balcony.

"No" sighed Josie "But I'll have to get the spare key now, because you've just locked us out mum".

Josie went and fetched the spare key from Carlos, before getting ready for their walk around the bay. They ate some beautiful fresh cakes and drank tea then explored the local market before making their way back to the hotel for their evening meal. Some of the guests who had also been at the Happy Days hotel had started to become friends and socialise together in the evenings.

Brian and Margaret were a couple in their late 60s with grey hair and were enjoying their regular winter break. They had worked most of their lives, had children and grandchildren but were now determined to enjoy their retirement as much as they possibly could. Paul and Karen were a couple in their 30s and were much more outgoing. They too had children but had left them at home with the grandparents to enjoy a holiday alone, and regularly took breaks with friends. Karen had voluminous black permed hair and always wore large hooped earrings and was usually heavily made up, no matter what time of day it was. Paul was slightly quieter out of the two, and always seemed to make sure he sat next to Josie whenever they were sat in a group.

One of the larger hotels in the area had a happy hour from 6pm-7pm and Paul and Karen encouraged the others to go. It had very grand entrance with a landscaped area out the front including a very large cannon which was sat as a decorative piece surrounded by a stoned area and assorted plants including several large cactuses. The bar area in the hotel was also very grand looking. Half the floor was carpeted and the other half was a black and white tiled dance floor where a black grand piano stood and was regularly played for anyone who wanted to listen or indeed to dance.

Karen smiled at the others as they all sat down on the sofas that surrounded a low glass table.

"I couldn't believe that other hotel you know, so rough" declared Karen, sipping on her half price cocktail " When I went into the shower, not being rude right, but I put the shower head down there" Karen pointed down at her groin area "And it suddenly went hot".

Paul chimed in "Similar happened to me in that dodgy hotel. I was stood in the shower when it suddenly got hot and I jumped back and burnt my cock".

Josie nearly spit out her drink and Margaret who was sat on the sofa opposite, pursed her lips in disapproval.

Rebecca then recounted the story of how she'd once nearly burnt her groin with the candle and essential oils in the bath, followed by the story of being videoed earlier by the man with the camera.

"Blimey, all happens to you doesn't it" said Paul, buying Karen another drink and who was fast having far too much alcohol to handle.

Josie agreed that lots of things did seem to happen to her mum all the time, but that was just the way she was. The group managed to fit in rather a lot of cocktails in the happy hour and as 7pm came and went they decided to make their way back to their own hotel.

"Does anyone want to see my tanned boobs??" asked Karen as they made their way to the hotel entrance to leave "I always show my friends my tan when I get home!"

Margaret gave Brian an elbow before he could answer and Paul managed to get Karen through the large hotel lobby without her falling over. As they made their way outside the hotel, Karen spotted the large cannon outside.

"Ooooh let's take a photo on the cannon" said Karen running drunkenly towards it "Someone help me on it".

Brian gave Karen a leg up onto the cannon before joining her astride it much to Margaret's disdain.

Paul took a photo quickly with his camera before gesturing Karen to get down "Come on love, we said we'd try and get through this year without getting arrested".

Brian swung his leg over the cannon, before dropping down onto the stony ground and held out his arms "Come on love I've got you!".

Karen slid off the cannon towards Brian who lost his balance as she bumped into him falling off and landed onto a nearby cactus.

"That's probably why the cactuses are there" offered Josie.

Some of the hotel staff came outside to see what the commotion was so Paul quickly led Karen away, followed by the rest of the group.

"I've been pricked" said Karen, rubbing her thighs and calfs as they walked down the street "What the bloody hell did I land on?"

"Apart from Brian you mean?" laughed Rebecca.

Paul began walking next to Josie, who felt a pinch on her bum. Surely that was a mistake. Minutes later in happened again, so Josie moved away to walk closer to Margaret who seemed the much safer option. As they made their way into their own hotel and into the lobby, they all said their farewells for the night. Paul and Karen were in the next room to Rebecca and Josie.

Josie and Rebecca went into their room and turned on their bedside lamps to give their room a nice relaxed glow. Josie made her way onto the balcony and looked out over at the busy town which was still full of noise and people socialising in bars and restaurants, their voices and the music carrying though the night air. Josie heard the balcony next door open and then close and looked over to see Paul out on the next balcony.

"Hey" said Paul, drinking out of a bottle of beer "you had a good night?"

"Yes" said Josie, smiling politely "Is Karen ok? She seemed to land right on that cactus earlier".

Paul laughed "Yeah she'll be ok, she's asleep on the bed now. She's always doing stuff like that. Last year she got arrested for streaking at the local cricket match after she got drunk on the free jugs of Pimms that they were serving in the refreshment tent. You ever been arrested?"

"No I haven't, funnily enough" laughed Josie awkwardly.

"So" said Paul, smiling over at Josie "Did you know that this hotel has a roof top area? Really nice this time of night...".

"Oh, no I didn't" said Josie "It sounds lovely, maybe I'll have a look before we have to go home".

"Why not look tonight?" said Paul with a wink, swinging his bottle of beer between two fingers "Could be fun".

Josie pulled a face "No thanks, maybe Karen might enjoy it with you tomorrow, goodnight!"

Josie quickly shut the balcony doors behind her and went back into the room, where Rebecca was in bed reading a book.

"Who were you talking to?" asked Rebecca.

"Paul, he asked me to meet him on the roof top!" replied Josie.

Rebecca looked over the top of her book "Pervert! Best keep away from him then, what is it with these men? Best not tell Karen, otherwise she'll probably slap you one".

Josie whole heartedly agreed and got ready for bed then spent some time going through some of her inboxes. There were lots of messages, mostly from older men, apart from one man who was two years' younger that had sent Josie a message. It read:

*'Hello, you're very beautiful, how do you feel about dating a younger man?'*

Josie rolled her eyes. Two years' younger than her and he considered himself a 'younger man'. He looked a bit like a scientist as his picture showed him wearing a white coat and thick rimmed glasses. Josie didn't fancy him and showed her mum the message and his picture.

Rebecca put down her book and looked at it "Younger man??
If you want a younger man go at least 10 years younger! He's
only 2 years' younger. Tell him that yes you do want a
younger man so if he can find one for you that would be great
thanks!".

Josie laughed and carried on looking through her messages.
There was another message from a guy called Steve who again
was 2 years' younger and didn't seem too bad. He was local
and looked normal which was always a good start. Josie
messaged him back and there were some chatty messages
back and forth before she fell fast asleep.

The next morning the sun streamed through the hotel room
window, peaking through the curtains and warming up the
room. It was a lovely feeling to have the sun on a January
day. Outside it was about 18 degrees and the locals were
wearing warm coats whilst the tourists were wandering
around in t shirts and much more summery clothes, who were
clearly used to much colder weather.

Breakfast was a buffet affair and Paul kept glancing over nervously towards Josie as they helped themselves to the selection of breakfast pastries, toast and fruit. Paul and Karen joined Josie and Rebecca at one of the long breakfast tables. Karen put her foot up on one of the chairs.

"Look at that! I've got holes in my leg and my bum from where I landed on that cactus. I thought that Brian would catch me better than that".

"Don't blame Brian love" said Paul, winking at Josie and Rebecca "he probably saw your arse coming and dived out of the way, poor fella haha".

Karen gave Paul a disgusted look then turned to Josie and Rebecca "Anyway ladies, what are you up to today, anything good?"

They had decided to spend their last full day exploring the island. Malta was a very beautiful island full of sandy stoned buildings and a capital town that housed many shops, restaurants and museums that reflected the Island's history. It was easily accessible by a bus service that serviced the whole island, and whilst a bit bumpy at times, provided quite a reliable service.

On the final evening the group decided to go back to the large hotel for a final happy hour, although there was much less alcohol consumed this time around. The piano was being played and Brian decided to teach everyone how to waltz properly and chose Josie for his partner.

"You know this modern dancing is just not intimate at all. With a waltz you can get quite close to your partner, much better" declared Brian, showing everyone the basic steps "I used to be a fireman you know" continued Brian, raising his eyebrows and briefly taking his hand away from Josie's waist to flatten his greying hair.

"Oh really" said Josie, her eyes wandering over to Karen and Paul who seemed to now be having a full blown argument in the corner. Rebecca intervened by taking Karen to the bar for an extra cocktail, whilst Paul drowned his sorrows by sitting with Margaret who was now knitting in the corner and appeared to be quite happy to listen to Paul's apparent woes of being with Karen.

The weekend had been fun and a very pleasant change from day to day life. Malta had been warm, friendly and welcoming, and was definitely somewhere that Josie would like to revisit. As the plane took off from the airport, Josie looked out of the window at the beautiful island and glistening blue sea that was slowing getting further away. Now it was time to get back to reality.

# CHAPTER NINETEEN

When Josie got back home and into her normal routine, she had carried on messaging Steve for a little while and had arranged to meet him for a date. He looked quite confident in his picture and had a bit of a smirk on his face but Josie thought she shouldn't judge him on that alone. He suggested that they meet for a meal in a country pub which Josie agreed would be rather lovely.

The night before, Josie met up with Jo, Katie, Mel and Aimii for a little bit of a catch up.

"Do you remember Hat Richard??" said Aimii, pouring everyone a drink "You remember him Josie, from ages ago?"

Josie nodded "Yeah you mean the one you didn't want to come to our town haha!"

"He is conman babes, look".

Aimii showed the girls an article that showed Hat Richard was indeed a conman, who had conned a woman out of £20,000 worth of savings and was now in prison as that wasn't his first offence. Josie slumped back onto the sofa. He had seemed a bit weird, but this was another thing to contend with, the fact that some men might be after what little money women had for their own gains and didn't want a relationship at all. At least most of the men who just wanted sex were a bit more honest about it.

Katie smiled and updated everyone with her news. She was still dating the guy who had broken his leg and things seemed to be going really well in that direction. Mel hadn't been having a lot of luck. Most of the guys she had been messaging seemed to ghost her after a while or were only after one thing. It was quite a common theme in the online dating world.

Josie braced herself for her next date. Dating shouldn't be something you have to brace yourself for, but Josie was having so many disasters she felt it necessary.

The pub that Steve had chosen was a very traditional looking pub in the middle of the countryside. It had a small gravelled car park, and lanterns lit up the archway into the garden and to the main entrance.  When Josie pulled up into the car park, Steve was already stood there waiting by his car.  His was wearing a billowy white shirt, dark blue jeans and brown shoes.  His face was true to his picture and he smiled broadly as Josie approached.  She'd decided to wear a flowery tea dress with a cardigan and boots and her blonde hair was looking smooth and shiny.

"Hey you" beamed Steve, kissing Josie on the cheek "you look amazing, let's go in and get a drink and decide what we should eat".

Steve led the way into the pub which had low beamed ceilings and wooden floors throughout.  They sat down at a thick oak table which was lit up by small candles.

"Very romantic" declared Steve, picking up the menu "So Josie, how have you been getting on with the online dating stuff?"

It was always a weird question to have asked, because Josie always felt that discussing other dates probably wasn't the best way forward with a new potential partner and surely if it was going well, she wouldn't be still online. But Josie carried on with the theme, as sometimes it was interesting to see what their answer to the question was.

"Not too great" said Josie, honestly "Bit of a mixed bag. How about you".

Steve smirked "Well I must confess that I've had a bit of luck".

Josie looked up from her menu, which she then placed back on the wooden table.

"What do you mean 'a bit of luck' " asked Josie. It sounded like something a man would say to one of his mates rather than his latest date. Steve looked briefly panicked, obviously having revealed too much already. He dug himself further into a hole.

"Well you know" said Steve "I've had a few flings. Not that I intended them to set out that way of course I should add".

Josie felt disheartened. These type of guys were actually worse than the ones who sent dick pics and blatant requests for sex - at least they were honest. The Steve-types got their own way by buying a few meals if you were lucky, making out it was going somewhere, then after getting you into bed, moved onto the next one. It wasn't pleasant and felt dishonest.

Josie kept being polite and listened to Steve talk about himself and his job for most of the meal. As the restaurant area filled up, the air became quite warm so Steve opened a window to get some fresh air. As the cool air filtered through into the room, Josie could smell the distinct smell of cow dung and farmyards seeping through the window.

"You can really smell the countryside out here" remarked Josie at the strong smell.

Steve laughed "Well excuse you Josie, what a fart" inferring that Josie had made the smell.

Jokes like that were never funny. Rude and not funny, especially on a first date.

"So" said Steve, leaning in slightly "I think me and my brother must have a thing for older women as he's seeing an older woman too".

Josie was 2 years' older than Steve, hardly anything ground breaking. Again, it was rude, thought Josie, and he was rather full himself. Josie made it through the rest of the meal and insisted on paying for her half at the end of it, so that Steve definitely wouldn't think that she owed him anything if he paid for it all. As they made their way out to the car park, Josie made sure that they kept a reasonable distance to avoid Steve making any attempts to kiss her.

"Night then young man" said Josie unlocking her car.

"Night then old lady" laughed Steve, going towards his own car "Thanks for a lovely evening".

Josie didn't reply to his rudeness and instead sat in her own car for a while, reflecting on yet another disastrous date. After a few minutes, her phone beeped with a message. It was a message from Steve already.

*"Were you wearing any panties this evening? ;-) "*

Oh my god, thought Josie, how inappropriate was this?? She had obviously been too polite. Josie blocked Steve then made her way home.

February began a cold and snowy month and so began all the adverts for Valentine's day. It was a bit of a crappy time of year to be single, with all the shops full of hearts, cuddly toys and cards declaring undying notes of love to significant other halfs. Josie bemoaned her singleness on Valentine's day during her lunch break at work.

"I don't know why you get so hung up about it" said Nic, eating jaffa cakes on one of the sofas with Helen "I've been married for years and my husband never gives me anything, he's rubbish".

"Actually" confessed Josie "When I was married, my ex husband used to give me really rubbish presents for all kinds of occasions. He once bought me a toaster for my birthday. He did give me other stuff, but the biggest box, the one that looked most exciting, contained a bloody toaster!".

"Awful" agreed Marvin, joining in the conversation "My worst present was one of those joke thongs that looks like an elephant, it was waaaaaay too small for a start".

"Reminds me of the first time I saw a bollock" said Helen eating a jaffa cake whilst adjusting her flowery skirt over her leggings.

"Do tell" said Marvin, crossing his legs and pursing his lips.

"Well" continued Helen "I was about 10 and in a swimming pool, and as I swam to the edge of the pool, a teenage boy was stood there waiting to jump in. He was wearing speedos that were way too small and I could see a hairy bollock poking out the side".

"That pair of budgie smugglers has a lot to answer for" smiled Marvin "it started your journey to bigger and better things".

Helen laughed "it sure did".

Josie finished up her lunch and made her way through Reception where Bridie was sat with a very large bouquet of flowers sat on top of the desk.

"Wow, they're beautiful" declared Josie, going over for a closer look.

"Actually they're for you" said Bridie, reading the envelope that was attached to the outer wrapping.

"Are you sure?" asked Josie.

Bridie nodded and carefully handed over the large bouquet "You'd better take them upstairs for now, before it sets off my hay fever".

Josie carefully took the flowers upstairs and placed them in some water before tearing open the envelope. Who on earth could be sending her flowers, and such a huge bouquet. Josie opened the envelope and read the card inside.

*"My dearest Josie. I hope these flowers find you well. I know that you love flowers and hope that this bouquet gives you a smile. Kindest regards, Charles".*

Josie took a photo of the flowers and card and sent it to Aimii who was quick to respond.

*"Oh my god babes they are beautiful! And from Charles. But how did he know where you worked??"*

Josie thought carefully about the conversations she had had with Charles. She had told Charles what her job was but not where she worked. He must of searched her on the internet and found her listed on the company's website. She wasn't sure if it was a bit stalkery or romantic, but they were the biggest bunch of flowers she had ever seen.

*"That is so romantic babes"* messaged Aimii.

*"Do you think I should go on another date with him? I feel guilty now"* replied Josie.

*"No, he ate your face alive babes remember, you had to buy more wipes!"*

Josie recalled the feeling of the awful kiss which had enveloped her whole mouth and half her face, and had to agree. She would send Charles a text to thank him but reiterate very politely that he wasn't the one for her.

Josie placed the flowers in some water and pondered over her last few dates and where she had possibly gone wrong. It hadn't seemed to matter whether the men were the same age, or a bit young, the outcome had been the same - disastrous dates. She hadn't been on one date yet where she'd really really fancied the person or had come away thinking what a great time she'd had. Maybe it was her that was the problem and she set the bar too high. Or too low. Marvin interrupted Josie's thoughts.

"Penny for them" he smiled as he filled the kettle with water next to Josie's flowers "nice flowers, and for Valentine's day too".

"Oh I don't know about this dating crap any more, it's too hard work" sighed Josie, leaning back on the worktop and folding her arms "Don't men look for relationships any more? Maybe it's me??"

Marvin gasped in horror "Any man would be lucky to have you my darling, it's just unfortunate that you and your mother attract perverts far and wide!"

"My mum attracted another one the other day actually" said Josie, casting her mind back to a conversation with Rebecca the other day "She was in a book shop and some weird little man kept staring at her chest, so she went into the vegan section and he followed her there too.  Anyway I digress, where are all these lovely men?? Is it too late in my life to find a decent one?"

Marvin became serious for a moment "You, Josie my darling, will definitely find what you are looking for, because you deserve it.  All these beasts you keep meeting just don't deserve you, that's all".

Josie gave Marvin a faint smile and showed him her inbox.

"Look.  Mr Right isn't there is he??" stated Josie.

"You don't know until you try. Give the phone to me, let's do a random choice! Pick number 3 on the list and go on a date with him. Why not. Your selection criteria clearly isn't working" laughed Marvin.

Josie looked at the third message in her inbox. The guy had slightly ginger hair, was ten years' younger and was reasonably local. She showed it to Marvin who shrugged.

"Yeah him. Why not" said Marvin, adding three sugars to his tea "Tell him you'll meet him tomorrow, he's already asked you out look. Why waste time in all this chit chat only to go on a bloody awful date. Cut straight to the date and if it's crap, very little time wasted. Give me your phone".

Marvin grabbed Josie's phone and typed in a message, waited a few seconds, then smiled.

"All set. In your local pub tomorrow night at 7pm" declared Marvin, handing back Josie's phone.

"Oh bloody hell Marvin" said Josie, staring at her inbox "What have you done? And in my local pub too??"

"It'll be fine, means you can have a drink to steady your nerves and no wasted petrol if it's crap as usual".

"Thanks Marvin" said Josie sarcastically "Anyway I'd best get back to work, I'll be speaking to you soon!"

Josie didn't know if the last minute date arranged by Marvin was a good idea or not, but she thought that about most dates, so decided to go anyway. She did her usual thing of making sure Aimii knew who she was meeting and where, and made her way to the pub. It was a windy evening, so by the time Josie had walked to the pub, she was looking and feeling rather windswept. Matthew was already stood at the bar waiting for her. He was dressed in a black jumper and black jeans, and his hair seemed slightly more ginger in real life than in the picture, but apart from that he was a true likeness to his picture. He grinned when he turned around and saw Josie approach.

"Hello, hello, let me get you a drink, you look lovely" said Matthew.

"Very kind, but I'll get these" said Josie, trying hard to flatten her hair that had taken a battering in the wind "And you look like the Milk Tray man, all dressed in black".

Josie had no idea why she blurted that out, but Matthew grinned and appeared to take it as a compliment as he got them both a drink instead of taking Josie up on her offer. Josie decided on wine and they made their way to a table at the quieter end of the pub. Matthew was very chatty and keen to tell Josie all about him and his life. He worked as a administrator for a large snack company, had two dogs, enjoyed films, football and going on holidays. Josie tried to listen and pay attention as Matthew carried on chatting about himself. As she drank her wine she noticed that Matthew kept rubbing his thighs with the palms of his hands. Maybe he's nervous, thought Josie, still trying to pay attention to what he was saying.

Eventually Matthew stopped talking for a little while to find a little bit more about Josie. She was wary about giving too much information away, especially after Charles had managed to track her down and send her those flowers, which had been a bit disconcerting. The evening had been a reasonably pleasant one but Josie quickly came to realise that she didn't fancy Matthew, although he seemed to be quite flirty and chatty with her despite his weird habit of rubbing his thighs. As the evening wore on and as Josie had to walk home, she decided not to leave it too late before ending the date.

"I really should be getting home" said Josie, putting on her coat "Thank you for the drink and the company."

Matthew grabbed his black jacket "I'll walk you outside".

Josie and Matthew walked out onto the street and then Matthew began leaning in towards Josie, so she took a few steps back and began chatting, to avoid any unwanted kiss scenarios.

"I really must go you know, it's getting late and cold" said Josie putting on her gloves.

"Of course" said Matthew "Message me when you get home".

Josie nodded and pulled her coat tightly around her body before making her way back home, giving a couple of glances back to make sure that she wasn't being followed. Maybe walking to dates wasn't such a good idea, thought Josie as she walked more quickly towards the flats. Once inside her flat, Josie felt her phone buzz. It was a message from Matthew.

*"Hi Josie, thanks for a lovely evening, I'd really like to see you again".*

Josie replied quickly *"Hi, yes thank you for this evening, you're really lovely but not the one for me, I really hope you find what you are looking for".*

Within minutes a longer message came back from Matthew.

*"Oh my god I'm sorry that I was so nervous!! It must of put you off. But I think you are super hot and I'd really like to see you again!*

*I'm sorry that I kept rubbing my legs but I was nervous and I haven't had sex for ages! I'm desperate for sex!  Please let me see you again!"*

Josie looked in horror at the message. Hadn't had sex for ages?? Was he expecting sex then?? Josie felt annoyed, firstly with Matthew for being so bloody odd and secondly with Marvin for setting it up in the first place.  Josie went round to Aimii's flat and knocked on the door, hoping that she was still awake. Aimii answer the door in her pyjamas.

"You okay?  How was your date?" asked Aimii.

"Bloody awful as usual" declared Josie, making her way into the kitchen and pouring herself a glass of wine "Hope you don't mind but I need this!"

"Of course babes" said Aimii "What happened?"

Josie explained about the date and how he had acted oddly.

"I don't get why he was rubbing his thighs" said Aimii screwing up her nose "Was he touching himself??"

"Oh bloody hell I don't know. But afterwards he sent me a message saying sorry for acting weird but he really fancied me and was in desperate need of sex!"

"Oh my god he sounds so weird" said Aimii, reading the message for herself "What was the thigh rubbing about, is that a sign a man wants sex then??"

"Fuck knows" said Josie, swigging the wine "Has anybody got any good news??"

"Jo is still seeing Danny and he's a stud in bed apparently" laughed Aimii "Anyway do you remember that guy Todd, who me and Katie tried to set you up with in the pub that time? You know, I messaged you his picture and you said no and cried?"

"Umm yeah" said Josie, vaguely recalling that day.

"Well he went out with that Sammy, you know the girl who works in the chip shop in the high street? Well apparently he's a crazy man, and when she ended it he threw a drink over her and now she has a restraining order on him. Proper nuts babe".

"You tried to set me up with that!" said Josie indignantly, finishing her glass of wine "I wanted good news, not news of yet another pyscho in our midst".

"Sorry babes" said Aimii "I've given up on this dating stuff for now. It's too hard work and I quite like being on my own at the moment. No complications".

Josie thought that might actually be a plan. At work the next day, Josie found Marvin in the staff room talking to Nic and Helen.

"I want a word with you!" said Josie, pointing at Marvin "That man you selected for me turned out to be a weirdo".

"Was he gay?" asked Nic, looking at Marvin accusatorily.

"No, well I don't think so!" said Josie sitting down next to them "He was really chatty which was fine, but then there was thigh rubbing going on"

"Rubbing your thighs?" asked Nic.

"No, let me finish" said Josie "He was rubbing his own thighs and then afterwards said it was because he was desperate for sex".

"Was he rubbing his thighs like this?" asked Marvin, demonstrating his question "was he rubbing his hands down his groin, palms facing inwards and around his genitals as he moved his hands down, or was he rubbing them up and down the length of his thighs with the bottom of his palms?"

"What's the difference?" asked Helen "Does it mean different things?"

"No" laughed Marvin crossing his legs and folding his arms as he shook with laughter "I just wanted to picture it correctly!"

Josie threw a teabag at Marvin "Idiot! Anyway that's the last time I listen to you!"

## CHAPTER TWENTY

Josie decided to pay Jane a visit.  She hadn't seen her for ages, and was wondering if she was keeping up with the online winks every day in the hope of getting some back.  The thatched cottage looked as cosy as ever and Josie knocked on the door firmly.  Jane answered it dressed in a dressing gown and wellies - quite an interesting combination thought Josie.

"Hello hellooo" shrieked Jane "You always catch me feeding the bloody chickens.  Come in, let's have a cuppa and cake, it's lemon drizzle, hope you like it but that's all I've got".

The smell of baking filled the air, and a freshly baked loaf of bread sat on the kitchen counter next to the beautifully moist looking lemon cake which had a crust of sugar on the top.  Jane boiled the kettle and began making a pot of tea for them both.

"So how's it going then?  Found anyone gorgeous yet?" asked Jane hopefully.

"Nope" said Jane, walking towards the kitchen table "Lots of dating disasters though, just one after the other. It's terrible".

Josie looked for a clear chair to sit on, as each one had stacks of paper on, except one which had a single piece of paper.

Jane munched on a piece of cake as she walked over and picked up the piece of paper.

"Schedule from my ex husband for next year" explained Jane "When I can expect my maintenance, when he's on holiday, when he wants the kids. Very precise".

"Oh you'd better keep it somewhere safe then" said Josie, sitting on the chair now it was empty.

Jane scrunched up the paper and threw it on the floor for the cat to play with.

"Oh he can fuck off, he changes it about 10 times anyway, not sure why I printed it off. He's getting remarried you know".

"Remarried? Who to?" asked Josie in surprise, as Jane placed the pot of tea on the table and fetched some matching red cups.

"Oh some woman from another country who needs a fucking visa I think. Why else would anyone want him?"

Jane poured out two cups of tea and continued "anyway I've been filling my time my messaging someone, but it's not going to go anywhere so I stopped it".

"How come?" asked Josie, sipping her tea "Do you not fancy him?"

"Nah" said Jane, cutting into the large lemon cake "Anyway he's married.  His wife looks like a fella and he says they haven't had sex in years".

"Why message him then?" asked Josie.

Jane shrugged "Was something to do I guess?  He's not very attractive really, but it passed the time.  He offered to help sort my loft hatch out".

Josie nearly spit out her cake "you mean your actual loft hatch or did he mean something else?"

Jane laughed "No my actual loft hatch!  I stopped messaging

him then he got all funny and started sending me really weird messages, saying how he had been paying for sex with prostitutes and how did I feel about that".

"Was that supposed to make you jealous?" asked Josie, continuing to eat cake.

"Who knows" said Jane "Anyway I think I've found someone who you should go out with".

Josie sighed. It did feel that when you were single, lots of people were keen to match make you to anyone else who they knew, in the belief that it would instantly work.

"Who's that then?" asked Josie.

"Well" explained Jane "You know my kids are involved in the youth group? At the moment they are being helped out by some sailors! One of them is a single pringle like you. He's about 17 years younger than you, but I think you could get away with it".

"Thanks" laughed Josie "I'll take that as a compliment then".

Jane showed Josie a photo of a slender man, with large ears and a pale face, he was wearing a life jacket and standing with a group of children next to some canoes.

"I don't think so" said Josie "I mean he looks ok I guess, in an interesting way, but if he's in the forces then he's going to be travelling about a lot and I'd prefer someone who was actually going to be around".

"Fair enough" said Jane "I did show him your picture and he said he was very busy but he could meet you by the river when he was canoeing one evening if you wanted to".

"So romantic" laughed Josie "If that's all he can stretch to then I think I'll give him a miss, but thanks anyways".

Jane smiled and cleared away the cups and plates "More cake? More tea?"

"No thanks" said Josie standing up "I must go and see my mum, I haven't seen her for a few days so will pop in there on my way back home. Thanks for the lovely cake though".

Jane smiled and let Josie out the door of the cottage.

"Let me know if you find your Prince Charming" called Jane from the door.

"I will!" laughed Josie, getting into her car.

When Josie got back home she decided to have another look at online dating again. She decided that she had to have another try before possibly giving up all together and rely on fate to take a hand. Josie had decided that she still didn't want an older man, but maybe one the same age or possibly a bit younger. With online dating you could usually choose an age bracket of what you would be interested in and you could choose the radius of within how many miles you wanted your ideal partner to live. Josie kept her age bracket choice quite wide to try and keep her options open a little. One particular site seemed to have a lot of men in their twenties and thirties and another seemed to have a lot of over 50s despite claiming to be for all different ages. Josie browsed through the site that had the slightly younger men on it, having had a slight confidence boost from Jane that she could "get away with" someone who was 17 years younger than her, not that she was looking for someone in their twenties.

Often younger men weren't looking for someone in Josie's age bracket, but Josie had a browse through. One man in particular caught her eye. His username was 'FitnessFootball'. She usually went for dark haired men but this particular man had dark blonde hair and she noticed that he had a small dog in the background of his profile picture. Liking animals was never a bad sign. Josie looked through his profile and his 'likes' and hobbies. He enjoyed sport, especially football including playing it, liked 80s music and enjoyed watching films. Josie had a look at his age. He was in his early thirties which made him 13 years younger than her. Not ideal, but she was rather taken with his whole persona. She had a look at his preferred age bracket which was stated at 28-35 years, and she immediately felt slightly disappointed, as she clearly wasn't going to be the somebody that he was looking for.

As she carried on scrolling through different profiles, she noticed that she had a notification that someone had looked at her profile. It was "FitnessFootball". On this particular website, you got notified every time someone looked at your profile, even if it was the same person, and over the next few days, Josie got regular notifications that "FitnessFootball" was taking a look at her profile. Maybe he was interested, thought Josie.

Eventually a message came through from "FitnessFootball" asking her questions about her pet dog and what films she liked, which meant that he had actually read her profile properly which made a nice change. "FitnessFootball" was chatty and funny. Josie broached the subject of her not being within his preferred age group which he glossed over, and eventually asked Josie for her number which she was very happy to give to him. Not long after she did, a text came through.

*"Hey guess who?"* said the text message.

Josie smiled and replied immediately *"FitnessFootball!"*

*"Haha it is! But you can call me Lance"* came the reply.

The texting continued and this progressed to a phone call which had also gone well. Lance eventually built up the courage to sort of ask Josie out on a date via text.

*"So maybe I'll see you around town then at some point?"* messaged Lance.

*"Yes let's leave it to chance, because that'll happen lol"* replied Josie.

*"I'd really like to meet you"* said Lance *"Let's arrange to meet up"*.

Josie smiled and messaged her agreement. She'd suggested her local pub as she felt so comfortable about him, but Lance said he'd prefer to meet in one closer to town which Josie said was fine. It all seemed to be going rather well. On the next girls' night out, Josie was keen to show them who she was going on a date with.

"I recognise him" said Katie, drinking her prosecco. Katie was dressed in skin tight leather look trousers and a printed top, partnered with wedge heels. She always turned heads whenever they went out.

"I know him" said Mel, peering more closely at the picture "he used to work in one of the bars down town a few years ago".

"Did he seem ok?" asked Josie hesitantly.

"Yeah" said Mel "I used to talk to him a bit.  He used to come into the local pub with his grandad. Nice pair of blokes actually".

Josie felt relieved that he seemed to be ok. She was fed up of finding strange men, desperate men, rude men!

"When are you meeting him?" asked Aimii "He looks nice".

"Tomorrow" replied Josie "Just for a drink".

"Good idea" said Aimii "Then if it doesn't go well you can just leave".

Josie nodded.  Jo came and sat down with the girls and handed everyone a glass of champagne.

"I've got news for you my gorgeous peeps" declared Jo "Me and Danny are engaged to be married!"

"Oh my god!" shrieked Aimii, jumping up and giving Jo a massive hug "That is so quick, oh my god how exciting!" Josie, Mel and Katie also stood up and gave Jo a big hug, congratulating her on the news. Jo had never been married before, and her face was glowing with the excitement.

"I know it's quick, but you know when something just feels right?" explained Jo "I just bloody love him so much. We're going to have a Disney themed wedding! And all our guests are going to be asked to dress up too. And ladies, I'd like you all to be my bridesmaids!"

"Aww that's amazing" said Josie, smiling "I'm sure we'd all love to".

"Wait a minute" said Mel "If it's a Disney theme, what are you expecting us to dress up as??"

Jo laughed "Well I'm keeping mine a secret, but I was hoping that you could all come dressed as Disney princesses for your bridesmaids outfits. I was thinking Katie could be Snow White, Aimii could be Sleeping Beauty and Mel you could be Elsa from Frozen".

"What about me...?" asked Josie.

"Cinderella" smiled Jo.

"She's kissed a few frogs already, and one that sucked her face off" laughed Aimii.

"That was a different princess" laughed Josie "But I will take Cinderella".

The girls raised their glasses to Jo.

"Here's to a Happy Ever After" said Katie.

"Happy Ever After" agreed everyone, clinking their glasses together. All were glad that Jo had found what she was looking for.

Josie was careful not to drink too much, as she was looking forward to her date with Lance and didn't want to be hungover or looking too rough. As the date approached, Josie became a bit more nervous and couldn't decide what to wear. She tried on different options and took photos which she sent to Aimii.

*"I like the dark green dress babes"* said Aimii.

Josie agreed. It had capped sleeves and a high neck but stopped mid thigh, and she partnered it with a waterfall cardigan and matching dark brown boots. She looked at her watch. She was a little early but decided to leave and drive so that she could wait in the car park until Lance arrived as she hated waiting in pubs on her own. Not long after she parked up, a message came through from Lance and Josie immediately thought that he was going to cancel. He wasn't cancelling but instead was telling Josie that he was going to be about 20 minutes late and was going to have to take the bus. Josie felt so nervous, she offered to go a collect him rather than keep waiting in the pub car park.

*"You're a superstar"* replied Lance *"Can you collect me from near the post office on Hammond Avenue?"*

Josie agreed then checked on her phone exactly where Hammond Avenue was. It was about a 10 minute drive away. As Josie drove towards the Avenue she could see a man who looked very different from Lance's pictures. He was very tall, in his mid twenties, wearing earphones and had a long goatee beard. Josie glanced over to see if he was looking out for anyone who was driving along, but to her relief he carried on walking with his head down to his phone. Then just ahead, Josie could see a figure that looked like Lance next to the post office. He was wearing a shirt and jeans and was quite nice looking. She hoped he wouldn't be disappointed with how she looked. As she pulled up, Lance got into the car and Josie noticed that he had the most beautiful green eyes that she had ever seen. He strapped himself into his seatbelt and looked over at Josie and smiled.

"You alright?" asked Lance with a grin.

"Yes I am" said Josie, turning the car around to head back into town.

She felt relieved that he looked like his photos. In fact she thought that he was slightly better looking in person which was always a bonus.  They decided to go to the original pub where they were going to meet and Lance bought Josie a drink.   It turned out that that when they were married to their previous partners they had actually only lived about 100 metres apart from each other as the crow flies, though bizarrely their paths had never crossed.  Lance used to be good mates with the lads who lived next door to Josie in her ex marital home and they both knew lots of the same people. Lance was funny, in a quick witted kind of way, and Josie enjoyed sitting back and listening to him chatter.  As they sat at their table, Lance had said hello to a few people that had walked by.

"You seem to know quite a few people, is this your local pub?" asked Josie.

"No" laughed Lance, his green eyes twinkling as he looked back at her "I just know loads of people.  I used to work in bars down town and did some d-jaying too so I know lots of faces".

Josie remembered that Mel had said he used to work in some bars.

"So are you going to pie me tomorrow?" asked Lance smiling at Josie.

"Pie you? What does that mean?" asked Josie, hoping that it wasn't a sexual reference.

"When you pie someone, it means that you don't want to see them any more" explained Lance, drinking his beer then placing it back on the table "So what do you think?"

Josie smiled at Lance and didn't reply, instead she simply enjoyed the rest of the evening with someone who she felt she had been looking for, for quite some time.

Josie went into work for the next few weeks with quite a big smile on her face. Lance had initially sent her a joke text the next day after their date saying *you've been pied* before having to quickly explain that he was only joking.

"You're looking happy" commented Marvin "What's up with you?"

"Charming" said Nic, before picking up her phone to answer it.

"I've met someone I really like" explained Josie "We've just clicked. We get on really well, he's really funny and I actually find him quite attractive. Only thing is, he's going away on holiday in a couple of days' time for a week with some of his mates to Spain".

"Oh my god" said Helen "You can say goodbye to that one then. Lads holiday, he'll be chatting up all the women over there, you know what blokes are like on that sort of holiday".

Josie felt slightly deflated. Maybe Helen was right and she needed to not get her hopes up. They were going out for a meal that night so maybe that would be the last time that Josie saw him. They went to a buffet type restaurant and Lance was the one who broached the subject of him going away on holiday.

"I know we've only been going out for a few weeks, but are we exclusive?" asked Lance.

Josie didn't know if he was asking this because he wanted to know if he was free to do what he wanted on holiday or if he wanted her to wait for him until he came back. It was the latter.

"Thing is I really like you" explained Lance "I will still ring you when I'm over there".

Josie tried to contain a big smile, but couldn't quite do so "I really like you too" she replied "I will be here when you get back".

The evening turned out to be a very late one, as Josie and Lance sat in the car and talked until 2am in the morning. As they were sat there, a fox walked down the middle of the road without a care in the world. It was quite surreal. The night sky was clear, and the moon shone down onto the houses below, reflecting in the windows. The streets were empty and silent, except for Josie and Lance who felt like they could sit and talk forever.

Lance's plane had left early in the morning the following day, and Josie hadn't had a chance to speak to him properly before he'd left. He sent her photos of him and his friends at the airport and was giving a thumbs up. The group all looked happy and excited to be going away. A few days went past without any further communication from Lance on holiday, except one photo that he had sent of him on a sun lounger wearing massive oversized joke sunglasses, and Josie had a sinking feeling that it was done and dusted, so against her better judgement she sent him a text.

*"Hi, hope you're having a good holiday. If you're not interested any more, can you let me know, thanks".*

It was a bit needy but Josie didn't want to be hanging around and kept wondering if he didn't want to see her any more. There was no reply to the text but at 4am in the morning, Josie's phone rang. It was Lance.

"Hi Josie, how are you??" shouted Lance. He sounded slightly worse for wear, and sounded like he had been drinking, but sounded pleased to hear Josie's voice.

"I've lost my mates!" explained Lance. Josie could hear his feet on the ground as he walked along and was slightly out of breath.

"Are you okay??" asked Josie sleepily, still waking up "I hadn't heard from you. I sent you a text".

Lance laughed "Yeah I know you did. You thought you'd been pied didn't you?? I had no signal. And, well I've missed you".

Josie's heart skipped a slight beat "I've missed you too actually".

Lance continued to chat as he walked along the sea front, trying to find his mates, then Josie could hear him talking to somebody.

"Hi, I'm ok thank you..... no, no thank you..... please don't kick me, that's very rude!"

"What's going on?" asked Josie as Lance sounded more out of breath and sounded like he was now running.

"Oh I just had a transexual prostitute asking me if I wanted any business, then when I said no, he kicked me and chased me down the road. Luckily he was wearing really high heels, and I'm not so I was faster haha".

Josie laughed nervously "Are you ok? Sounds very odd. Anyway, what have you been up to?"

"Well" began Lance "You get these clubs over here and in the day time they are like really normal places with like bingo and karaoke, then after about 10pm it all goes a bit weird and turns into sex shows".

"You watched a sex show?" asked Josie "They have sex shows in Spain?"

"Well yeah, they're quite common actually" said Lance "My mate Ryan took us in there. It started off with some dwarf strippers, then this couple came on the stage on a pair of

Segways. As they were spinning round, she was giving him a blow job. If you and I did that, we'd end up taking out the front two rows of the audience, knowing your balance skills haha".

"Thanks for that" laughed Josie.

"Then when they got off the Segways, the fella blew up some balloons and the woman fired arrows out of her fanny and popped them.....hey I found my mates" declared Lance suddenly in the midst of his sentence "They are all here in the fried chicken shop, got to go!"

And with that, Lance hung up.

# CHAPTER TWENTY ONE

Work had been quite busy and Sandy was still desperately trying to sell tickets to BobbyB's ball. She had started advertising the event on social media, including pictures of BobbyB's jewellery that he was offering as prizes in the raffle if people wanted to pay an extra £250 on top of the price of £50 for a regular ticket. Sandy had booked a band to play at the ball and put down a deposit to reserve the date.

"Are you sure you don't want to come to the ball?" asked Sandy, who was wearing a tight white dress, tanned tights and white shoes "You could bring your fella, Josie, what's his name? Lance isn't it?"

"Yes his name is Lance, and I think we'll have to decline your invitation Sandy" replied Josie, continuing to type on her computer "Lance is away in London that weekend and I'm busy too".

Josie wasn't busy that weekend at all, but didn't want to be involved in any of Sandy's dealings with the ever increasingly shady BobbyB. Sandy sauntered off, just as Marvin approached Josie's desk. Marvin had started following BobbyB on social media and showed Josie his latest status. "Look at this, he's put '*Banksy, give me a call mate*' on his profile. Surely to god if he knew Banksy, he wouldn't be having to put out a request on social media" said Marvin shaking his head "The guy's a fruit loop. Seems to have a few followers too who believe all his stuff. Some deluded woman has offered to put a shout out to find Banksy on one of the Bristol pages. Madness. And Sandy's involved in all that".

Nic looked around to check that no one was listening, which meant she was about to gossip.

"She told me that she was dating some man that she met on her recent holiday" said Nic in a lowered voice "She'd sat next to him on the plane and they chatted for hours. Then it turned out they were staying at the same resort! Spent most of the holiday with him apparently".

"I heard that she had sex with him in the sea" added Helen, joining in the conversation.

"I don't know about that" shrugged Nic "But he was travelling alone and so was she. I thought it might just be a holiday romance but I heard that she had been seeing him since she came back off holiday as he doesn't live too far away from her".

"Let's have a look at her social media then, catch up on the goss" declared Marvin, who seemed more keen than ever to avoid doing work that day "ooh actually it does say on her profile here that she's in a relationship. He's called Lee apparently".

Josie, Nic and Helen looked at Lee's photo that Sandy had tagged him in from her holiday.  He was in his 50s,  and had short, dark but greying hair.  Sandy was sat on his lap in the photo, with no make up on and she was wearing a bikini and a sarong as a cover up on her bottom half. Sandy's hair looked slightly tousled and she actually looked quite beautiful with very little make up on and a slight tan which had brought out some freckles on her face.

"She looks normal!" said Marvin pursing his lips "She ought to try out that look more often instead of the 'put it on with a trowel' look".

Marvin stopped talking just as he spotted a white dress heading back in his direction. It was Sandy walking back into the office.

"Hi Sandy, you ok?" smiled Marvin.

Sandy appeared slightly tearful "No not really, I've just had a massive row with Lee and I think it's all over".

Marvin grabbed Sandy's arm to lead her to the staff room, and gestured to Josie to follow him. It was worth another few minutes of taking up his day without doing any work.

Marvin put the kettle on "What happened then? I thought you'd just tagged him in a relationship on social media??"

"I had" said Sandy, looking quite miserable "We'd had a lovely time on holiday but when we came back things started to go a bit wrong?"

"What had been happening?" asked Josie, taking over from making the tea as Marvin was too intent on listening to what Sandy had to say.

"Well we kept having arguments over silly things, like the tv remote and then he would storm off home, or he'd say that he had to be up early in the morning so couldn't stay over" explained Sandy "Then something really bad happened today".

Josie handed Sandy a cup of sweet tea "Here you are. Come and sit down".

Sandy sat down on one of the sofas and continued her story "Well last night I kept getting annoyed because he's never made any declarations about us on social media or anything. I have him in my profile picture, tagged him in a relationship and our picture is even on my messaging app too. Anyway, last night he came over and as usual said he couldn't stay over which was fine, but then today he sent me a ranty message saying that his messaging app had a picture of us together on it as his profile picture and his friends were asking who I was. That's hardly my fault is it??"

Marvin and Josie looked at each other, feeling slightly confused.

"Wait a minute" said Josie, trying to clarify the situation "His messaging app photo had been changed without him knowing about it? How could that happen?"

"I don't know" said Sandy, looking slightly guilty "But now he's all angry and says it's over".

Sandy took a quick sip of tea "Anyway I've got to get back to work as Mrs Wilshire is due in the office any moment".

Josie rubbed Sandy's arm to comfort her "Ok, well if you need anything then let me know".

Sandy grabbed a tissue from a nearby box and dabbed her eyes, taking special care not to make her mascara run.

"Thank you Josie, I'll speak to you later".

As Sandy walked out of the room, Marvin grabbed his phone from his back pocket.

"Something very odd going on there" said Marvin, beginning to scroll through his phone.

"What do you mean?" asked Josie.

"Well how can someone's profile picture on their messaging app change without them knowing about it?? Sandy must of got his phone and changed it without telling him. Thing is you can't see your own photo unless you go into your settings. I can understand him being mad about to be fair, but then why was he cross that people were then asking who she was? What's the big secret?"

Marvin began searching on his social media and quickly got the answer.

"Aha! I bloody knew it, look", said Marvin showing two social media profiles for Lee. One was the one that Sandy had tagged Lee in and the other was also Lee but had pictures of him with another woman. A profile that clearly Sandy didn't have access to.

"He's married??" said Josie, looking to see that a woman with the same surname had been tagged in his second profile picture "oh my god".

"And" added Marvin "It makes sense as to why he was always going home early due to arguments or poor excuses. I mean, so what if you have to get up early in the morning?".

"Are we going to tell her?" asked Josie cautiously "I really don't want to be the bearer of bad news".

Marvin shook his head "It sounds like it's over anyway to be honest, so why twist the knife. If she gets back with him then we should probably have a word about the cheating git, but for now I think it's best to keep quiet."

Josie agreed wholeheartedly and spent the rest of the day trying to avoid Sandy as she knew she'd find it very hard not to say anything if Sandy started saying what a wonderful man Lee had been. As it was, it seemed that Sandy wanted to throw herself into her efforts to make the ball a successful occasion for the enigma that was BobbyB.

Josie was glad to get home that day. Dealing with other people's love lives was more stressful than dealing with her own. She sat down on the sofa and heard her phone go off with a message. It was a message from Lance. Not a written message but a link to a music video that Josie clicked on. It was a song entitled "I love you always forever". Josie was taken aback a moment as she looked at the song lyrics coming up on the screen. She tried not to read too much into it, maybe it was a just a song that he liked. Josie replied with a heart then later that evening rang Lance up. He sounded a little cautious.

"Hi you ok?" he asked.

"Yes, I am" said Josie "That was a nice song that you sent me earlier..."

There was silence on the other end of the phone for a moment

"Yes it is" replied Lance "you do know what I was trying to say to you?"

This time it was Josie's turn to pause.

"I was trying to say that I love you" said Lance "I know it's quite early on to say it but I know what I feel in my heart, and I know that I love you".

"I love you too" replied Josie, feeling like she was going to cry. Lance was a bit younger than Josie but they had so much in common. They enjoyed similar films, had the same sense of humour and got on well.  Lance had wiped away Josie's tears and danced with her in the kitchen when she was sad, he'd made her cups of tea in bed and he was always making her laugh.  These were the little things, but important things, about being happy with someone.  Josie had trawled a long way through the dating sites to find Lance, but finally she felt it was worth it, and was so happy that he was clearly feeling the same way.

Josie had a long overdue catch up with the girls at Aimii's flat.

"Well I have some news" declared Katie, producing a bottle of champagne "I'm getting married".

"Oh my god" squealed Aimii, giving Katie a hug "That's two of you getting married, that is so exciting. Another one bites the dust haha!"

Katie showed everyone her beautiful engagement ring. It was a large solitaire diamond set in a plain gold band, that set off Katie's dainty fingers beautifully.

"I can't believe that the one and only guy that you found on a dating site is the one you are marrying" laughed Mel "That is just so you Katie".

"Maybe we could have a double wedding" laughed Jo, looking at the ring.

Katie smiled "As much as I love Disney, I'm not dressing up as a Disney Character for my wedding.  It's going to be a classic English affair, with old fashioned bridal cars, a big white dress and lots of handsome men in suits!"

"Sounds lovely" agreed Josie, clinking champagne glasses with everyone.

"Are you getting married again then Josie?" asked Aimii.

Josie laughed "I'm not sure. I do want to be with Lance forever but I think he has an aversion to wedding cake since he got divorced - I always joke that he has an allergy to marzipan!"

"I'm never getting married again" said Mel, sipping her champagne "I did it once and that was enough. Was a whole big white wedding affair so many people invited. Then the awful divorce. That definitely was enough for me".

"I had a big white wedding" said Josie reminiscing "I had the whole shebang, the horse and carriage, loads of bridesmaids, white meringue dress, church, the lot. I remember arriving at the church and a bee flying under my veil and the photographer had to rush to get it out before it stung me. Then I got my massive meringue dress stuck on the end of a pew when I started walking up the aisle. If I did ever get married again I'd be happy doing it in jeans and a t-shirt to be honest then splash the cash on a big lovely holiday".

"And a party when you got back" added Jo.

"Yeah maybe" laughed Josie "Anyway, how are your wedding plans going Jo?  Only a couple of months until your wedding now".

"Yeah bit of rush but why wait" said Jo "I always felt that Danny was the one for me. I've never been married before so am going to do it exactly how I want it.  Actually we need to sort all your costumes out for your bridesmaids' outfits soon".

"Where are we going to get them from, not like I can get an Elsa outfit from a Bridal shop" said Mel quizzically "Are you sure about this theme?"

Jo nodded "I know somewhere, don't worry. I love Disney and so does Danny, this is my dream wedding! And his mum and dad are going to pay for us to go to Disney World for our honeymoon. I love it there, am so excited".

Josie was pleased for both Katie and Jo. They had found their ideal men and were getting married and whilst marriage wasn't in Josie's plans, she was happy in what she'd found with Lance. Lance had gone away to London for the weekend with his dad and Josie was missing him. She decided to have a nice long bath before going to bed early to read a book. She hadn't bothered to take off her make up before getting in the bath as she was on her own and enjoyed a long luxurious soak in the hot water surrounded by bubbles that smelt of lavender to help her relax.

Just as Josie was getting out the bath, Josie could hear her phone buzzing, with an incoming call, which she'd left on the floor next to the bathmat. She stood dripping wet and answered the call. It was Lance, and Josie had answered the phone in such a hurry that she hadn't realised it was a video call. She could see her own image in the bottom corner of the screen, mascara having run down her face and bare shouldered - beyond that she was completely naked. Josie shrieked and ran into the dark bedroom, holding the phone as she ran, probably giving Lance and everyone around him quite an interesting view. Luckily Lance had had a few pints of beer and was dancing around whilst holding his phone in the air, oblivious to Josie's panic of her nakedness on the video call.

"I LOVE YOU" shouted Lance to Josie before the call ended as quickly as it began.

Josie smiled and began cleaning the smeared make up from off her face. It was a sweet but brief conversation with Lance and Josie would be glad when he was back. He was always good at keeping in touch, they saw each other regularly and Josie was never left wondering how he felt about her. She rued all the time she had spent meeting men who were a complete waste of time. But then how would you know what a good relationship was until you'd had a bad one she concluded.

Jo's wedding plans were in full flow.  The girls met up to have a look around a hotel which had been reserved as a venue for the ceremony and reception.  It was a grand country hotel, set in established landscaped grounds, with a fountain in the rear gardens and a terrace which overlooked a lake in the distance.  As they drove up the sweeping driveway in Katie's car, Aimii let out a gasp at how picturesque it all was.  As they got out the car, Aimii looked up at the imposing building.

"Oh my god Jo, this is so nice!  It must be so expensive though!" commented Aimii "It looks amazing!"

Jo nodded "Yeah this whole wedding is going to cost a pretty penny but Danny's mum and dad said that they are going to pay for it luckily".

The 5 women entered into a grand, marble tiled hallway that had a large staircase that went up by about 15 steps and then split into two different directions to the second floor. They were greeted by a young woman in her 20s who was dressed in a smart grey skirt suit and whose brown hair was tied back into a very tight smooth pony tail.  Her make up was very on point and her eyebrows were the most perfect that Josie had ever seen.

"Hello, I'm Elizabeth the hotel wedding planner. Which one of you is Jo?"

Jo moved forward and shook Jo's hand "Hi that's me".

"No Danny today?" commented Elizabeth, looking over the 5 women "Oh, unless one of you ladies is Danny..?"

Jo laughed "No no, he's not here today, he works too many shifts.  He's left it all up to me to decide, he says as long as we get married he doesn't care".

"Oh how lovely" chirped Elizabeth, holding her clipboard "And are these ladies with you going to be part of the wedding party?"

"Yes" said Jo, feeling slightly nervous at how real it was all becoming "This is Aimii my Chief Bridesmaid, and this is Katie, Mel and Josie who are going to be my bridesmaids".

"Nice to meet you" said Elizabeth, giving them all a limp handshake "It will be a wonderful day  can assure you.  You haven't given us too much notice with all this but we can bring this all together for you.  Let me show you our main function rooms and where you can take photographs after the ceremony".

Elizabeth walked perfectly in her high heels to one of the main function rooms which had floor to ceiling windows and two sets of large double doors that opened onto the terrace.

"This is the reception area where you can have your main reception followed by your evening reception" explained Elizabeth "Hopefully it will be a warm evening so that your guests can spend time out on the terrace.  The fountain area is a lovely place to take photographs or if the weather isn't kind, we do have beautiful areas inside the hotel where you can take pictures, but hopefully that won't be the case.  Are you planning on having an evening disco?"

"Yes definitely" answered Jo, looking around the room "And a karaoke too, I love a bit of karaoke".

"How lovely" said Elizabeth writing everything down on her clipboard "If you look over there, we do have a small staging area where we can do that for you".

Jo spent time with Elizabeth sorting out the final details as the others managed to carry on looking around. They then went to get some drinks at the bar and sat outside for a while in the sunshine. It was a beautiful spring day and the birds were singing in the nearby trees.

"Bridesmaids outfits next" said Jo, finishing off her drink "Let's do this!"

Katie drove them to a small workshop, just outside of one of the villages which housed a small business that specialised in theatre costumes. It was a plain wooden two storey building from the outside that was like an Aladdin's cave inside. There were rows upon rows of expensive looking costumes, and trunks and shelves full of props and accessories. Aimii's eyes widened as she looked around the room.

"This place is amazing babes, how on earth did you find it?" asked Aimii.

"Danny's sister is a costume designer and designs for allsorts really. Plays, film productions, weddings, etc. This is her gift to us" explained Jo "She's already made up the basics of your costumes, she just needs to do a fitting with you all to make sure it fits like a glove, so no losing weight or putting it on!"

"What are you wearing?" asked Mel, looking over a suit of armour on a stand in the corner "We know we're Disney princesses but what are you going to be?"

"It's a secret" laughed Jo.

"And why I am Sleeping Beauty?" asked Aimii, trying on a jewelled tiara.

"Because you're always napping" laughed Jo.

"Oh this is so exciting, I can't wait for you to get married! I'm so glad we're all part of this together" said Katie.

Jo smiled "Yeah me too".

# CHAPTER TWENTY TWO

Easter had come early that year and the weather was unseasonably warm. Lance and Josie had spent Easter day together, and it was nice to to have some planned time to spend alone together over the holidays. Lance had accidently bought Josie a dark chocolate egg instead of a milk chocolate egg which she preferred and had insisted on going to change it on Easter Saturday. Josie said he could wait until after Easter, but Lance wanted her to have it for Easter day.

"You deserve to have a gorgeous Easter egg" explained Lance on Easter Sunday, presenting Josie with a large box which contained a beautiful chocolate egg, decorated with a yellow bow and surrounded by individual chocolates.

Josie gave Lance a kiss "Aww thank you, it's beautiful" said Josie, and gave Lance a large chocolate rabbit and a big box of chocolates in return.

Lance smiled and gave Josie a big hug and a kiss. She planned on cooking a Sunday roast for the two of them with all the trimmings and then have a few days off work and spend time just being together, doing things like having long lie-ins, watching films and long country walks. It had sounded like heaven.

"Do you mind if I watch some football upstairs?" asked Lance.

"No that's fine" said Josie "This roast will take me a while to prepare and cook, so I'll give you a shout when it's done".

Josie's speciality was cooking roast dinners, her roast potatoes were always lovely and crunchy and the gravy was made with juices from the meat. When the food was ready, she gave Lance a shout and they sat down and ate the large meal together. Lance seemed rather quiet and once the meal was over, Josie asked him what was wrong.

"Oh it's nothing" said Lance, getting himself a drink, but seeming overly subdued which was really not like him.

"Is it me?" asked Josie nervously, not deep down thinking that it was, but just questioned it.

"Not really" said Lance.

Josie's stomach lurched. That meant that it was possibly something to do with her. She took him by the hand and sat down next to him on the sofa.

"What's the matter?" asked Josie "you know you can tell me anything".

"I'm not sure this is what I want" blurted out Lance "You know, moving in together and all that".

"But I thought that just might happen one day" explained Josie feeling sick "Where has all this come from?"

Lance shrugged "I don't know, I just don't know if I feel the same any more, and I might want loads of children one day, who knows??"

Josie began to cry as she knew that she couldn't do anything about any of it. Slowly and painfully as she sat on her sofa and she let go of Lance's hand, her heart began to break.

"I'm just so stupid" Josie said crying "Not knowing you felt like this, and thinking all this would work".

"You're not stupid" said Lance standing up "I think I'd better go".

Lance went upstairs and packed his small bag and looked as sad as Josie had ever seen him. As tears rolled down both their faces, Lance gave Josie a kiss and hugged her goodbye. As the front door shut, the sound echoed through the hallway. Josie sat on the door mat and began to cry harder than she had ever cried before.

A few weeks passed and there had been little contact between Lance and Josie. Josie had been through the flat and gathered any belongings of Lance's that she could find and they met to swap keys. It felt a very sad ending to what had been a really lovely relationship. Josie had never felt that way about anyone before and was still confused as to why it had all happened.

Even though Jo had been busy planning her own wedding, she was there to comfort Josie in her time of need. Josie spent a few occasions crying at her desk at work and been sent home early on more than one occasion, much to Marvin's dismay. He hated seeing his friend so unhappy.

"You deserve to be happy" said Marvin one day, giving Josie a big squeeze "You will find someone".

"I thought I had" said Josie, trying to wipe away her tears with her sleeve "But you know, I'm not interested in anyone else, I'm giving up. This is just too painful".

Marvin put his hands on her shoulders. He looked at Josie in the eyes and looked very serious.

"You, my gorgeous Josie" began Marvin "Are a kind, bright and beautiful woman and he has made a very very big mistake. You were both very happy together and he will never find another person like you, or indeed another relationship like you two had".

Josie hugged Marvin and thanked him for his kindness.

"Thanks Marvin, that really does mean alot to me" Josie smiled

at Marvin, feeling grateful for all the good friends that she

had.

"Anyway we need to go downstairs now" said Marvin,

shoving a tissue in Josie's hand and showing a sense of

urgency "Something's going on that we need to check out".

"What do you mean something's going on?" asked Josie

pulling herself together and wiping her eyes "How do you

know??".

"There's a police car that's just pulled up outside, which of

course means that something's going on" Marvin tugged

Josie's arm "if we go to the lift area, we'll be able to hear what's

going on as it overlooks reception. Come on, hurry up".

Josie and Marvin made their way towards the lift area and

overlooked the glass barrier down into Reception. They could

see two policemen talking to Bridie who was on a telephone

call and looking flustered at the uniformed men in front of

her. As one of the policemen turned round, she recognised

him as Danny, Jo's fiancée.

"I know him!" whispered Josie to Marvin "That policeman there, he's going out with one of my friends, they're getting married soon".

"But what are they doing here??" whispered back Marvin, keen to know what was going on as usual.

"How would I know?? Oh wait, Bridie has come off the phone and is talking to them".

Marvin and Josie strained their ears to listen to the conversation but couldn't hear any details. Suddenly it went quiet for a few moments and then the lift doors opened and Danny and his police colleague walked out of the lift towards Josie and Marvin who tried to appear casual.

"Hi Josie! Didn't know you worked here, how are you? Got your glass slippers ready?" said Danny with a wink.

Marvin looked at Josie quizzically.

"Disney wedding" said Josie by way of explanation "anyway PC Wilkins, what are you doing here today?"

"You can probably help actually" said Danny "I'm looking for a Miss Sandy Peters, do you know where her office is?"

"I do!" interjected Marvin, walking forward and opening the door "It's this way Mr Policemen, follow me".

As Danny and his colleague walked through the door, Marvin gave a whisper to Josie.

"Love a man in uniform".

Josie rolled her eyes and took over with an attempted air of professionalism "Now is not the time Marvin. Right officers, this way, follow me".

Josie led them to Sandy's office, where she was deep in work for once at her computer.

"Not now Josie, I have reports to finish for Mrs Wilshire" said Sandy, then as she looked up she saw the two policemen behind Josie.

"Oh I'm so sorry, I didn't know that we had company, I do apologise" Sandy stood up and went to shake their hands "I'm Mrs Wilshire's assistant, nice to meet you. How can I help you?"

"Are you Sandy Peters?" asked Danny, suddenly going very serious.

"Yes, yes I am" said Sandy cautiously "Is there a problem?"

"I am arresting you for dealing in stolen property......" began Danny's colleague.

The officer read Sandy her rights as Josie and Marvin looked completely stunned at the developments.

"Stolen property?? I don't know what you are talking about! Would somebody like to explain to me what is going on??" exclaimed Sandy "This is ridiculous!".

The two policemen took Sandy out of her office, back into the lift, out of reception in front of a stunned Bridie and put Sandy in the back of the police car.

"Oh. my. god" said Marvin very slowly "This time she has got herself into some serious trouble, maybe we should help her?"

"But how?" said Josie, staring at the police car as it drove away with Sandy in the back.

"Jonathon!" said Marvin beginning to stride away "I know that he has an exceptional lawyer who gets him out of all kinds of trouble, including financial stuff".

"How do you know that??" asked Josie, quickly following along the office corridor, struggling to keep up with him.

Marvin briefly stopped and tapped his nose "I know lots of things my darling Josie! Now come on, let's find Jonathon".

Marvin had a brief word with Jonathon's assistant before going into his office. Jonathon was sat at his large desk, glasses on, going over an awful lot of paperwork that was spread all over desk. Jonathon peered over his glasses.

"And how can I help you two today? If you're chasing up staff rises, you're a bit too early. Budgets have only just gone in and

Mrs Wilshire wants all the finance reports by the end of the week".

Marvin sat down and crossed his legs, and Josie gingerly sat down in the seat next to him.

"Sandy's been arrested" said Marvin "And I really think you should help her".

Jonathon slowly took off his glasses and placed his arms on the desk, grasping his hands together.

"And why should I do that?" asked Jonathon.

"Because" explained Marvin, glancing over at Josie "I know that you have talked a lot about your financial dealings with Sandy and asked her to do things for you that might not have been by the book as it were. I think Sandy may have something to say to Mrs Wilshire or possibly the police if you don't speak to her first in this situation".

Jonathon sat back in his leather chair, deep in thought for just a moment.

"I have no idea what you mean of course" said Jonathon, standing up and putting his suit jacket on, giving him back his debonair air "But I will contact my lawyer and go and help Sandy. Meanwhile can I ask you to keep this to yourselves?"

"Souls of discretion" said Marvin, pursing his lips "Aren't we Josie?"

Josie nodded in agreement before adding quietly "Yes of course".

Jonathon grabbed his briefcase and his phone before hurriedly making his way out of the office, making a quick phone call and then driving away in his car at speed. It was a few long hours before Jonathon made his way back to the office with a rather dishevelled and upset looking Sandy. Jonathon summoned Marvin and Josie to his office.

"All sorted, my lawyer got her out of that hole. You'd best go and see her to confirm this but in the meantime can we agree that nothing else is said?"

"Yes yes" said Marvin hurrying out of the office with Josie "all forgotten! We'd best go and find Sandy".

"I can't believe you dragged me into this" said Josie crossly "Jonathon is not happy!"

"Oh who cares" said Marvin, making his way towards Sandy and Mrs Wilshire's offices "We'll probably get a good pay rise too haha!".

They went into Sandy's office to find her sitting at her desk with her head in her hands. She looked up as Josie and Marvin walked in to reveal her mascara stained face.

"Oh my god, I've just spent several hours being interviewed by the police then Jonathon came to save me with his solicitor!" cried Sandy, grabbing a tissue out of a box on her desk.

"Why were you arrested in the first place?" asked Josie.

"It was BobbyB's fault" cried Sandy "The jewellery that he was putting up for the raffle at the Ball I was helping him arrange, wasn't stuff that he had made at all, it was from some bloody

jewellery heist that he'd arranged from prison! Then when he

came out he needed somewhere to store it. He was that

arrogant and full of himself, keen to show how wonderful he

was, he didn't think that anyone would recognise the jewels.

He was planning to keep them for himself of course and

replace them with fakes".

"And what's happened to BobbyB now?" asked Josie feeling

concerned.

Sandy shrugged "I don't know.  He had several fake profiles

apparently which have all disappeared and most of his stories

were fake too. He didn't know anyone famous at all.  And he

landed me right in it.  I've lost my deposits for the ball too, as

he never ever paid me back.  Thank god that Jonathon and his

lawyer came to help me today".

"Yes thank goodness" said Marvin, winking at Josie "Well be thankful that you're not ending up in prison and perhaps you should go home early. I'm sure Jonathon can explain something to Mrs Wilshire".

Sandy nodded and packed her work stuff away before going home. It had been a long and eventful day.

Over the next few weeks' Josie gave herself time to grieve the loss of her beloved Lance and as time went on, started to feel a tiny bit better. Having a broken heart was horrible, because only time could mend it and she wished that she had a magic wand to move time forward to a place where her heart didn't hurt any more. As that wasn't an option, Josie worked hard to pull herself together. She told herself that one of her best friends, Jo, was getting married in less than a month, and Josie wanted it to be a happy time for her so really had to pull herself together. She began running again and became fitter and also lost some weight, which didn't particularly please Jo as it meant two extra fittings and visits to the costume workshop.

"Don't lose any more weight" said Jo, as Josie tried on her Cinderella outfit for the last time "At least you still have your boobs" laughed Jo, eyeing Josie's full chest that was heaving out of the top of her shiny blue ball gown.

Jo gave Josie a massive hug "Please enjoy my wedding day, don't think about him. Have you got anyone else for your plus one?"

"Yes I can bring Marvin from work? He's a good mate and I think he'd love to dress up for the day".

"Of course!" said Jo "I'll add him onto the seat plan. This will be so much fun, I can't wait!"

The day of Jo's wedding dawned bright and sunny. The initial clouds in the sky had faded away, leaving a bright blue sky and a calm day. Aimii's flat was a buzz of activity as all the girls had decided to get ready there except for Jo who was getting ready at her mum's house before making her way to the hotel.

"Do I look okay?" asked Mel, straightening down her Elsa gown and trying to fix her long plaited blonde wig in place which kept looking crooked.

Katie was getting away without a wig, as her character was Snow White and she already had dark brown hair, instead just needing to place a headband on top of her shiny hair that had been straightened and set in place with spray.

"Where's my apple?" asked Katie, hunting around.

"This is no time to be hungry babes" said Aimii, trying to fit her gold tiara on her head, and straightening out her golden gown .

"No, my poisoned apple" said Katie, continuing to look around the flat "you know, the one that the witch tries to kill her with".

"I think Mel ate it earlier" said Josie, trying to do up her Cinderella gown "Bloody hell this princess business is hard work, can someone help me do this".

"Sorry I forgot you needed an apple" said Mel "Was nice though, sorry!"

Aimii held up the front of her long gown to walk over to help Josie do herself up.

"You look gorgeous babes" declared Aimii "you shall go to the ball!".

Josie laughed "As shall we all!  Mel don't forget your gloves otherwise you'll freeze everything over!"

The friends stood and looked at each other in their princess gowns.

"Bloody Disney wedding, my arse" said Mel, trying to straighten out her wig again "Did you say that the car is picking us up about 11am?"

Josie heard a horn beep outside the flats "Oh bloody hell, I think that's the car, is everyone ready??"

Mel nodded, making her wig shift out of place again, and the women quickly put on their shoes before making their way out of the flat.

"I'm going to need help going to the loo today" said Aimii, locking her front door "Right let's go".

Outside was an beautiful old wedding car decorated with a ribbon on the front bonnet and in the front seat was a chauffeur dressed in a black suit and black cap. Aimii took out her phone and took a few selfies and pictures in front of the car before everyone managed to get in. The car began its journey to the hotel.

"I'm so nervous" said Josie.

"You'll be fine" said Aimii reassuringly "I spoke to Jo this morning and she is really really nervous but excited".

"Can you hear that funny noise?" asked Mel, straightening her wig and looking around "the car sounds a bit dodgy".

At that moment that car's engine made a large bang and ground to a halt.

"Oh bloody hell" said Katie "We've broken down! What are we going to do now??"

"I don't want to get out of the car" declared Mel as the chauffeur opened the door.

"Why not??" said Katie.

"Because I'm dressed like fucking Elsa that's why!" said Mel, crossing her arms over the lace snowflakes that decorated her dress.

"Have you not got a spare car??" asked Aimii to the driver "We really need to get to this wedding, we are the bridesmaids".

"Disney wedding" added Josie unnecessarily.

"Not for another hour or so" said the chauffeur "We'll have to wait".

"No no" shrieked Aimii "It will be too late by then, what are we going to do??"

Josie had an idea "I'll ring Marvin, his uncle has a black cab which we could all fit in, I'll give him a call. I'm pretty sure that his uncle was taking him anyway, because Marvin likes a drink at this type of occasion. I should warn you that he is quite flamboyant though".

"I don't care" said Mel "Just say it's an emergency".

Josie gave Marvin a quick call who was only too ready to leave slightly earlier to come and give them a lift.  It wasn't long before the black cab appeared and out of it came a figure dressed as Peter Pan.

"I'm forever young!" declared Marvin holding out his arms in a theatrical manner "And I'm going to be looking for some Lost Boys tonight haha!"

"Behave" said Josie rolling her eyes and feeling extra nervous "Thank you so much for helping us out.  Right this is Aimii, Mel and Katie, also known as the bridesmaids for today so we need to get there in one piece please!  We're meeting everyone else at the hotel, does your uncle know where it is?? And nice costume by the way!"

"Thanks" said Marvin "I knew it would come in handy one day. Right, let's get all you princesses to the wedding!"

# CHAPTER TWENTY THREE

Josie enjoyed going to weddings but they also made her feel nostalgic and made her think back to when she was younger and her own wedding. Her grandfather had given her away as her own dad had passed away before she got married, which had made it even more of an emotional occasion. Josie remembered standing outside the old village church, holding on to her grandfather's arm who had then turned to her and said "You'll remember this day for the rest of your life". Josie had had a full on white wedding and the day had mostly been a happy occasion until the speeches when the groom said "I'd like to thank my beautiful bride... but where the hell's Josie??" It was supposed to of been a joke, but no one at the reception laughed. The groom wasn't supposed to make jokes out of the bride's usual state of attractiveness at the wedding, if ever at all. They'd also attended a pre-marriage course where Josie's ex husband had told the vicar that he didn't believe in god, so it was probably a true miracle that he had married them at all.

Josie looked around at her friends in the taxi as they made their journey to the hotel. Katie had never been married before and was looking forward to her own wedding in the Summer, Mel was divorced  as was Aimii and Josie. Divorce was an odd thing.  Even if you wanted it all to be over, when you got the final papers it still felt  like all your hopes and dreams for the happy future that you'd hoped for had ended with a disappointing piece of A4 paper that dropped through your letter box one day.  Josie had cried when she'd received her decree absolute, not because she was sad that she was finally divorced but just sad that things had to end that way at all.

"Are you okay babes?" asked Aimii, taking a sneaky puff of her vape that she was keeping in her bra in a very non-princess way "Thank god we got this taxi in time, Jo would of killed us if we were late!"

"When get there, we've got to go and find Jo who should be getting ready in a room in the hotel somewhere" explained Katie, feeling very organised "Then when it's time I think Elizabeth, the wedding coordinator will let us know when to make our entrance".

"Can't wait to see what Jo's wearing" said Mel "and has anyone seen my gloves??"

The black cab drove up the driveway to the hotel and pulled up outside the main entrance. As everyone got out, Mel found her gloves on the back seat that Aimii had been sitting on.

"I'm going to the bar" declared Marvin "I shall see you lot later, be good!"

Josie smiled "Don't drink too much Marvin, at least not before the ceremony. Afterwards it probably won't matter so much as Jo will probably be on the gin by then anyway!"

Marvin gave Josie a kiss on the cheek "I know today is hard for you but enjoy" he told her softly.

"I will" smiled Josie.  She had been thinking about Lance but had managed to push him out of her mind for a while during all the wedding chaos.

The photographer began taking some photographs and after a few minutes, Elizabeth the wedding coordinator came out onto the front entrance steps to hurry the bridesmaids along. She was wearing her normal skirt suit, but today was also wearing a headset to help her coordinate everything through the day.

"Oh I'm so glad you are here ladies, 10 minutes behind schedule though!" said Elizabeth tapping her list on her clipboard and wrinkling up her nose "Never mind, at least you are here now, although I was expecting a wedding car and not a black cab".

"Our car blew up" said Aimii, taking out her vape "It went bang and so we had to get a taxi here".

Elizabeth looked at the vape disapprovingly "We are of course a no-smoking venue but if you wish to smoke, we have a small gazebo within the grounds where you can do so".

"I'll put it away now" said Aimii, placing the vape back in her bra and rolling her eyes "I think I'm too old for this bridesmaid shit anyway. And I'm so tired already".

"Can I ask if any of you ladies know the gentleman sat in the bar dressed as Peter Pan?" said Elizabeth "He's drinking cocktails and if he's not involved in the wedding then we may have to move him".

"Yes he's my plus one" explained Josie "He'll be fine".

"Hmmm ok" said Elizabeth "Right let's get you all inside with Jo, she's nearly ready but I think she would like to spend a little time with you all before the ceremony".

Elizabeth gestured for the bridesmaids to follow her into the hotel. The whole hotel was hired out for Jo and Danny's wedding and the Disney theme appeared to be everywhere.

Josie peered into the reception room where every table was decorated with the crockery from Beauty and the Beast, including the teapot, cups and candlestick. Each table was covered with a large white tablecloth and all the chairs had white covers and were finished off with red and white polka dot bows.

"It looks amazing" commented Josie "At least now we feel dressed for the occasion".

"I love your Cinderella outfit" said Aimii, admiring Josie's blue gown.

"Come along, come along" said Elizabeth "Jo's upstairs, follow me".

Everyone followed Elizabeth up the grand stair case and along a corridor to one of the guest rooms. Elizabeth opened the door to reveal Jo stood by the full length window, dressed as Jasmine from Aladdin and looking incredibly beautiful in her turquoise outfit.

"Didn't want to do a dress" said Jo by way of explanation

"And you lot look bloody amazing!"

"Thanks" said Mel "We felt like twats earlier but I think we feel better now that we're here and everyone else will be dressed up".

"Marvin's the one dressed as Peter Pan" explained Josie "He's currently in the bar chatting up the barman and drinking cocktails so you might not see him at all to be fair".

"Doesn't matter, as long as you lot are all here, I don't care" said Jo, embracing them one by one.

They posed for a few photographs out on the balcony, where the view of the landscaped gardens could be seen bathed in the sunshine.  It was a great day for a wedding.

"Right ladies, time to go downstairs, your Aladdin has just arrived" said Elizabeth, adjusting the microphone on her headset.

Jo took a deep breath and looked around at her friends "Right this is it then".

"Yep" said Josie also taking a deep breath "You'll be fine".

Elizabeth handed Jo and the bridesmaids their bouquets of flowers. Whilst it was a themed wedding, there were also some traditional touches too.

Elizabeth led the women to the top of the stair case.

"Right your wedding starts here. Walk elegantly down the stairs and into the ceremonial room, where everyone is waiting for you. Best of luck".

Jo walked down the stairs with a big smile on her face, followed by Aimii, Katie, Mel and then Josie. They carefully placed each foot down onto every step, being careful not to trip and make a fool of themselves. As they entered the room, Jo could see Danny standing at the top of the aisle in his Aladdin costume, which included a sleeveless jacket which revealed a nicely tanned body including a 6 pack. He gave a big grin as Jo walked up the aisle to meet him, the chairs either side full of brightly costumed guests. The bridesmaids stood to the side and listened to the registrar conduct the ceremony and hear Jo and Danny say their vows. The large windows of the room had been opened slightly to let in some fresh air, which was making the full length curtains billow slightly into the room but added a lovely effect to the ambiance of the occasion.

When the ceremony was completed Jo and Danny kissed and the room cheered, along with several of Danny's colleagues who were sat at the back dressed as animals from the jungle book. Every guest had come dressed as a character and it made for a very special and colourful occasion. Even the hotel staff had joined in, with the master of ceremonies dressed as the Mad Hatter from Alice in Wonderland and on everyone's table there was the odd riddle for everyone to answer. If you could answer a riddle, then you got to have an extra treat at the table. Aimii was keen to get one right.

"Answer this one before that Hatter man comes back" said Aimii holding up the riddle on her card "It says 'what has teeth but cannot bite' ?"

Josie had had a couple of glasses of wine and it had gone to her head slightly so couldn't think of the answer, so messaged her mum Rebecca for help.

*"Mum, can you answer this riddle, What has teeth but cannot bite?"*

Rebecca replied *"False ones"*.

Josie laughed as Katie came up with the correct answer "I think it's a comb".

"Makes sense" laughed Josie as the master of ceremonies returned and left a large bag of sweets at their table.

Jo and Danny's wedding day was going exceptionally well. The happy couple spent most of the day together, chatting and laughing with their guests and looked really happy together. It had been a bit of a whirlwind romance but both Danny and Jo had known quite quickly that they were made for each other and had decided not to waste any time in spending the rest of their lives together.  Some had been a bit cynical of their decision, but their love was clear for all to see and had made Josie realise that sometimes true love really does exist.

As the day wore on, the music began to play and after Jo and Danny had had their first dance, the other guests began dancing in their various costumes and filled up the dance floor.  The full length windows in the room had also been left wide open in order to let in a cooling breeze make its way across the room.

Josie sat on her own at one of the tables with her drink, watching her friends dance in their princess costumes.  The master of ceremonies briefly announced  that the karaoke would be starting soon, before letting the music continue for a while.  Mel quickly made her way over to Josie.

"Have you seen that Lance is here??" said Mel.

"What??  It can't be" said Josie "I know he was going to be my plus one, but I haven't seen him since I gave him his key back".

Mel shrugged "All I know is that he's over there, look".

Mel adjusted her wig and pointed across the darkened room to the doorway, where a figure that did look like Lance, stood in a costume.  As he made his way over, Josie could see from the way he walked that it was indeed Lance.

"Hey how are you" said Lance with a grin, his green eyes twinkling "How have you been?"

"I'm ok" said Josie, looking at Lance's costume "What are you dressed as?"

"Prince Charming" replied Lance sheepishly.

"No irony there..." said Josie raising her eyebrows, and drinking some of her drink.

"Thanks for that. Well I knew you would be dressed as Cinderella so I had already hired a Prince Charming outfit and it seemed a shame to waste it" explained Lance "So how about a cup of tea some time? Would be good to just catch up".

At that moment the music stopped and the Master of Ceremonies asked for the bride and all the bridesmaids to come forward.

"Ladies and gentleman, the bride would like to sing a song with her friends, so can I please have Jo, Aimii, Katie, Mel and Josie to the floor please".

Josie stood up and looked at Lance "Looks like we're singing now, I'd better go".

Lance laughed "Can't beat a bit of karaoke. See you later for the cup of tea."

Josie smiled and nodded, then made her way to the dance floor and held onto one of the microphones. Up on the screen came the words to the song "*You've got a friend in me*".

Jo looked at all her friends "This song seemed the most appropriate for us to sing together. You lot mean everything to me".

They all smiled and hugged, including Mel who had to readjust her wig for the last time. Josie looked around at the friends dressed in their princess outfit and thought about what they had all gone through together, with all the fun nights out, divorces, hideous dates, broken hearts and finding love again. Josie felt a moment of happiness and realised that as long as she had her friends with her, she would always be ok.

Printed by Amazon Italia Logistica S.r.l.
Torrazza Piemonte (TO), Italy

12952827R00283